The Widows of Paradise Bay

JILL SOOLEY

BREAKWATER BOOKS LTD.
www.breakwaterbooks.com

LIBRARY AND ARCHIVES CANADA CATALOGUING IN PUBLICATION

Sooley, Jill, 1968-
The widows of Paradise Bay / Jill Sooley.
ISBN 978-1-55081-330-2
I. Title.
PS8637.O58W53 2010   C813'.6   C2010-903558-5

© 2010 Jill Sooley
Cover Design: Rhonda Molloy
Layout: Alison Carr

We acknowledge the support of the Canada Council for the Arts which last year invested $1.3 million in the arts in Newfoundland. We acknowledge the financial support of the Government of Canada through the Canada Book Fund for our publishing activities. We acknowledge the financial support of the Government of Newfoundland and Labrador through the department of Tourism, Culture and Recreation for our publishing activities.

PRINTED IN CANADA

The WIDOWS *of* PARADISE BAY

For my grandmother, Ruth, who loved a good read.

CHAPTER ONE

Prissy

I don't want to have sex with my husband tonight, but I don't think I'll be able to get out of it either. It's been nearly six months since we've slept together and Howie seems intent on resuming relations with me this evening, dropping a series of not so subtle clues as to his intentions. For starters, it is Friday, he has arranged for our son to spend the night at a friend's, and he refers to us needing to talk later. But we both know that Howie is not much of a talker, and that "talk" is most often a euphemism for screw or fuck or whatever else he has on his mind, as if I'm too delicate for him to actually come out and say it to me directly.

The morning sun is strong and I squint against the light, tucking the bed sheets under my chin like a nervous bride, although I am in no danger of being ravished, not yet. Howie is at least two hours into a busy morning schedule that has already included a short run, a shower, a handful of text messages, one and a half cups of black coffee and scrambled egg whites that come in a container resembling a milk carton. I turn away from the stench of his workout clothes, a pile of nylon and spandex that still holds the shape of Howie's thighs and calves. They are, not surprisingly, piled in a heap on the floor just inches away from the hamper. I'm tired of asking how much extra energy he has to expend to toss them an additional six inches.

I am hoping to stay in bed long enough to avoid him altogether this morning, but he seems to linger purposefully, waiting for me to get up and get Quentin ready for school. I can hear him clear his throat from the kitchen, a guttural sound more reminiscent of a dying cancer victim than a forty-seven-year-old man, who, for all accounts, is in such excellent health that he boasts about his cholesterol levels as if they were gifted children. I think of the sounds he makes when we're having sex, the grunts and moans that accompany his exaggerated facial expressions as he lies on top of me, his hairy chest slick with sweat on my bare skin.

I don't want to think about that right now, but I can't help it. My head automatically swirls with potential ailments, ranging from an upset stomach to a yeast infection and a host of other illnesses I might possibly feign. I close my eyes against the morning sunlight, remembering another lifetime, when neither of us could keep our hands off each other, and I swallow a painful lump in my throat at the realization of how much has changed.

It's perfectly normal, I assure myself. Our marriage has simply evolved from passionate to practical, as most marriages eventually do. Sex no longer ranks up there with what I consider to be the better aspects of marriage, like having someone on hand who can unclog the toilet, bring in my car for an oil change every 6,000 kilometres, shovel the driveway after a snowstorm, or reach things on the high shelves of cabinets and closets.

It's not that I don't love my husband or that I don't like being married. To the contrary, I can't imagine not being married to Howie. I like referring to him as "my husband" in a way that still makes me feel like a little girl playing house. Whenever a letter or a card comes in the mail addressed to Mr. and Mrs. Howard Montgomery, I suspect I feel much the same way as someone who first sees the word President, Principal, or Partner after their name. The formality of being Mrs. Montgomery makes me sound grand, important even, like a character that someone thought up.

After sixteen years of marriage, whenever someone calls me Mrs. Montgomery, I feel a thrill reminiscent of the first time we were introduced as Mr. and Mrs. Howard Montgomery at the Legion in Paradise Bay. I'd been so happy that day, dressed in a white silk gown that I purchased from The Model Shop on Water Street after my Aunt Sade, who claimed to be psychic, told me she had a vision of me in a white dress with a sweetheart neckline and a tulle skirt. I had already purchased a simple antique white gown with beading along the bodice, but my mother insisted I return it after Aunt Sade's vision. Mom dragged both me and Sade to every bridal shop in St. John's until Sade could verify the one that most resembled the one she'd seen, and then my mother performed a series of alterations on the dress until it was an exact match. I didn't love it as much as the one I returned, but who was I, I thought, to tempt the fates? I was just thankful that Howie was in Sade's vision in the first place, or else my mother would have objected to the wedding altogether.

I remember the way my tiny jewelled hand disappeared in Howie's firm grasp, while aunts and uncles, cousins and friends gathered around to wish us well. I remember admiring the handsome profile of my husband as he nodded at something my father said. I wanted to imagine Dad sounding protective, telling Howie to take good care of his little girl. More likely though, my father was offering advice to Howie of a more practical nature, giving directions to the hotel in St. John's and urging him to get to the airport at least two hours before our flight was scheduled to leave.

The sound of Quentin dragging his feet into the shower awakens me from my reverie and I drag my feet over the side of the bed, any hope of avoiding Howie dashed for the moment. After accumulating two late slips so far this month, Quentin needs to get to school on time for once. I glance at the clock, the LED display telling me it's 7:23, and my motions immediately go from sluggish to hurried.

Howie is quietly reading the newspaper and sipping orange juice at the kitchen table when I walk into the room in search of coffee. He briefly glances up but otherwise ignores my entrance. He does not say good morning or ask me how I slept or if I heard the thunder in the middle of the night, nor do I ask the same of him.

Howie's hair is still slightly wet on the sides from his morning shower and he's clean-shaven. I know if I put my arms around his shoulders and kiss his neck, the woodsy scent of pine mixed with the fresh smell of an impending rainstorm would envelop my senses, but it's been so long since I nestled my face in his neck that I feel awkward even thinking about it now.

He's wearing a navy suit with a crisp white shirt fresh from the drycleaners, which he paired with a tie that bears a sailboat pattern. It puts me in mind of what members of a yacht club must wear when they are not out sailing, although what Howie knows about sailboats is negligible at best. I think of a yellow t-shirt in the back of my dresser that has "Surf Hawaii" emblazoned on the front, even though I've never been to Hawaii, or surfed for that matter. I bought it because I thought the yellow complimented my blonde hair and golden tan, and the carefree message made me feel youthful. Howie looked dubiously at me when I wore it, so I hid it away afterwards, too embarrassed to ever wear it again.

I don't know why his approval of my t-shirts even matters, but it does. I resist the urge to call him a hypocrite now, not because I don't want to start an argument but because he'd have absolutely no idea what I was talking about. He would surely have forgotten the entire incident, oblivious as he is to every hurtful comment or look he happens to send my way.

Sailboats or not, at least Howie looks pulled together. In contrast, I look every bit the image of someone who has just crawled out of bed. My hair is pulled back into a hasty ponytail with knots of tangles matted along my scalp. I haven't brushed my teeth yet and the sleeve of my faded blue bathrobe showcases stains of coffee and strawberry jelly.

I pour myself a cup of lukewarm coffee and reach for Quentin's backpack, which is hanging on the back of a chair at the kitchen table. I tuck a ten-dollar bill into the backpack for lunch from the school cafeteria and find a pack of cigarettes wedged inside his math binder.

My first inclination is to hastily dispose of them before Howie notices. In an effort to avoid a conflict between my husband and my son, I carefully pull out the cigarettes and throw them in the garbage, concealing them with a notice about an end of year PTA luncheon. A more responsible mother would probably confront her son, lecture him on the negative health effects, warn him of the perils of addiction, but I know Quentin and I know he won't listen to any of it. He'd sigh, tell me he's heard it all before, which he has, swear they aren't even his, and then he'd buy more cigarettes with his lunch money. I would have done the same thing at fourteen — did, in fact, do the same thing. I steal a sideways glance at Howie and try to imagine him in the throes of teenage rebellion and almost laugh outright at the implausibility of my husband doing anything he isn't supposed to. He never does anything fun or crazy anymore, not like the first time we met.

I watch him now, irritated at the way he folds his napkin into a perfect square and places it on top of his half-eaten plate of scrambled eggs to signify he's done — his period at the end of a sentence. I notice the smeared ketchup on the rim of his plate, his latest health obsession being all things tomato in a last ditch attempt to salvage his prostate. He eats tomatoes of all varieties now — beefsteak, grape, cherry, plum, vine, heirloom. He guzzles tomato juice and squirts ketchup on almost everything. I wonder when he became so old. He has twelve years on me, but sometimes it seems more like twenty-five.

"I have to go," Howie announces, throwing on his suit jacket. I pretend not to see the piece of pulp stuck between his front teeth and wonder how long he'll go before someone points it out to him or he figures it out on his own. I feel a mild pang of guilt for not bringing it to his attention, but at the same time it gives me some satisfaction to know he's not as perfectly pulled together as he thinks he is.

"Remember, I'll be home early tonight," he reminds me, as if I need reminding. "Quentin is staying at Jake's so we can be alone. We really need to talk, Priss."

"Yes," I snap, sighing. "So you've mentioned one hundred times," I say more quietly.

He deposits his empty glass in the sink, the remnants of the pulp sticking to the sides. I'm past telling him to rinse his glass out so the pulp will not stick and I won't have to pick it clean with my fingernails, the same way I am past telling him to put his dirty clothes in the hamper or to hang his towel up to dry. He never listens anyway. I sigh heavily, roll my eyes and proceed to rinse the glass myself with far more force than necessary. He ignores my exaggerated movements, and my momentary guilt for not pointing out the pulp in his teeth is replaced with smug satisfaction.

I watch the broad expanse of his shoulders escape through the narrow kitchen doorway. Before he's gotten to the front door I am already refining my list of excuses to get out of this evening's romp. I've become something of an expert in evading sex, finding that excuses focusing on a woman's private troubles prove the most successful. A headache, a cold, or other common ailments never work, but the mere hint of a yeast infection can put a swift end to any advances.

Often, I lie shamelessly about being on my period because I know it embarrasses Howie. All I have to do is mention the word period and his face becomes red. Sometimes I don't even have to say anything. I simply leave a box of super-absorbent overnight maxi pads out on the bathroom countertop and that keeps Howie at bay for at least a week and a half. Every time I go to the drugstore for toothpaste, shampoo, soap or aspirin, I find myself browsing the family planning section, picking up Monistat, Vagasil, Summer's Eve and feminine wipes to leave out on the bathroom countertop. I wonder what the checkout girls at the drugstore must think about me, the way I am always getting irritated down there.

For Howie's birthday last summer, I wanted to surprise him with some racy lingerie that I purchased on impulse from the Bay. But when I tried it on in the bathroom that night, it made my breasts look more lopsided than usual, showcased cellulite and stretch marks, and draped the buttocks right where I was harbouring a huge pimple. I rolled the offending garment into a ball, hid it in my underwear drawer next to all the beige cotton panties and bras, and then I presented him with a new dress shirt and tie.

Three months ago Howie came home from work one day and locked himself in the bathroom for nearly half an hour. He did the same thing for four days straight and I was beginning to think he was suffering from a horrific stomach ailment. It was only when I went to retrieve the towels for the laundry one morning that I noticed the telltale stain on the bathroom rug and I knew what he'd been doing in the bathroom all week. I rolled up the rug and threw it in the laundry basket in disgust, feeling almost admirable for not taking him to task for leaving the stain.

I wonder when I started feeling such dread at my physical relationship with Howie. Certainly, it wasn't a conscious decision on my part. At some point, sex had become just another household chore. I made dinner, washed dishes, did laundry, helped Quentin with his homework, and then when he was finally asleep, Howie's hands would be on me. In the early years, I relished the attention but after a while I just wanted to relax at night and Howie's advances became one more task to perform before I could go to bed and start all over again. After a while, I approached sex with as much aplomb as emptying the dishwasher or folding sheets.

Lately, I've been noticing things about my husband that never bothered me before. He picks at a tiny mole on his neck when he reads the newspaper. He has a propensity to chew his food almost exclusively on the left side of his mouth to the point I wonder why every tooth on that side is not rotting out of his head. He hardly ever covers his mouth when he yawns, and when I catch sight of his stringy saliva connecting his teeth together, I have to look away.

Once Howie has left for work and Quentin for school, I move about the house with my usual efficiency. I strategically put dirty dishes in the dishwasher, stacking plates and coffee mugs in close proximity so as to maximize space without overcrowding too much. I feel slightly pathetic knowing that my expertise in loading the dishwasher has become something I'm proud of and one of the few things I can claim superiority over my husband. *Not that way! You're doing it all wrong!* I chastise him simply because I need at least one thing I can do better than him.

I go about the rest of the day making beds, doing laundry and running errands. In the check-out line at the grocery store, my attention is drawn not to the supermarket tabloids but to a rack filled with bags of candy, and it reminds me of the first time Howie and I met. I pick up a bag of Swedish fish and smile wistfully as I think about that long ago day. Back then, I needed no excuse to avoid sleeping with Howie. In fact, I was stark naked within fifteen minutes of meeting him.

Seventeen years earlier: I'm sorting penny candy into groups of ten and twenty-five so I'll be ready when school lets out and all the kids come into Hayward's General Store with their dimes and quarters, eager for a taste of gummy bears, gobstoppers or sour rings. I'm so absorbed in the task that I don't notice Howie in his expensive suit and tie until he's standing directly in front of me like an apparition. No one in Paradise Bay wears a suit unless they're going to a wedding or a funeral. I know right away that this strange customer is not from a 100-mile radius of this place. He's clean-shaven, his hair is cut short even though longer hair is in fashion, and he's wearing cologne that smells like pine trees and a well-beaten dirt path. Although he smells like he's just spent all day communing with nature, he looks as if he'd be completely lost the minute he stepped out in the woods. He's unlike anyone I've ever met, and handsome in a way that takes my breath away.

I am still a girl myself, and have spent most of my time in the company of boys. One look at this man and I know he wouldn't snicker at the ferocity of his own farts or play air guitar to "Stairway to Heaven." He's older than me, although it's hard to judge by how much. At first I figure he's from St. John's, but when he speaks to me, it's quite obvious he's from the mainland, maybe Toronto or even as far away as Calgary. This fact immediately intrigues me since Paradise Bay rarely attracts tourists, especially in March, and business travellers are practically unheard of. He smiles down at me and I look away shyly at first, but then I smile back.

"You made me lose count," I accuse him, but I'm smiling when I say it, his offence already forgiven.

"I'm sorry," he says playfully. "I'm just going to grab something to drink," he says, pointing to the coolers at the back of the store. He lingers for what seems like an interminable amount of time in the snack aisle, picking up bags of potato chips, cakes and cookies, and placing them neatly back on the shelves. By the time he decides on a jar of orange juice and a bag of dry roasted peanuts, he's surveyed just about every item in the tiny store.

"Beautiful day," he says as I ring him up.

"If you like getting soaked, I s'pose," I answer, over the sound of the wind whipping the rain against the windows.

"Yeah, that's what I meant," he says awkwardly. "I like the rain," he says as if only now noticing the puddles forming in the parking lot, although it has been raining on and off all day.

"Stick around then since it rains a lot," I say, surprising myself with the sweetness of my own flirtatious tone. I smile shyly and I feel him staring back at me deliberately and unapologetically, his eyes taking in everything about me. Oddly, his gaze doesn't make me feel awkward or self-conscious. Instead, it sends my pulse racing and I stand taller under his inspection.

"It's a really beautiful town you got here," he says.

"God's country." I cringe at the way I sound more like my father than an eighteen-year-old girl. If he thinks it strange, he doesn't show it.

"Are you from here?"

"Uh-huh."

"Are all the girls from here as pretty as you?"

This makes me embarrassed so I look away, my face reddening at the compliment. "Nah," I say, trying to sound modest before realizing it might have the opposite effect.

"I'm Howard," he says, extending his hand.

I've never shaken anyone's hand and I have to think for a moment which hand to hold out.

"Howard Montgomery," he says, grasping my hand.

I marvel at the way my hand disappears into his, warm and strong. "Prissy," I say, feeling my heart beat faster. "Well, that's not my real name. It's just what everyone calls me. My real name is Priscilla."

"Well, Priscilla," he says, "it's been my pleasure meeting you."

"So what brings you to Paradise Bay?" I ask because I don't want him to leave just yet.

"You."

I shoot him a look that says, as charming as he may be, I am not foolish enough to fall for such a line. "Is that right?"

"Actually, I was surveying some buildings over in Carbonear. My firm is interested in acquiring a warehouse in the area." It strikes me as absurd that people go about shopping for things like warehouses.

"Since I'm the junior partner, they sent me, but I think I have the last laugh since you, Priscilla, have most definitely just made this trip worth it."

"I sure hope I'm better looking than a warehouse," I say, and he laughs in agreement. He makes his way slowly to the door, stopping halfway to look back, as if he's reluctant to go. The way he stares at me makes my face redden and my fingers tingle. I liked the way my name sounded when he said it, and my hand is still warm from his touch. My heart beats faster and my breath is caught in my throat. I am aware of a warmth in my middle and I involuntarily flex my thighs, while reminding myself to breathe. I look around. There's no one else in the store and the parking lot is empty except for Howard's rental car. School won't let out for at least another hour and Mr. Hayward is in St. John's for the day. I walk over to the front of the store and flip over the sign that reads "Back in 30." I make my way slowly back to him until I am standing directly in front of him. He's tall and I have to tilt my head back to see his face.

"Welcome to Hayward's. Can I help you?" I whisper. It's an invitation he accepts wholeheartedly. When he leans forward to kiss me, I nearly explode with excitement. Whatever force has consumed me seems to have consumed him as well. He's practically panting when he pulls my panties down over my wobbly legs, lifts me up onto a shelf of hard tack and peppermint knobs and begins making love to me with hurried, frenetic movements.

He needs only a few minutes and then he's done, looking down at me with utter disbelief that he's just committed such an act. He awkwardly tightens his belt and gathers his car keys, muttering something about how nice it was to have met me, before he darts out of the store, red-faced, without so much as glancing back.

Later, as the children come through the doors eager to spend their quarters, I wonder if the entire event happened at all. I'd never done anything like that before and it all seems so surreal.

I've only had sex twice before, both times with Ryan Hiscock. I've only told Lottie about it, but God knows who Ryan has told — probably half of the Bay. *How's Hiscock?* Lottie is fond of saying to me before she dissolves into a fit of laughter at what she thinks is such a clever double entendre, but Lottie ought to talk, especially given her own set of circumstances. I told her it was magical, because that's what Lottie seemed to want to hear, but in truth it was awful. It hurt; I was freezing and uncomfortable and found the entire ordeal humiliating. I don't know how making love to a complete stranger amidst a pile of jam jams can be less humiliating than having sex with my high school boyfriend on a bench in his family's shed, but it isn't.

I relive the moment over and over again, and each time I feel the same tingle in my belly and the shallow breathing that accompanied the actual moment when I felt his lips on mine. I decide not to tell anyone about it, not even Lottie, because I want it to be all mine.

I don't expect to see him again, so when he shows up at Hayward's

General Store two weeks after our first encounter to announce that he's just acquired a warehouse and would I like to have a celebratory dinner with him, I decide right then and there that I am going to be Mrs. Howard Montgomery. This requires a complete change of behaviour from our initial meeting. I decide not to have sex with him again, at least not until he asks me to marry him. But I let him put his hand up my shirt and I rub him through his pants until the seams of his trousers look like they might split apart. The more I tease him, the more attention he lavishes on me. He takes me to St. John's where we dine at real restaurants with tablecloths, a wine menu, and the kind of napkins that you rest across your lap.

I am completely in love and I tell anyone who will listen that we're going to get married and settle down in Toronto. Lottie doesn't believe me, and I get the distinct feeling she is jealous since Ches hardly turned out to be the man of her dreams. She insists Howie is probably already married since he's so old. I don't get upset with her because I feel sorry for her that she got knocked up by the likes of Ches Crocker, and when Howie asks me to marry him, I ask her to be my maid of honour.

By two o'clock in the afternoon, I am conveniently nursing a headache, which makes the whole ordeal of coming up with an excuse easier. I imagine sitting on the sofa with Howie, my head in his lap while he rubs my temples and massages my scalp. I take the extra-strength Tylenol from the medicine cabinet, swallow two pills and leave the bottle on the kitchen counter where it can be seen. When it's almost five-thirty, I draw the curtains closed even though it's the middle of June and there are almost three hours of daylight left. I lie down on the sofa and place a warm washcloth on my forehead and wait for the sound of Howie's car to pull up in the driveway.

But when Howie comes home he doesn't look like he's ready for romance at all. He stands in the centre of the living room, staring at me, but I feel like he's looking right through me. He doesn't seem to notice that I'm lying in a dark room or that I'm wearing his U of T sweatshirt even though it must be 28 degrees outside. The lines around his eyes seem to have grown deeper since he left the breakfast table that morning. When he begins pacing up and down the living room, I sit up and remove the washcloth from my forehead. For the first time all day, it occurs to me that Howie actually does want to talk to me about something important. Judging from his troubled expression, it's something bad. I look expectantly at him.

My first thought is that Howie is sick, maybe dying. On the surface, he's the picture of health. He doesn't look like most men approaching fifty. His hair is mostly grey now, with streaks of dark brown, but it's still full. He has also avoided the paunch around his middle, the result of his morning jogs three times a week and his refusal to indulge in anything sweet, sticky or flavourful. Still, I've always thought I'd be a widow someday. That possibility, no likelihood, comes with marrying an older man, but I'm not ready to face such a possibility just yet. Howie's not even fifty, but lots of people have heart attacks, cancer and all sorts of other ailments in the prime of their lives. Howie's own father died at fifty-two, which is why he puts so much effort in trying to be healthy.

I'm panicking now at the possibility of life without him. Whatever it is, I am going to be there for him. I resolve to drive him to chemo treatments, keep track of all his medicines, hold the straw steady for him while he sips water through parched lips, even help him get to the bathroom if it comes to it. I'll be his rock, his inspiration, the person he thanks for his recovery when he's well again. I stand up and go to him, wrap my arms around his neck and rest my head against his shoulder. I breathe in his familiar scent, which has an instant calming effect on me. My gesture is loving and supportive and conveys all the things I'm thinking. *We'll beat this. I am here for you. I'll do whatever it takes.*

I'm surprised to feel him stiffen under my embrace and even more surprised when he pulls away from me. When he says the word divorce all I can do is stare blankly at the sailboats on his tie. I picture myself sailing and then suddenly sinking to the bottom of the ocean. I can feel my lungs fill with water and I wait to be pulled back above the surface.

CHAPTER TWO

Lottie

I sit on the edge of the bed and watch my husband sleep, although there is nothing tender or loving in my demeanour. He's been in bed for nearly three straight days now and I notice that the room is beginning to smell of his unwashed body. I make a mental list of all the things I hate about him, starting with the noises. As if on cue, a nasally whine escapes through his nose, followed by a ferocious snort. I hate most things about my husband, from the way his breath smells in the morning to his annoying habit of biting the skin on his knuckles until they're raw and pink. I suppose I should hate that he's a drunk but I don't. There are good drunks and there are bad drunks, and Ches most definitely belongs in the former category. If he was the type of drunk that slurred insults and raised a fist in anger, perhaps then I might hate his taste for whiskey. As it is though, Ches is the kind of drunk who laughs and sings and places an arm around anyone who happens to be next to him. It's only in those moments of complete sobriety that he becomes bitter and angry and sneers at me with such contempt I can feel the weight of it on my chest.

In fairness I try to make a list of qualities I like and admire in my husband. He can fix things; that's for certain. Of course, the downside is that I never get to purchase anything new because Ches manages to make just about anything functional. My washing machine is held together by two wire hangers and a clothespin and yet it works perfectly every cycle. I dream of the Sears truck pulling up in front of my house with shiny new appliances, but as long as Ches is around I'll be using the same ancient almond-coloured fridge and stove that my parents left behind when they followed my sister and her husband to Calgary.

I strain to think of some other redeeming quality about my husband but I can't think of anything except that he has a soft spot for animals. He cried when we had to put the dog down last year, like it was the only thing that had ever truly loved him, and it probably was. Ches never even seemed to mind the foul smell that clung to the dog's hair, its breath, even its paws, which always surprised me since Ches is so sensitive to odours. He never seems to mind things that smell truly bad though, only the artificial sprays and deodorants meant to conceal. He once told me he'd rather stand the smell of his own shit — that he rather liked the smell of his own shit — but the orange blossom air freshener I plugged into the bathroom outlet made him gag and retch. Years earlier, he insisted I buy unscented maxi pads because he claimed the smell from the deodorant ones was making him sick. But that disgusting dog could climb up on Ches' lap and he'd think nothing of the odour, only the Glade I sprayed afterwards.

I wrinkle my nose, wondering how someone with such a keen sense of smell can stand the stench of stale cigarettes and liquor and his own body odour. I sigh heavily, wondering when I gave up on Ches, or more to the point, when he gave up on himself. I think Ches can fix just about anything but himself.

"Ches, come on, get up," I whisper as I try to nudge him awake again. I wonder why people whisper when they're trying to wake someone up when it's probably far more efficient to clang pots and pans and shout out that person's name at the top of their lungs. Of course, if I did wake Ches up in such a fashion, he'd be in too foul a mood to do me any favours. Still, I've been whispering at him to get up for a half hour now and my patience is waning.

He sleeps almost all the time now. Entire days go by without Ches making an appearance, not for breakfast, not for dinner, not even for *Hockey Night in Canada*. Sometimes, he'll head over to the Legion where he'll drink until closing, stumble home singing and giggling and demanding I get up and cook him something. At three in the morning I'm bleary-eyed and dog-tired but I get up anyway and fix him a sandwich because I'm afraid he'll turn on the stove and then pass out on the couch and burn the house down. I've seen the safety videos from the fire department on the CBC and it scares me half to death to know how fast and furious a pot of fat burns.

I study my husband's face. He has a slightly upturned nose and a narrow jaw, the same features that our daughter has. They are beautiful on her, but on him I think they make him look weak in character. Men are supposed to have square jaws, but Ches doesn't really have a jaw at all; he has a pointy triangle. He hasn't shaved in more than a week and his beard has grown in patches, lending him a sickly look. His neck is dotted with tiny bumps that remind me of the skin of a freshly plucked chicken. Sleep is supposed to soften even the harshest features but Ches looks anything but restful with shadows under his eyes and deep lines around his mouth.

It's only 10 am, and under normal circumstances I wouldn't even dream of awakening him at such an early hour, but today is anything but normal. I am tempted to drive Ches' truck myself, but I don't know how to drive a standard and Ches won't teach me because he says I'm too uncoordinated to master control of the clutch, the pedals and the steering wheel at the same time, and he's probably right. How many times have I forgotten about the roast in the oven to tend instead to the pot of boiling vegetables?

"Ches?" I say again, louder this time since I'm losing patience. "Come on, we have to go into town today to bring Marianne to the university, remember? Today's the science fair." Ches is still sleeping and I'm trying not to envision the possibility that Marianne might actually miss her chance to show off her invention. "You promised," I say meekly, childlike. "You know how much Marianne has been looking forward to this."

In fact, it's all our daughter has talked about for months. Marianne came home from school one day flush with excitement about how she was going to invent a special new perfume for the science fair. Every afternoon for the past three months she tinkered with the lupins that grew wild on the side of the Trans Canada Highway, blueberries, sea salt and dried up kelp that had washed ashore during high tide. When I asked her what on earth kind of perfume she was making, Marianne turned to me and cupped her mouth before whispering, "It's fresh air," as if the executives from Chanel were nearby, waiting to steal her idea. "Daddy says if you could bottle the smell of the air in Newfoundland, you'd make a fortune." Sometimes I think the whole endeavour is Marianne's way of getting her father's attention, a sad plea for approval on a subject Ches has always been so opinionated about.

Marianne did end up concocting a fragrance that was fresh and surprisingly sweet. It held a hint of dampness, not like the musty odour that seeped into basements, but the faint moisture present on a spring morning. It was good enough to earn Marianne a trip to St. John's for the provincial science fair and a shot at a scholarship to the university.

I dressed for the event a full three hours earlier and I am already so uncomfortable in these fancy clothes that I can't wait to take them off again. I hope not to be too much of an embarrassment to Marianne, but when I look in the mirror I am still just a tired-looking middle-aged woman who looks far older than my thirty-five years. My tan suit fits me too tightly across the middle, emphasizing my large waist and hips. The material is cheap and it itches my skin, but I avoid scratching. My hair, fine and silky and streaked with grey, grazes the tops of my shoulders. I'm wearing the sensible black shoes that Marianne says are ugly, but my feet are so wide, I can't really wear anything more stylish. I wear no makeup since it makes me feel silly, as if a sweep of colour on my cheeks and glossy lips could make me into someone more appealing. I know Marianne is embarrassed by me because I'm fat and unfashion-able, but at least I'm awake and showered.

I get more aggressive in my efforts to rouse Ches, grasping him by the shoulder and shaking him. "Ches, come on," I plead. "Today's the science fair in St. John's. You know how much Marianne's been looking forward to this." I cross my fingers and hope Ches gets up without an argument.

He rolls over and draws the covers over his head. "I can't," comes his muffled reply.

I watch his back, looking for some sign of movement but there's none. I can tell by his breathing that he's awake.

"Ches!" His name is a screech on my lips. I am so angry I can feel sweat pool between my breasts, and I'm clenching my fists so tightly I know I've left fingernail marks in my palms.

"I can't do it today," he sighs. "I thought I could but I just can't get up and go anywhere right now."

"You can't get up?" I repeat stupidly. "You've been sleeping for three God-damned days! You smell, you're dirty and you disgust me. Now get up!" My voice is shrill now and I'm almost certain Marianne is listening on the other side of the door.

"Some Chinese kid is gonna win anyway," Ches mumbles. "They always do. You're so stupid sometimes, Lottie. Do you think they're really going to give a scholarship to the kid who made perfume, or to one of the Asian kids in town that's found a new way to save the fucking rainforest? May as well just save Marianne the disappointment of seeing someone else win."

I don't know how to respond to this since he's probably right but that's not the point. I rifle through Ches' jeans on the floor, grabbing the worn leather wallet from the back right pocket. It contains only twelve dollars and I shake my head in confusion. Ches' disability check only came in the mail four days ago and he'd been in bed for the past three.

I whip the wallet at his head, but it misses its mark and bounces off the headboard and lands softly on the green carpet next to a sock that's inside out and a book of matches. "You're pathetic," I say, the disgust in my voice evident. Ches pulls the bed sheets up over his head as if to agree with me.

I could yell at him, take him to task for being a poor provider, a lousy husband, father and human being, but all of that has already been said. There was a time when Ches and I traded cruel barbs and insults on a daily basis. He used to chastise me for being too fat, for burning dinner, or for being clumsy. In turn, I called him lazy and useless, even taunting him for being drunk enough to slip on the ice on the way home from the Legion and break his back. "Who's the clumsy one now?" I'd ask him as he lay in our bed writhing in pain while I yelled at him that if he was going to fall on the ice at least he should have had the common sense to do it at work, at the rink, where he could at least get better benefits. "You can't even slip and fall down right," I spat at him.

I don't love my husband the way most wives do, although I tried over the years, sometimes even pretended. I'm not sure how to act really, since Ches is the only man I've ever known.

Eighteen years earlier: Prissy has dragged me out here on the beach so she could meet up with Ryan Hiscock at what's turning out to be a full-fledged party. It's one of those rare summer evenings, the one night a year that you could be unencumbered by a jacket after the sun went down. By the time me and Prissy arrive there are no less than a dozen bonfires hissing and cracking, sending sparks flying. I recognize most of the people here from school and they all look as if they're having the time of their lives. They are dancing, a beer in one hand and a smoke in the other. Prissy squeezes my hand as if to say, "I told you it'd be fun!" I'm convinced they'll all be puking at the water's edge by the end of the night, but right now the mood is definitely euphoric.

It doesn't take Ryan Hiscock long to spot Prissy's blond head amidst a sea of brown-haired girls, and he whisks her away into the woods so he can feel her up. I am left alone, sitting on a piece of driftwood, watching the fire. I sit for so long the backs of my legs ache, but I don't want to leave just yet because I'm afraid I'll draw too much attention to myself. I watch the boys and girls pair up and go off to their own corner of the beach to make out and I wish I was anyone but myself. When Ches sits down beside me, I am sure he's made a mistake and stumbled upon my driftwood by accident.

I don't know Ches personally, but I know of him because he was expelled from school last year for calling in a bomb threat because he didn't want to take his math final. My mother specifically warned me to stay away from Ches, vowing he was going to end up in jail at some point within the next five years.

I wonder if Ches is going to drag me into the woods and rape me, and the thought sends my pulse racing with a primal sort of excitement. But he doesn't hold me up with a knife, threaten me or anything of the sort. Instead, he offers me a taste of his beer and I swallow it thirstily, enjoying the frothy taste as it slides down the back of my throat.

"Whoa, Jesus, slow down before ya gets sick," he says, reaching back for the bottle. "You don't look like you're used to this stuff."

I shrug because I don't know what to say to that. He's right, I'm not used to drinking beer, but I don't want him to know that.

I must look insulted because he walks over to a case of beer, opens a bottle with his teeth, which impresses me, and hands the whole bottle to me.

"Here then. Have at it."

It is the equivalent of buying me a drink and I'm flattered, especially since beer is perhaps the most valued commodity of any teenage boy. I drink it quickly and my head starts to spin. He smiles approvingly at me and my cheeks burn. He doesn't look so scary. On the contrary, if you take away the ripped jean jacket and the long stringy hair, he might even look sweet. He has a dimple on just one side of his face when he smiles and his brown eyes put me in mind of a homeless puppy. I'm not sure what possesses me but I suddenly feel it's the most important thing in the world for Ches to like me in the same way that Ryan Hiscock likes Prissy. I'm not thin and pretty like her, but I have other attributes.

"Do you think I'm pretty?" I ask him before I burst out in a fit of embarrassed giggles under the effects of the beer. I hide my face in my hands but I know that Ches is sizing me up because I can feel him staring at me, thinking about the question. I wonder how he can arrive at a conclusion without looking at my face so I come out from hiding behind my hands. He's staring at my breasts.

"You got big tits," he says matter-of-factly. "Most fat girls got nice tits."

I am deep in the throes of adolescent insecurity so I take the vulgar comment as a compliment and blush. He takes me by the hand and leads me to a pathway in the woods, away from Prissy and Ryan and all the other couples. I follow him with my heart in my throat until we get to a small clearing of grass. In the darkness, I see in black and white. I know Ches' shirt is red and blue, but it looks one hundred shades of grey to me. He asks me to show him my tits and I willingly oblige, hiking up my t-shirt and lifting my bra up over them so they spill out in the moonlight. Ches eyes them hungrily and asks if he can touch them. I let him and then he asks if he can take more liberties. I think he's very polite to ask since Prissy told me Ryan just sort of did it to her before she even knew what was going on. He takes off his denim jacket and lays it out underneath the tree for me to lay my head on and I think it's downright chivalrous. By the end of the night, I'm pregnant, although three months pass before I know it for certain.

When I find out the consequences of my foolish act, I'm sick with regret. I lie in bed, pressing my fists into my belly in the hope that I might somehow force out this horrible thing growing inside me. I think if I fall down the basement stairs I might get rid of the problem, but I teeter at the top step, too afraid to make myself lose my footing lest I do more damage to myself than to my unborn child.

I tell Prissy first and she acts as if everything is going to be okay. She doesn't judge me, doesn't look at me with pity or shake her head in disappointment. She hugs me, tells me I'm going to be a great mom and asks if she can be my Lamaze coach. I try not to be offended since I imagine she thinks Ches is going to shirk that particular responsibility, but I have other expectations. When it's time to tell Ches, she doesn't warn me not to be disappointed if he pretends he doesn't know me, even as I know she's thinking it.

I know exactly where to find him, which is at the hockey rink where he drives the Zamboni on the weekends. I search the entire rink and finally find him outside by the storage shed, leaning against the faded blue siding and smoking a cigarette. I haven't spoken to him since that night but I think about him a lot. I imagine us getting married, taking Sunday drives along the shore and stopping for a soft-serve ice cream along the way. His hair has grown longer since I saw him last and he's sprouting a growth of facial hair on his upper lip.

"Hey," I call out. "Can I talk to you about something?"

He doesn't look like he's all that happy to see me. He takes a final draw from his cigarette and expertly flicks the butt on the ground. I don't know if the puff of smoke that trails out of his mouth is from the cigarette or the cold. He shoves his hands in his pockets and we both stare at the smouldering cigarette butt. The moment is more awkward than I imagined.

"Come back for more, are ya?" He pulls me toward him, presses his pelvis into mine and places a cold hand up my shirt. I jump back, startled.

"I'm pregnant," I blurt out. "Three months now." He steps away from me as if this news has suddenly made me a pariah. I see the colour drain from his face and the fear in his eyes. I feel a jolt of sympathy for him since I've had three months to digest the news, and he's had only seconds.

"It's gonna be okay," I say, trying to reassure him. "I mean we don't have to get married or anything, least not right away. Times have changed. I'm gonna be one of those modern working mothers, maybe even go to the career academy. I was thinking about going in for either a travel agent or a dental hygienist." I know I'm babbling but Ches hasn't said anything and the silence is too uncomfortable.

"Congratulations," he says, reaching into his pocket for another cigarette. "But I don't know what you're telling me for. Good luck to you, I s'pose."

He lights a match and cups it in his hands but the wind blows it out before he can bring the flame to the tip of his cigarette. I know Prissy thought he'd act this way by the way she promised to be home baking brownies for us, as if I would need cheering up, but I'm still in shock. I recall the way he explored my body. He was slow, gentle, and it made me feel as if I knew something about him that no one else did. But I feel foolish now, standing behind the rink, pregnant and more alone than ever. I bite my lip to stop from crying but I feel the hot tears spill down my cheeks anyway. I start running but I have no idea where. My house is in the opposite direction but my feet are hell bent on taking me away as fast as possible. I can hear Ches running after me, yelling at me to wait up, but I don't want to see him ever again, so I press on, ignoring the heat in my lungs and the cramp in my side. But at the end of the day I am a fat pregnant girl and Ches is a skinny teenager so it isn't long before he catches up to me. I don't know if I fall or if Ches tackles me but I know I'm on the cold ground surrounded by tall grass and wildflowers when I find Ches lying next to me, apologizing for being an asshole. He brings his mouth to mine and he tastes of stale cigarettes and diesel fuel.

I am twelve weeks pregnant and I have just had my first kiss.

I sit at the kitchen table wondering how I'm going to break the news to Marianne, nearly the same age now that I was when I met Ches. I use the pile of unpaid bills as a coaster for my teacup, leaving a brown ring on the envelopes. I look up and spy Marianne in the doorway watching me. In one hand, she's clutching her poster board, pasted with boxes and arrows of pictures and words. A flow chart, Marianne had called it. She holds a small glass container of her perfume in the other hand. Marianne looks at me knowingly, shrugs her shoulders and turns away. Not a word has passed between us, but everything has been said. It isn't so much the flicker of disappointment on my daughter's face that breaks my heart so much as it's Marianne's attempt to conceal it.

CHAPTER THREE

Prissy

It's slow at Lawlor's, part gas station, part convenience store, but mostly a diner. It's three thirty in the afternoon, too early for supper, too late for lunch. I sit across from my son in a booth at the back of the restaurant and wait for our deluxe hamburger platters. I take in the dated decor, the panelled walls dotted with oil paintings of various ships and lighthouses, and I feel out of place, even though I'm just minutes away from my childhood home. I couldn't wait to get back to Paradise Bay all day, but now that I'm here I wish I were anywhere else in the world, especially under these circumstances.

Our waitress sets our plates in front of us. "Enjoy your meal," she says enthusiastically, as if she were thankful we've given her something to do. "If you needs anything else, give me a shout."

I smile vacantly and thank her. Quentin can barely conceal his disgust at the meal and plugs his nose as our waitress turns her back.

"What's the matter with you?" I ask.

"Nothing," he mumbles, which is pretty much his answer to everything these days.

"Eat something." I nibble on a french fry.

"I can't. It's so freakin gross."

"What's gross about it?" I am dumbfounded by how a fourteen-year-old can find a hamburger and french fries gross.

"Everything is too thick," Quentin says, as if it were so obvious he can't understand why I can't see it for myself.

Quentin is accustomed to shoestring fries and McDonald's

hamburgers. These fries are thick and golden and the burger is actually visible between the two buns.

"Well that's how a burger is supposed to be," I counter.

"Says who?"

"Says me. My hamburger is delicious," I say with conviction, even though I've only taken one bite and I'm already feeling the stomach acid rise up into my chest. I haven't consumed this much grease in years, not since Howie began watching everything he consumed, always studying the labels first. Still, I feel compelled to defend the food simply because Quentin is being critical of it. I feel like a petulant child arguing with my son, and not at all the understanding mother I imagined when I pulled into the parking lot a half hour earlier.

I was hoping to have a last-minute heart-to-heart chat with Quentin. Despite the long day of travelling from Ontario to Newfoundland, we've hardly spoken about why we're suddenly in Paradise Bay without Howie in the first place, especially considering there's still a week of school left. I was hoping that the meal would give us both a chance to open up about things.

But as soon as the waitress offered Quentin the children's menu, he wore such a scowl that I knew it was going to be next to impossible to have a civilized conversation with him. Several times during the flight, I tried to talk to him about the reasons behind our unexpected trip, but it's difficult since I am reluctant to talk about them myself. I purposefully avoid the word divorce but find myself struggling for a proper euphemism. There isn't any easy way to say it. *Your father and I are going through a rough time right now, but things are going to get better.* I repeat this phrase several times throughout the flight, hoping that if I keep saying it, it might actually be true.

Quentin's response is a casual shrug of his shoulders, followed by a mumbled, "Whatever."

I watch as Quentin tears open a package of ketchup and squeezes it out onto the edge of his plate. He pours salt in his ketchup pile, and then sugar, before running his straw through the mess. He plays with his food when he's uncomfortable, a habit he picked up from his father, and the gesture irks me simply because it reminds me of Howie.

"Stop playing with your food," I snap, and immediately regret my harsh tone. I have to take a deep breath to keep from crying.

"I'm sorry, honey," I whisper in an effort to keep my tears at bay. "You can talk to me about anything, you know that, don't you? None of this is your fault. Your dad and I, we both love you and … neither one of us—"

"Oh my God, Mom, can you just stop talking?" Quentin says, cutting me off. "Please stop talking to me about this." Quentin rolls his eyes and lets out an exaggerated sigh.

He looks every bit the rebellious teenager with his shirt emblazoned with a marijuana leaf and baggy pants with rips in both knees. He wears a wool hat and his long hair sticks out by his ears. Quentin's hair is naturally blond like mine, but he's dyed it a horrific shade of bright yellow that reminds me of the yellow yarn on a doll's head. A silver chain hangs from his belt loop down the length of his thigh, completing his ensemble. I imagine my mother's reaction to his clothes.

"Why did you have to dress like that today of all days?" I ask, as if he didn't dress like this every day. "What am I supposed to say to your grandmother?" I don't expect him to answer me, at least not seriously.

"Tell her I'm battling a heroin addiction and I sold all my vests and pleated pants so I could get high." Quentin blows through a straw, sending air bubbles sizzling through the glass of coke.

"Tell her yourself," I say, tired now and feeling older by the minute. I take another deep breath and try to collect my thoughts. "At least have some dessert then." I longingly remember a time when ice cream could fix all of Quentin's problems.

"No thanks, I'm full," Quentin says, dragging the straw through his ketchup mountain and drawing red lines on the paper placemat featuring crude sketches of bears, moose, caribou and other wildlife found in Newfoundland.

I'm not sure what I expect from my son, but I know what I want from him — a promise that no matter what happens, he will choose me over Howie. It's selfish of me, deplorable even, and the only thought that brings me any sort of peace of mind. I want so badly to tell Quentin that this is all his father's fault, that Howie cheated, lied and betrayed us. I want to tell him so badly that I have to take another bite of the burger to stop the words from coming out of my mouth. I'm exhausted from the flight, the drive, and the entire awful ordeal, and I just want to lie down and sleep until this whole nightmare is over.

I shudder with shame as I recall how I cried and begged Howie not to leave me. I told him I could forgive him if only he'd forget this ridiculous talk about divorce. How pathetic I must have looked with tears streaming down my face, begging my cheating husband to take me back. It's not supposed to be that way. The man who strayed is supposed to grovel and beg for his wife's forgiveness, not demand a divorce. Howie balked at the suggestion we go to a marriage counsellor, but that was Howie. Once he made a decision, he stuck to it and he had obviously decided he wanted to divorce me.

I knew he'd been with another woman by the way he tried to evade the question. I wanted to know every detail about his affair and about the woman who had slept with my husband. *What was her name? How old was she? Where did you meet? When did you first have sex? How many times? Was the sex good? Was she better than me?*

"Stop torturing yourself," Howie had pleaded, his discomfort obvious.

"I'm not torturing myself, you're torturing me!" I yelled back.

He assured me his indiscretion was limited to just a few occasions and that it was over, which begged the question why he needed a divorce in the first place. "Neither of us has been happy for a long time," he said, and I winced against the pain his words brought. Howie seemed mildly surprised by my reaction. "Come on, Prissy," he said. "You and I both know our marriage has been dying for months, maybe even years." But I knew nothing of the sort.

I didn't sleep at all that night and lay in bed sobbing as quietly as I could into a pillow in an attempt to preserve a modicum of dignity. Howie slept in Quentin's bed and I silently cursed him for having the audacity to sleep in a warm bed when at the very least he should have slept on the sofa, the bastion of all cheating husbands. The following morning Howie left under the ruse of having to work even though it was Saturday. I knew he was lying but I wondered if he was simply too uncomfortable to be near me, or if he'd run to his mistress claiming, "I've done it. I've left her. Now we don't have to hide our love anymore."

I called my mother because I didn't know who else I could tell. I waited to hear "I told you so," even though Mom had told me no such thing. If anything, she doted on Howie so much I was convinced she was more enamoured with my husband than I was. Still, my mother was the type of person who predicted that she knew something would happen moments after she heard that the event had already occurred. *I could have told you that was gonna happen* was one of Mom's favourite catchphrases. But after barely a pause, she said only, "Come on home. We'll take care of it."

And like an obedient daughter, that's exactly what I did. By the time Howie came home from work, mine and Quentin's suitcases were packed and the arrangements were made. "It's just for a couple of weeks," I said. "I think it's best for everyone." Howie looked almost relieved.

I drive through Paradise Bay like I'm getting reacquainted with an old friend. Route 80, or The Baccalieu Trail, hugs the coast of Newfoundland, along the North Atlantic. It's dotted with tiny communities settled some 400 years earlier, its first inhabitants lured by the promise of abundant fishing grounds. It's a veritable postcard of scenic coastline, rugged cliffs and quaint cottages.

Towels, bed sheets, undershirts and tiny baby clothes stained with milk flap in the wind from clotheslines. ATVs travel on the side of the road, their helmetless drivers navigating around makeshift signs for firewood. I see Hayward's General Store up ahead and grimace, trying in vain not to recall the first time I met Howie. In neon letters the sign outside boasts the coldest beer in the Bay and claims the Atlantic Lotto Jackpot is now $3 million. I concentrate on the curve of the road and focus on finding the turnoff to my mother's house.

I wonder why it always seems to take a crisis to get back home. The last time I visited Paradise Bay was to bury my father two years earlier. Howie had driven this same route in the cold October rain while I pressed my face against the window of the rental car, feeling horribly guilty for not being there when it happened, but there was really no way of knowing. My father wasn't sick. He just ate dinner, sipped a cup of tea with my mother and then lay down on the couch to watch the local CBC newscast. He closed his eyes just before the weather forecast and never woke up.

While everyone, Mom included, took comfort in the suddenness of his death, I wished that he could have gotten sick first, not a long painful ordeal, just some warning so I could have at least come home to say goodbye.

It's suppertime when I pull up the steep driveway of my childhood home. The house is a typical saltbox with a high sloping roof in the back. It's more than a hundred years old, and never has it looked its age more than it does right now. The paint is peeling, several shingles are missing from the roof and the light fixture on the porch is rusted. I look sadly at the pair of identical rocking chairs on the back porch, recalling the way my father would sit outside on summer mornings, drinking tea and squinting out into the horizon as if he were stranded on a deserted island, waiting for a ship to rescue him.

"Are we gonna go in, or are we just gonna sit in the car all night?" Quentin asks, his irritable tone forgivable under the circumstances.

"Come on then," I say, taking a deep breath. "We'll get our bags later. I'm sure your grandmother can't wait to see you."

I try not to cry at the sight of my mother stepping out on the back porch and making her way cautiously down the steep incline of the driveway. She's trying to run toward us but her knees are swollen and her legs can't keep up. I should walk towards her and save her the trouble of having to get down the steep driveway in the first place, but my feet are stuck to the ground as if they'd taken root right on the spot.

Mom bypasses me altogether and wraps Quentin into her tight embrace. She peppers his cheeks with little kisses the way she did when he was a toddler. "How's me old trout?" she asks, before taking him into another embrace. "You're my little squishy boy." The kisses continue, on the top of his head, his cheeks, his forehead, his lips. Quentin looks like a deer caught in the headlights and I am amused by his obvious discomfort. He stands several inches above his grandmother now, and I wonder whether the height difference can be attributed to Quentin getting taller or my mother shrinking. Quentin shoots me a pleading look that begs me to rescue him from what is clearly a violation of his detached teenage demeanour.

Mom looks smaller and more fragile than I remember. She is lighter and frailer and I can see the outline of her bones in her arms and legs. I confess I don't know how old she is, even though I think it's something I ought to know. I suspect she's approaching seventy since my father was seventy-two when he died two years ago.

The wrinkles around my mother's eyes and mouth are considerably more pronounced and her once golden hair is completely and unapologetically white now. But the most striking change is in her mouth. Once full lips that smiled and kissed my young cheeks have deflated into a thin line, making her look as if she's perpetually in a foul mood. She's wearing a plain cotton housedress in a faded hue of blue gingham with her trademark knee-highs, which are nowhere near her knees, but gather loosely around her ankles instead.

"Mom," I say loudly, interrupting my mother's attack on her grandson. "It's so good to see you." I realize this is true, and the enormity of how much I've missed her hits me.

I look up at the back door, left wide open, and half expect to see Dad run down the steps and volunteer to carry the bags. It's hard to see my mother without my father by her side. Not that they were the kind of couple that did everything together. In fact, as long as I can remember, my parents never did much of anything together. Dad spent his weekends fishing and hunting and playing cards while Mom made blueberry preserves, went to Bingo every Wednesday night, and knitted sweaters and blankets, which she continues to send in the mail for Quentin even though he's too old for them. "Nothing says I'm gay like a hand-knit sweater," Quentin says whenever one of Mom's packages arrives in the mail. "Can't you just tell her to send me money?"

"Well, come on in," Mom says. "We can't be standing out here all evening giving the neighbours something to gossip about."

Since the nearest house is nearly a kilometre and a half away, I don't know what my mother means by this.

"Lord knows," she continues, "we're gonna have enough damage control with you and Quentin coming here in the first place without that piece of shit you married."

"Mom, please," I plead. "Not in front of Quentin."

She shrugs. "Well I didn't mention any names now, did I?"

"Quentin knows who I married, Mom."

"All right, all right," she says, shushing me. "I got a surprise for you but you got to come in and see it."

I enter the kitchen to the smell of something savoury roasting in the oven. I know she has cooked for me and Quentin, and I'm afraid to tell her we stopped to eat already. The smell reminds me of Sunday afternoons and a wave of nostalgia washes over me.

I love my mother's kitchen despite the fact it's outdated with its faded wallpaper, yellow laminate countertop and linoleum floor. This room holds some of my happiest childhood memories, from raucous games of 120, where my mother insisted on bidding thirty for sixty on the ace of hearts alone because she hated to lose, to my Uncle Ted playing the accordion while my Aunt Luce and my Aunt Sade danced in circles around the kitchen table. I think of my own kitchen with the stainless steel appliances and granite countertops. I don't think me and Howie and Quentin have shared a meal there in years.

"Quentin, my love, I just can't get over you," Mom says for the third time, after we've sat and tried to eat supper for a second time. "You've grown up into such a handsome young man, although with that getup you looks like you're on the welfare. Your mother never could thread a needle to save her life, but I think I can fix it for you," she says while she inspects the rip in his jeans. Quentin protectively covers the tear while my mother retrieves her sewing kit.

"It's supposed to be that way," Quentin says. "It's the way people born in this century dress."

"Quentin!" I scold. I am about to remind him that all of us were in fact born in the same century but my mother is waving a dismissive hand at me.

"It's okay," she says, smiling and drinking in the sight of her grandson. It's been two years since she's seen him and he's undergone an incredible transformation from twelve to fourteen. "You're all grown up now," Mom says, smiling at him. "Next thing ya know you'll be growing whiskers over your lip and sprouting hair on your chest. It seems like yesterday you were in diapers, running around down to the beach screaming because you thought the crab was gonna pinch your toes. Oh Lord, how you bawled that day."

My mother is chuckling to herself at the memory but Quentin fails to see the humour. "Can I watch TV?" he asks, getting up before I've had a chance to say yes or no. "Do you even have cable out here?" He disappears into the living room.

I'm nervous now that Quentin has left us since I'm sure my mother will bring up my crumbling marriage and I don't want to talk about it.

"You still take one sugar?" Mom is standing at the sink, filling up the kettle to make a pot of tea.

"Yeah, that'll be fine." I feel awkward without Quentin as a buffer, and I think my mother does too. It's hard to know what to say really. I watch her fill up two mugs with boiling water, dip a teabag into one mug and then the other. She brings the tea over to the table and lights a cigarette, inhaling deeply before blowing a puff of grey smoke into the air.

"Still haven't given those up?" I don't mean to sound judgmental, but it comes across that way.

"Oh Jesus, we're gonna start that again, are we?"

"It's just that I worry about you. Especially now that Dad is gone."

"I should be so lucky," my mother says, rolling her eyes. "Smoking won't kill me. Sure, your Aunt Fran died of lung cancer and she never smoked a day in her life. She used to make me go outside for a smoke, and the closest I got to dying was freezing to death on her back porch."

I make a face at her.

"Don't you go getting smart with me. I've been smoking for forty years and I'm still going strong, aren't I?"

I nod. Better to agree with her than to pick a fight about smoking, which I know I can't win. Mom enjoys smoking and believes the only thing wrong with cigarettes is the high price tag.

"So what's new?" I ask, as if my visit to Paradise Bay is a purely recreational one.

"Aside from your husband leaving you?" my mother asks. "Come on, Prissy, nothing ever happens around here." She inhales another deep breath of smoke. I am desperate to change the subject to something less nerve-wracking.

"How's Lottie doing?" I ask, thinking about all the sleepovers at Lottie's house when we would lie awake next to one another, giggling and laughing until our eyes became so heavy we could no longer fight it. Lottie was the closest I had to a sister and yet we've grown so far apart, I feel as if I don't know anything about her anymore.

"Lottie is fat and miserable, but I guess I'd be too if I was married to that sorry ass excuse for a husband." She exhales another breath of smoke. "Not that you made out much better in that department."

I marvel at how she can make every thread of the conversation come back to my marriage. I watch the smoke escape from her mouth and nose.

"Me and Howie are just going through a rough patch, that's all." I look down into my teacup and wonder what made people think their fates could be deciphered by the arrangement of tea leaves in the bottom of their cups. I feel my mother's eyes on me but I don't look up.

"Oh, is that what you're calling it? A rough patch?" She stubs her cigarette in the ashtray as if to accentuate her point and gets up from the table to retrieve the newspaper from the kitchen counter.

"Read this. It'll make you feel better." She looks like the proverbial cat that swallowed the canary.

I look at the copy of *The Telegram*. There is a picture of a house fire on Lemarchant Road in St. John's on the cover. "The newspaper?" I say, confused. I'm tired and I'm not in the mood to read about the state of the fishing industry or to learn about the latest round of collective bargaining between the government and its unions. "I don't want to read the paper right now."

Mom ignores me and begins leafing through the paper until she finds what she's looking for. "For your information, Prissy, I'm talking about the obits."

My curiosity is piqued. "Who died?"

My mother wears a self-satisfied smirk as she places the newspaper on the table in front of me, her yellow finger pointing to the centre of the page. "Just read that," she says triumphantly, lighting another cigarette even though she just put out one less than a few minutes earlier.

I wonder who on earth could have died to make my mother so happy. I reluctantly look at the newspaper.

*Montgomery, Howard John, 1963-2010 — Passed away
peacefully at his Toronto home. Leaving to mourn, wife Priscilla,
nee Hallorhan, of Paradise Bay, and son Quentin. Funeral
services were held Tuesday in his hometown of Barrie. In lieu of
flowers, please make donations to the Canadian Cancer Society.*

I can't believe what I've just read, so I read it again. I am so confused that I momentarily wonder if Howie died since I last saw him this morning. Then I wonder if I am living in some parallel universe where another Howard Montgomery married another Priscilla Hallorhan and had a child they named Quentin. It didn't make any sense whatsoever.

"I don't understand. Howie isn't dead," I say, dazed.

"Well, I know that, but they all don't have to know that," my mom says, gesturing to the back door. "I mean, face it, this whole town would be abuzz with how Howard took up with someone else, leaving you and Quentin all alone. Why, you'd be the laughingstock of the town. Ever since you ran off with him all those years ago, people here have been waiting for you to come home with your tail between your legs."

My mother is still talking but I've stopped listening. "You did this?" I ask incredulously. "I can't believe you did this." I am shocked, although I shouldn't be. It's just like Mom to go and do something outrageous in the name of helping.

"Of course I did it," she says, looking proud of herself. "Cost me fifty cents a word too. That's why I didn't get too detailed. But I figure the less details, the less likely we are to be found out."

We? I ask myself how and when I became a co-conspirator in my mother's ridiculous plan. "Mom, it's not a shame to get divorced anymore. People do it all the time."

"I will not have my daughter be the butt of everyone's jokes because your husband left you for someone else."

My mother has always been blunt and her words pierce through me. "Mom, I will not go along with this," I say firmly. "Howie is not dead, and for your information he did not leave me for another woman. They aren't even together anymore. He just needs some time, that's all. Look, in a few weeks all of this will be blown over and Howie will come back for me and Quentin. It's just a thing he's going through, that's all. He'll get back to normal soon," I add with a conviction I don't necessarily feel.

"Don't be foolish, Prissy, you've seen the last of Howard Montgomery." Mom snuffs out her cigarette, which isn't even half smoked, with more force than necessary. "He may as well be dead."

"No," I say adamantly. "This is stupid. This might be the stupidest thing you've ever done and that's saying something."

"Don't be that way, Prissy," my mother says, her tone softening. "I hate that he hurt you so badly and I just want to help you. Lord knows he broke my heart as well as yours when you told me what happened." She sounds so tired and mournful that I feel bad for being harsh with her. In her own way, my mother is only trying to help. I take another sip of tea and wonder what it might be like if Howie actually was dead. I'm pretty sure I'd be sad, devastated even, but I certainly wouldn't feel like a pathetic reject. Surprisingly, the thought of being widowed actually makes me feel better.

CHAPTER FOUR

Georgia

I am known around Paradise Bay and up and down the Baccalieu Trail as the fudge lady even though everyone knows my name, or at least knows of me, although not because I make fudge but for another reason entirely.

I first learned to make fudge after Joseph told me how much he had a weakness for the sweet stuff. I purchased all the ingredients and made several different batches until I was satisfied I had made the perfect fudge. It was sweet, but not overly so; it had a smooth texture, a rich colour, and it literally melted in your mouth. Joseph endorsed my efforts by eating an entire block and then insisting I make more. I thought he was just being nice, but when he began handing them out to the girls at the depot for Christmas, and other people started making requests, I knew I was on to something.

I've been selling fudge at the Paradise Bay flea market for nearly three years now and I think Joseph would be proud. I've decided to sell pie this year too since Joseph loved pie, especially in the summer with a scoop of vanilla ice cream on top. I have a mental image of Joseph mashing his fork into the pie crumbs left on his plate and then licking the tines clean, and I feel a pang of longing that leaves me lightheaded. I concentrate on creaming together butter and sugar to the right consistency. The whirl of the beaters is familiar and relaxing and has an instant calming effect that is disrupted by the shrill sound of the telephone ringing. Confused, I look up at the wall phone. I can't remember the last time I heard the sound. No one ever calls here, not anymore.

"Hello?" I answer tentatively, cradling the phone on my shoulder as I rinse my hands in the sink.

"Georgia?" My name echoes loudly in my ear.

I don't recognize the voice, although the familiarity in the way the caller addresses me assures me it is neither a telemarketer nor a wrong number. Still, I answer formally. "Yes, this is she. May I ask who's calling?"

"No need to be putting on airs. It's Clara. Clara Hallorhan," the caller says, not bothering to hide the tone of annoyance in her voice when I don't immediately respond.

She sounds slighted, as if we talked on the telephone every day around this time and I ought to be expecting her call. I don't know Clara very well, although I know who she is. Joseph went to school with her daughter, but she had moved away before I even met Joseph. I see Clara sometimes at different places around town, at the pharmacy waiting for her pills while I shop for dish detergent or paper towels, or at Lawlor's where she sometimes eats breakfast with her son. We acknowledge one another with a casual greeting but we have never really stopped to chat about anything other than when the sun might show up or if the lilacs are ever going to flower.

"Of course. What can I do for you?" I can't imagine the purpose of her call, although I don't imagine it's to exchange pleasantries.

Clara clears her throat. "I'm calling about our family tragedy that you probably read about in yesterday's paper."

I pause because I don't know what she's talking about. I stopped reading the paper after what happened to Joseph. Every time I pick up the paper I see a picture of Joseph's mangled truck, no matter what's actually on the front page.

Clara must mistake my pause for shock because she elaborates. "I know it leaves you speechless, maid. I mean, what can you say when something like this happens?"

I still don't know what she's talking about but it's obviously bad news. I steel myself for the worst but then I chide myself for my foolishness, since the worst has already happened. Still, I feel my heart quicken and my mouth go dry as my body braces for bad news as if it were trained for such moments.

"I'm sorry, Clara, I don't read the paper," I say calmly. "Maybe you could tell me what happened."

"Well, you see, my son-in-law, he's the one in Toronto. You don't get to see him much cause they pretty much keep to themselves on the mainland. Haven't seen them myself since Artie died. Listen to me going on and on," Clara chastises herself. "My son-in-law passed away the other day and Prissy and the little one are staying with me for a little while, until she gets back on her feet and all."

I fight the urge to cry, even though I've only met Prissy and her husband once. It had to be ten years ago now when Joseph and I ran into them on the beach during an afternoon walk. Prissy smiled and hugged Joseph the way you embrace a friend that you haven't seen in a long time. I couldn't help but feel a tinge of jealousy when I saw this young beautiful woman, with sand in her fingernails and droplets of salt water sticking to the fine hairs of her arms, touch my husband in what I thought was an intimate manner. The little boy was hurling rocks into the ocean and Prissy was trying to teach him how to skip the rocks. Her husband was watching them with such a look of contentment on his face that I had an awful feeling come over me. It was the same feeling I had when Joseph wrestled with me in the yard until he pinned me underneath the maple tree and nuzzled the side of my neck with his warm breath in a way that left me shaking with desire. True contentment is fleeting and can only be followed by tragedy on the grandest scale. I have that horrible feeling again, not quite as raw, but enough to make my head hurt.

"Oh my God," I whisper, and I have to sit down at the kitchen table because my feet are too weak to support my weight. I am barely aware of the way my fingers grip the telephone receiver or the way my breath now comes in quick shallow pants, in time with the beat of my racing heart.

"Oh, Clara, I'm so sorry," I say, and my eyes well up in spite of my effort to keep the tears at bay, at least until I can hang up. "Can I do anything? How's Prissy holding up?"

I hated when people asked me that after Joseph died. Short of bringing Joseph back from the dead, no one could possibly do anything to ease the pain, and yet here I am, asking the same stupid questions. A sob escapes from the back of my throat.

"Jesus, Georgia. Sure, you're taking it worse than Prissy."

I take several deep breaths to calm myself.

"She's doing all right, all things considered. My daughter is strong and her priority right now is Quentin."

"Of course," I concur but I can only imagine. Joseph and I never had a child, so without that responsibility, I was free to spiral into a deep depression. "How is your grandson holding up?"

"Quentin? He's fourteen now, and he's bigger than me and Prissy. Truthfully he's having a lot of problems. He hasn't quite accepted it yet. He still thinks his father is alive and well in Toronto. Still in denial, I suppose."

I empathize since I know denial better than anyone. "What happened?" I ask.

"It was the cancer," Clara replies. "He put up a good fight, but in the end it was just too much. It's a horrible disease."

I wonder if it's worse to lose your husband slowly to cancer or to lose him suddenly, the way I lost Joseph. I mentally weigh the pros and cons and I can't decide. On the one hand, losing someone suddenly blindsides you and you spend countless days in a state of utter shock. I remember Joseph heading out the door, giving me a playful wink and promising not to be too late, and then the next time I saw him he was cold and pale and lifeless. But then again, I consider, it must be awfully hard to watch a man weaken and die before your eyes. At least I'll always remember Joseph as being big and strong and healthy.

"Howard was a very proud man," Clara continues. "He didn't want anyone to know he had any weakness whatsoever. Sure, he was at stage three before he even told Prissy what was going on. By that time, it was too late. All they could do was make him comfortable."

"What kind of cancer was it?" I ask, because I think this is what everyone seems to ask once cancer is mentioned.

"It was testicular cancer," Clara says after a pause. "They took the left testicle but by the time they caught it, it had spread to the right one. The poor bastard died with no balls at all."

It sounds like a peculiar thing to say but I know firsthand how grief can impair your judgment and make you say and do things you never dreamed of.

"Anyway," Clara continues, "he's dead and buried and there's no need to be talking about it now, although I'm sure we'll be having a small memorial service in the next week or so, so people around here can pay their respects. But it's Prissy I got to worry about now, which is why I'm calling. I thought maybe it'd be good if Prissy could talk to someone who's been through it all before. Maybe she could help you out at the flea market every now and then. Good to get her up and about, you know what I mean."

"Of course," I answer softly. "I'd love to see her … we could talk about things." By the time I hang up I am regretting my decision to talk to Prissy about being a widow since I don't think I'm in any position to help anyone. I am only just starting to let go of some of my grief and I'm afraid that being around Prissy might make me feel the rawness of it all over again.

I glance at the window to my cooling pies and feel the familiar ache in my chest. Strawberry-rhubarb pie was Joseph's favourite, and every time I make it now I can't help but remember the way he'd come home in the middle of the afternoon telling me he could smell that pie all the way from the depot. And then he'd cut himself a slice and eat it up in three bites before giving me a peck on the cheek with his berry-stained lips and heading back to work. I never told Joseph those visits were the highlight of my day and I wonder why not.

When he died I baked strawberry-rhubarb pie every day for weeks and placed them on the table to cool. I'd sit at the kitchen table and wait for him to come barrelling through the front door demanding I cut him a sliver, which by Joseph's definition was nearly one quarter of the pie. I'd sit there, motionless, in my stained apron for hours, listening for his truck to pull in the driveway and staring at the front door for him. I'd stay that way until it got dark, and then I'd get up from my perch in the kitchen and throw the pies in the deep freeze before washing up for the night. In the bathroom, I'd take the cap off Joseph's cologne and hold the bottle underneath my nose, sniffing in his scent. I'd dab the cologne behind my ears so I could smell him on me. Then I'd head on over to the bedroom and peel back the covers. I'd lie down in his spot because I couldn't bear for his side of the bed to be cold, and then I'd bury my face in his pillow and cry. The following day I would do it all over again.

I lost any desire to look after myself. I went almost two weeks without showering, or even brushing my teeth. As far as I was concerned, there was no point to anything anymore. Joseph was gone, the funeral was over, and all I wanted was to wallow in my own self-pity. People came by to check on me and bring me food but the visits were nothing more than annoying interruptions to the misery that I couldn't wait to get back to. I made them uncomfortable with my dishevelled appearance and the way I politely apologized that I couldn't offer them a slice of pie because I was saving it for Joseph. Only the most steadfast continued to knock on my door, but after a while even they gave up trying to engage me in idle conversations about Mildred Peach's blueberry preserves or Ches Crocker's two broken vertebrae from his fall on the ice.

I spent my days crying over the things Joseph and I talked about but would never do, things like drive across the country and spend at least one night in each province, see Joseph's beloved Maple Leafs win the Stanley Cup, witness the birth of our children. I cried over all the holidays that were yet to come, Christmases, birthdays and Easters that I'd be alone. Sometimes, completely out of the blue, I would think about all the times I yelled at him for leaving his dirty plate on the coffee table, and the guilt would wash over me like a tidal wave and render me incapable of even getting out of bed.

It was like that for so long, I lost track of the days. They were all the same anyway so what did it matter whether it was Sunday or Friday? Then I lost track of the months. I nibbled on stale crackers and dry cereal. Three days after I'd eaten the last tin of tomato soup from the pantry, I ventured all the way into St. John's for groceries instead of trudging over the hill to Hayward's so I could avoid the sympathetic looks. At a mammoth Sobey's on Ropewalk Lane, I purchased all of Joseph's favourite foods, double-stuffed Oreo cookies, pork and beans and frozen breakfast sausages — all items I never allowed in the house when he was alive. It's bad for you, I'd scold him, and yet he was dead all the same.

On the way back home I stopped for what I thought might be an accident since I counted four cars parked on the shoulder of the road. My palms grew sweaty at the thought of seeing twisted metal, broken glass and worse, but it wasn't an accident at all. It was Fred Bishop, larger than life and selling turnip greens, potatoes, carrots and other produce out of the back of his pickup truck on the Trans Canada Highway.

I stopped and stared and felt my hands shake with anger. That Fred Bishop had the audacity to park his truck and make a profit not three kilometres away from the place where he killed my husband made me seethe with anger. I wanted him put in jail, locked up, but the police told me he wasn't culpable. It was an accident, they said, but it didn't make a bit of difference to me.

I know that Joseph would scold me for laying the blame on Fred, since Joseph would have forgiven Fred anything, even his own death. They were best friends, practically brothers. Their fathers crewed on the same fishing boat, and their mothers would get together for tea and sandwiches daily. They were on odd pair. Where Joseph was lean and muscular, Fred had poor posture and a slight bulge of belly fat. Joseph was blessed with a crown of golden hair, whereas Fred was bald, save for the semi-circle of dark hair that framed the back of his head. Joseph was everything Fred wasn't and yet there were no apparent jealousies. "He's my best bud," Joseph would say of Fred, and Fred of Joseph. "He's got a heart of gold, give ya the shirt off his back, he would. You'll never meet a nicer man."

At first I didn't know why I didn't share my husband's enthusiasm for his best friend. Fred wasn't like most annoying male friends. He never drank heavy volumes of beer, didn't encourage Joseph to spend more time away from me, never made crude comments about the female anatomy, and he hardly ever showed up unannounced. In fact, he was quite the opposite. Fred apologized for interrupting whenever he called; he was overly polite, almost formal around me. I thought maybe he was jealous that I was monopolizing all of Joseph's time, but it turns out I was the jealous one. I grew tired of hearing every sentence begin with, *Remember the time when* ... and ending with fits of laughter and some comment on those being the good old days, as if the present fell short of the life Joseph used to lead before he met me. I resented the fact that Fred knew what Joseph was like as a boy, that he had accumulated more shared memories than I did, had countless shared jokes, and held a shared frame of reference that was lost on me.

But most of all, I hated that Fred was the last person to see Joseph alive. It was Fred who got to ride the ambulance with Joseph, hold his hand, and hear his last words when it should have been me. By the time I got to the hospital, all I got was a corpse.

When I saw Fred selling produce out of the back of his pickup truck, my first inclination was to run to him, hit him and scream and rail at having killed my husband. I wanted to do it at the funeral, but I held my emotions in check out of respect for Joseph. But I could not resist any longer and I got out of the car, slammed the door shut and ran screaming toward him.

"What the hell do you think you're doing?" I yelled, knowing all the while I was making a scene. People stopped sifting through bunches of carrots to stare at me, my face red and filled with anger.

"What are you doing here, Georgia?" Fred's tone was curt and I was incensed that he had the nerve to act as if I was doing something inappropriate. "You should go home," he said, the way an angry parent might speak to a child.

"No, you should go home," I screamed, near hysterics.

Fred bit his lip as if he were thinking about the best way to phrase something. "I think it's best for you to go back to St. John's. You don't need to be running into me any more than I need to be running into you." I could scarcely believe he had the audacity to tell me to leave when it was he, I thought, who should be banished from Paradise Bay.

Still, I turned and left and I could almost feel Fred's sigh of relief on the back of my neck, but the following day I returned with fifty bricks of fudge that I placed in a box with a *Homemade Fudge for Sale* sign I scribbled in black marker. He was so angry when he saw me his face turned a shade of purple.

"Go the fuck home out of it, Georgia, and stop tormenting me. I'm just trying to make a living!"

I looked him straight in the eye and told him that I would be there every day to remind him of what he'd taken from me. I expected him to yell some profanity back at me, to call me something awful that might drive me out of town, but he grew silent instead and I could almost see the anger leave his body, and in its place was despair that might have matched my own. He adjusted the brim of his baseball cap and cracked a few knuckles.

"You don't have to remind me. I think about it every God-damned minute of every day."

And then he left. He got back in his truck and drove away with a cab filled with fresh produce that would probably rot in the sun, leaving me alone on the side of the Trans Canada Highway with a box of melting fudge. I stayed in my car for four hours watching traffic drive by before I went home, defeated. But I returned the following day and so did Fred, filled with new determination. He ignored me and I him.

From the locals we attracted curious stares and plenty of gossip. But at the end of the day, I was always sold out. It was this fact that lit a fire under the entrepreneurial spirits of the residents of Paradise Bay. One particularly chilly summer morning, Ellie Briggs showed up with a box of hand-knit sweaters, which sold within a few hours. Others followed. It seemed everyone in Paradise Bay had something to peddle: placemats, woollen socks, jarred fruit preserves and bird-houses in the style of a St. John's row house. The police threatened to shut down the impromptu marketplace, claiming it was causing traffic jams. I figured it would be the end of it, but Fred had the Paradise Bay flea market, as he called it, moved to Powers' Field. He lobbied the transportation minister to put up two signs on the Trans Canada Highway, at the exit to Route 80 near Whitbourne, and another at the Veterans Memorial Highway. He even managed to coax the tourism minister to put it in the visitor's guide, and this year he applied and received a grant to buy open-air tents so that it could go ahead regardless of the weather.

It was the flea market that finally got me motivated about something after Joseph died, albeit for all the wrong reasons. I mimicked Fred's easygoing nature and made conversation with perfect strangers about the weather, the fishery and all sorts of nonsense that I could not have cared less about. To anyone, I must appear perfectly normal, a young woman who experienced a terrible tragedy but had the strength to build a new life.

I wonder if this is what Clara thinks of me, the way she asked me to speak to Prissy. I haven't got the heart to tell Clara that most of the time I only pretend, that I return home from the flea market most days cloaked in the silence of the living room. There is no one here to ask me how my day was, or to cajole into picking up the fish and chips, or to pass commentary on the news. It is an existence so sad and miserable, and so incredibly lonely, that I wonder what I was thinking in agreeing to talk to Prissy. How am I to help her get over her own grief when I can't even get past my own?

CHAPTER FIVE

Prissy

I pull the covers over my head and turn toward the wall in an effort to block out the noonday sun. I wish it was raining or drizzling outside, but the sun is shining so brightly, I can see the dust swirling around in the streaks of light that filter through the muslin drapes.

I am in my childhood bedroom, which makes me feel like a child again since my mother has done little to change it, despite the fact I have been gone for more than fifteen years. The walls are painted a softer shade of yellow, and the posters of playful kittens have been removed, but everything else is the same. Raggedy Anne is propped against the folded patchwork quilt that my mother and I made together the winter I caught chicken pox and the flu, one right after the other. Aside from a rustic shelf displaying a certificate of achievement in poetry, yellowed now with age, the walls are bare. I try to nestle deeper under the covers but my hair snags in the wicker headboard and I have to sit up to untangle myself.

I catch sight of the alarm clock. It's 12:02 pm and I glance at the doorway, expecting my mother to come barging through at any moment to take me to task for wallowing in self-pity till lunchtime. It's only 10:30 am in Toronto, and I vow to use this fact in my defence when my mother comes yelling at me. I know I need to get my act together, especially for Quentin, but all I can think about is that Howie doesn't love me anymore, and it strikes me with an intensity that feels like an explosion inside my chest.

I sit on the edge of the bed to study my reflection in the mirror.

My eyes are swollen from crying half the night and the dark circles under my eyes make me look gaunt, but I know they're only temporary and will subside once I get a good night's sleep. All in all, I know I've aged relatively well, although at thirty-five, I'm still too young to feel the full effects of time's wrath. My skin possesses barely a wrinkle, and I've never had to colour my hair. The style could use an update but I like being able to pull it back into a youthful ponytail or secure it loosely with a clip. Howie told me it was my smile that first bewitched him, and I try to replicate it now, but my lips tremble instead and I erupt into a new round of tears.

Howie didn't have an affair because I'd grown too fat or let myself go. I imagine he was just bored with me. "Oh God, what am I going to do?" I whisper to my reflection as if I were confiding to someone real, someone capable of dispensing sound advice. The enormity of my predicament is only now starting to sink in. I have no career, no work experience and no college degree to fall back on.

I'm not exactly well-versed in legal doctrine, but I know I'm probably entitled to some form of financial compensation from Howie. He said as much the night he asked me for a divorce, as if that might make everything better, which is precisely why I don't want it. I have something to prove now and I feel something slight stir inside me that I recognize as motivation. I'll need to find a job, open a bank account and buy an RRSP. I will show Howie exactly how capable I can be without him. I don't know why but this thought brings a fresh wave of tears.

I hear the phone ring, but I ignore it. It has been ringing on and off since eight this morning, as has the doorbell. I can't remember my mother ever being so popular, but I remind myself that this is Paradise Bay, where people are always dropping in on one another. I lie back down and try to shut out the ringing.

"Prissy!" my mother calls from downstairs. "Phone for you. It's Howard."

My heart jumps in my throat and I dart out of bed so fast, I feel slightly dizzy. I run out into the hallway and sit at the old telephone table. It strikes me as oddly fascinating that there was a time not so long ago when people purchased furniture specifically so they could sit and talk on the phone, and have a place to store the monolithic telephone books published by the phone company. The table is only fifty or so years old and already a relic. A week ago I had thought much the same of my husband. I stare for a moment at the shiny black rotary telephone and take a moment to catch my breath. The telephone receiver feels heavy in my hands.

"Hello," I say, trying my best to sound cheerful, as if I'd just been sitting around the kitchen table chatting and laughing and catching up with family and friends. My heart is suddenly beating faster and I can feel the beads of perspiration form under my arms and in the spot between my breasts.

"Prissy," Howie says evenly. "You were supposed to call me when you got in yesterday. I have been trying to reach you all morning, but obviously you don't have your cell on."

I feel a little bit like a child being reprimanded. "I'm sorry," I say. "Airport security asked me to turn it off when I got on the plane and I must have forgotten to turn it back on."

I start to pick at the same corner of wallpaper I did sixteen years earlier when Howie and I talked so long on the phone my parents would have to yell at me to hang up. But that was back when long distance calls were a luxury reserved for holidays and birthdays, and when telephone etiquette dictated that the receiver of the call end the conversation with the phrase, "I'd better let you go. This must be costing you a fortune."

"How's Quentin doing?" Howie asks in a tone filled with fatherly concern, to which I feel a prickle of annoyance, since this is all his fault in the first place.

"He's great," I answer defensively, but I offer no details since I've been too preoccupied with my own misery to inquire after my child's. I picture Quentin, probably still asleep in my brother's old bedroom.

There's an uncomfortable pause, at which point I study the brown stripes on the wallpaper. I am waiting for Howie to say something. Specifically I am waiting for him to admit that he was a fool, that he loves me, and to beg me to take him back.

"When are you coming home?" he finally asks, and just as I am contemplating whether to make him suffer by staying a few more days or to get back on the next plane, I can hear Mom's voice echoing from the phone in the kitchen.

"She is home, you sonofabitch," my mother says.

"Mom, will you please hang up!" I yell, feeling like a teenager again. I wait until I can hear the click of the kitchen phone being placed back onto the receiver before continuing. "I just got in last night, Howie. What is all this about?" I am positive he must miss me terribly and I am barely aware I'm holding my breath.

"It's just that you left rather … abruptly and we didn't get a chance to talk about the arrangement." Howie sighs like he is about to say something but doesn't know quite how to phrase it. "Look, I know that you want to be home with your family right now and you have every right to, but we have to deal with this eventually. I need to know that we have an understanding … something in place to make sure that … I have Quentin's best interests at heart right now and I need to feel that he knows he can come home any time."

I am stunned because I'm pretty certain Howie is trying to say he doesn't want me to steal his child. I am shocked, disappointed and angry all at the same time. I think about all the things I want to say, but I don't trust myself to speak so I just place the receiver gently back in its place because I'm simply feeling too defeated to slam phones or kick walls.

I am crying heavily again, barely able to breathe through my own sobs. I can hear Mom climb up the stairs, cursing her bad hip with every step, and I wipe my tears away, annoyed at my mother, of all people, for the intrusion. I just want to be left alone to wallow in self-pity, and the mere thought of my mother telling me to forget about him, as if he were just another bad date rather than my husband of sixteen years, makes me cringe.

"Come on, Prissy, I'll have none of that," Mom yells from the landing. She is too winded to make it any farther and I feel guilty for being the cause of her discomfort. "I told you you're better off without him," she continues. "Quentin needs his mother to be strong right now, Prissy, so stop wasting good tears on the likes of that no good sonofabitch and come down here or else I'll drag you down myself."

The last thing I want to do is go downstairs but I'm afraid my mother will make good on her promise, so I yell down to her, "I'll be right down," in a high-pitched, shaky voice. It seems to work because I hear the wood on the stairs squeaking under her slippered feet.

Reluctantly, I pull on a pair of sweatpants and an old sweater and make my way downstairs, but I am not prepared for what awaits.

To my astonishment there are stacks and stacks of casserole dishes on the kitchen counter, and on the kitchen table. Quentin is helping himself to a rather large plate of what looks like chicken pot pie and my mother is sampling cocktail weenies out of a crock-pot. A fully cooked turkey is covered in plastic wrap in the middle of the kitchen table. There is enough food to feed an entire town on the countertop alone.

"What is all this?" I ask. At first I think Mom must be helping out with St. Augustine's annual turkey tea, but I don't see the divided styrofoam trays, and I know for a fact that lasagna does not come with a turkey tea.

"Well, look who it is," my mother says in mock surprise. "C'mere. Try one of these." She waves a cocktail weenie in front of my face. "Come on, they're nice and tangy."

I gulp down the weenie and work hard at keeping it down. Mom is watching my face for my reaction. "It's good," I lie, although I might care more for it on another day when the mere thought of food doesn't make me nauseated. "Mom, what's going on here?"

"Oh, nothing really," she answers, but she averts her gaze so I know immediately that it is definitely something.

"It's just that a handful of people came by to pass on their condolences, that's all," Mom says dismissively. "We got plenty more in the fridge." She hands me a plate and a fork. "Eat the potato salad first. That's most likely to go bad."

"Oh no," I say, shaking my head at the realization. "You mean this is for Howie?" I mouth the question to her so Quentin won't hear, although he seems so absorbed in his chicken I'm not sure he's even aware I'm in the room.

"No," my mother objects. "Howie is dead so how can it be for him?" She says this as if she really believes her son-in-law has just lost his battle with cancer. "This is for you and Quentin now."

I look around the kitchen at all the Tupperware containers with the names of the owners printed in masking tape along the sides and on the lids. On top of the microwave, there is a neat pile of sympathy cards with my name on the envelopes. I am both horrifically appalled and genuinely touched. "Mom, this is wrong. I can't accept all this." My eyes are beginning to well up again. I hardly know these people anymore and yet it seems that every single member of the community has selflessly contributed to the bounty before me.

"Sure you can," Mom says. "When you taste some of Georgia's homemade fudge, you won't be able to think about anything except how it melts in your mouth. She was kind enough to bring over a big batch this morning and she's also agreed to take you under her wing for a little while. Maybe you could help her out at the flea market."

There's a cloud of confusion over my head, since I have no idea who Georgia is or why she might be interested in taking me under her wing. "Who is Georgia?"

When my mother tells me she is Joseph Reid's wife, I can picture her immediately from the time we met along the beach all those years ago. She had the palest skin and the blackest hair I'd ever seen and she put me in mind of an English heroine from a nineteenth century novel.

"Why on earth is Georgia taking me under her wing?" I ask, but I already know what my mother is getting at.

"Because you're both young widows and she knows what you're going though."

"How does Georgia know what I'm going through?" I ask, exasperated. "Her husband died and mine just left me!"

"Don't be nasty to me. I'm only trying to help," my mother answers defensively. She opens each Tupperware container and sniffs the contents. "Georgia sells fudge at the flea market and she says she's going to sell pies this year too. You're going to need someplace to go every day, Prissy, or else you'll be lying in that bed feeling sorry for yourself."

I try to think of an excuse to get out of flea market duty — other than the fact that I'm not a widow — but I can't think that far ahead. I just wanted to come here for a few days to let the news of Howie's announcement sink in and to gather some composure, and now my mother has me widowed and selling fudge in the middle of Powers' Field.

My mother wrinkles her nose at a container of baked beans. "Those'll give you the shits for sure," she mumbles, although she places a spoonful of them on my plate all the same. She piles fried chicken next to the beans and a heap of potato salad and macaroni and cheese.

Surprisingly, my stomach grumbles in response. I haven't eaten much of anything over the past two days and I am only now realizing just how hungry I am. I am gnawing on a chicken wing when my brother Charlie appears in the back door of the kitchen.

When he sees me, he runs to me, giving me a bear hug that leaves me gasping for breath. I laugh with genuine joy and hug him back. He looks the same as I remember, long and lean. His hair is the same golden shade as my own and nearly the same length. He's grown a goatee, which lends him a slightly dangerous air, although anyone who knows Charlie knows he is completely harmless. That he looks happy to see me surprises me almost as much as my own joy at seeing him.

"Hey, Miss Priss," Charlie says, and I smile back at him, nostalgic for the nickname I despised growing up. "How the fuck are ya?"

My brother has a foul mouth but not in a bad way, if that's possible. He doesn't tell people to fuck off or to go fuck themselves. Charlie uses the f-word more or less as a universal adjective to describe just about everything. It's either fuckin hot out or fuckin cold; he claims to be fuckin hungry or fuckin tired; he complains about never having enough fuckin money, and when he sits at the table to eat he's likely to ask you to pass the fuckin salt. After a while you don't notice, but then I hear Quentin snicker and I know he's laughing at the profanity. I think about telling Charlie to watch his mouth around Quentin, but I know it's never going to happen. It's just the way Charlie speaks.

If Charlie is surprised to see all the food laid out, he doesn't show it. He simply helps himself to a plate and begins piling an array of food on it. "I'm so fuckin starved I could eat the leg off the lamb of God right now," he says between bites of a buttered roll and a turkey leg. I forget he's one of those people with an incredible metabolism. He's downright scrawny and yet his plate is overflowing with rich foods. He would eat the entire tray of fudge for dessert if my mother would let him. I think my son looks like Charlie when he was the same age, and this thought makes me smooth my brother's hair lovingly. Charlie looks suspiciously at me and I can tell that the one gesture of affection has made him uncomfortable.

"How ya holding up, Priss?" Charlie asks. He looks sorry for me, which makes me feel completely pathetic. I am, after all, the big sister, the mature, sensible sibling.

"Whatever," I say, trying to belittle it by making a face. I try to laugh it off, and I wave a dismissive hand, as if being left by my husband of sixteen years was the best thing that could have happened to me, like losing a job I hated in the first place.

"I can't believe that about Howie," says Charlie, obviously not getting my hint that I don't want to talk about it. "I mean, when Mom told me I was like, 'No fuckin way!' But what can you do? I bet it wasn't the first time either. He's probably been cheating on you for years." Charlie's words put a hasty end to my appetite and I push the plate away.

My mother swoops in for my defence, giving Charlie a slap on the back of his head that echoes off the walls of the kitchen. "What the hell is wrong with you? I swear, Charlie, sometimes I think you have shit for brains. This is why you don't have a girlfriend, because you haven't got the first clue how to talk to a woman."

"It's okay, Mom. Just forget it. Please." I hate having it talked about at the kitchen table and I want to talk about anything else in the world except this.

"I didn't mean anything bad by it," Charlie says.

I take a sip of warm tea so I have something to do with my hands. "It's okay," I say again. "I really don't want to talk about it anymore."

Charlie looks like he's more than happy to let it drop, and he resumes shovelling forkfuls of potato salad into his mouth. "So how long you sticking around for?"

I wonder why everyone has to ask me that question. I recall my telephone conversation with Howie and fight the wave of nausea, which is made more difficult by the smells of so much food. I concentrate on my hands, fingering my engagement ring and wedding band.

Howie had surprised me with the engagement ring on board the tour boat he chartered for a whale watching excursion. In front of all my family and friends he sank down on one knee and then a wave hit the side of the boat and he went "arse over kettle," as my father would have said, before he had the chance to reveal the diamond. He endured a boatload of ribbing and laughter at his lack of sea legs, but in the end he managed to get down on one knee and ask me to marry him. There was a chorus of oohs and ahhs, but I remember the singsong sound of the humpbacks the most, urging me to say yes, as if there was ever any doubt. I was the happiest I'd ever been in my life and I never imagined this day would ever come.

"Stop crying now, Prissy," Mom says, although until that point I wasn't even aware that I was crying. "You'll feel better after the memorial service. The Reverend promised me a tasteful tribute."

"A memorial service?" I repeat dumbly. "What memorial service?" But I already know what my mother has planned and I cringe at the mere idea.

"Oh, it's just a quiet service, Prissy," she says. "A few friends is all. I already picked out the hymns and Barb Donovan is going to sing 'Amazing Grace.' That one's got a voice like an angel."

My mother continues to amaze me. She's always loved Howie dearly, fussing over him at every chance she could get. Part of me even feared telling her about my failed marriage in the first place, in the chance that my mother would somehow lay the blame with me, and yet she's done nothing of the sort. She has simply snubbed out Howie's very existence and I actually find the gesture touching in a perverse way.

"Mom, I appreciate what you're trying to do, but you have to tell the Reverend, and everyone else for that matter, the truth. I feel terribly guilty already just for eating this potato salad that someone made for me out of sympathy."

"Sure, that's nothing," Charlie says between bites of what looks like quiche. "I heard down to the post office this morning that they were thinking about donating the collection from this Sunday's service to Priss and Quentin."

"Can we get X-Box here?" Quentin asks, his face beaming with hope since I refused to let him pack up the one from his bedroom to bring on the plane. It was the one thing he was upset about, not that his parents' marriage was shot, or that we were en route to Newfoundland, but that he was going to be without X-Box for the next couple of weeks.

I am mortified by a collection being gathered for me, more than I can possibly imagine. "Oh, God, no," I mutter, hanging my head in shame. "Mom, please, you have to straighten this out."

Judging by the look on her face, she is not going to yield. "Christ have mercy," she says, not bothering to mask her tone of annoyance. "Why do you have to be so ungrateful?" She takes a seat at the kitchen table and lights another cigarette, exhaling two lines of smoke from her nose. "Everything I have done has been to protect you and Quentin, and all you can do is sit there and act all high and mighty. I am trying to salvage what's left of your life and the least you could do is say thank you."

My mother is genuinely upset with me and I feel hopeless. I can't seem to please anyone these days. "Thank you," I whisper in defeat. I have been home less than twenty-four hours and already I am in a bigger mess than when I arrived.

CHAPTER SIX

Lottie

I think Ches is having an affair, but I don't care one way or the other. I try to make myself feel all the emotions I should — shock, anger, betrayal, hurt — but I don't feel any of them. If anything, I feel the slightest bit relieved that at least he's out of the bed and planning to get out of the house and I don't have to listen to him whine about the pain in his back or the pounding in his head.

He hasn't come out and said he's having an affair but I can't think of any other reason for his appearance this morning. I hardly recognize him standing before me. He's shaved for the first time in a month and he smells of either soap or cologne, I'm not sure which. Whatever it is, it is definitely not the stench of stale cigarettes that I have come to associate with Ches. He's wearing brown trousers and a fisherman's sweater I purchased for him at the flea market last year.

"Where the hell are you off to?" I ask suspiciously.

"St. John's," he says, and I know that something is up because Ches hates driving around St. John's with its trafficked streets and stoplights. He's carrying his tool box, a large, awkward metal rectangle which he opens now to retrieve a handful of tools. I am too surprised to say anything as Ches moves about the house, fixing all the things I've been asking him to fix for months. He tightens the cold water faucet at the kitchen sink so I no longer have to hear the incessant drip of water against steel. He tightens the doorknob of our bedroom, applies weather stripping to the front door to keep out the draft and replaces the light bulb in the refrigerator. This only serves as proof of his infidelity, for why else would Ches do something for me other than guilt?

When he finishes he jingles his keys in his pocket. "Well, I'm gonna go now," he says and I think I hear the slightest tremor in his voice. I sense his nervousness, which I interpret as first-time jitters. I think about questioning him about his intentions, imploring him to think about what he's about to do, but I don't say anything.

"Okay, go on then."

"Don't wait up for me," he says as he leaves, which I think is a strange thing to say since it's only nine-thirty in the morning and I wouldn't wait up for him in the first place. Oddly, he's taken his toolbox with him, and he stops at the front door to stare at a school picture of Marianne hanging in the hallway.

I am alone in the house now and despite my best efforts to enjoy the solitude, I am lonely. I decide to make Prissy some macaroni and cheese and stop by to pass on my condolences. I know Prissy loves macaroni and cheese because that's all she ever asked her mom to make whenever I stayed over there for dinner. Prissy used to insert the elbows on the tines of her fork and dip them in ketchup, which meant it took her forever to eat a plate, and by the time she got halfway through, it was freezing cold. I figure her tastes are a little fancier now so I get to work on a recipe I tore from a woman's magazine in the doctor's office. I grate three different kinds of cheese until the skin on my knuckles is scraped from the dull blade of the cheese grater. I make a roux from flour and butter, simmer whole milk and then melt the cheese before pouring the sauce over the elbow macaroni and placing it in the oven for thirty-five minutes, until the top is brown and the sauce bubbles.

I think a lot about Prissy while the casserole is baking. I'm trying to summon sympathy for her loss, but I'm finding it hard in the same way I'm finding it hard to be jealous that Ches is having an affair. I think I must be emotionally stunted since I can't feel anything I'm supposed to. I love Prissy like a sister, but at the same time I've always been envious of her. Prissy was blessed in ways I could only imagine. She was pretty and thin regardless of what she ate, and it seemed to me that Prissy possessed a horseshoe or a rabbit's foot or some other omen of good luck. That she'd managed to screw a complete stranger in the snack aisle at Hayward's was one thing. That he would turn out to be well off, handsome and completely smitten was something only Prissy could pull off. Even though she's lost Howie, I'm fairly certain that he was the type of person to take care of things and make sure that she and Quentin were financially secure. If Ches died, I can't imagine the mess he would leave behind for me to sort out.

When the macaroni and cheese has cooled sufficiently to handle with my bare hands, I walk it over to Prissy's house. It's hotter out than I anticipated and by the time I make it up the steep hill to the back door, I am sweating and slightly out of breath.

Clara greets me at the door, a cigarette in one hand and a damp dish towel hung over her shoulder. As she inhales deeply from her cigarette, her cheeks deflate and her lips disappear. "Hello Lottie," she says. "I figured you'd be stopping by today."

"I made some macaroni and cheese. It's for Prissy," I clarify, as if I were in the habit of stopping by Clara's on a regular basis bearing trays of food.

"Someone already brought macaroni and cheese earlier," Clara says, "but we could always use more, I suppose."

"There's three different kinds of cheeses in this," I say defensively, eyeing my scraped knuckles. "It's not Kraft dinner, you know."

"What's wrong with Kraft dinner? I made Kraft dinner for you and Prissy many times and you didn't complain."

Clara intimidates me the same way she did when I was a child. "I didn't say there was anything wrong with Kraft dinner," I stammer. "I just thought Prissy might like to have something fancier."

"Prissy is still the same person she always has been, Lottie," Clara says as she stubs her cigarette on the back porch and relieves me of the heavy glass baking dish. "But I'm sure she'd love to try this fancy macaroni of yours."

"Can I see her?"

Clara shakes her head doubtfully. "Not today, I don't imagine. Prissy is very upset as you can well imagine. I don't think she's up for visitors quite yet. Sure, she aint even out of the bed."

I swallow hard. I used to be Prissy's best friend. It should be me protectively ushering people away from the door. "Of course," I whisper. "Please pass on my condolences." I turn to go down the hill feeling heavier than I did on the way over, despite having been relieved of the heavy glass baking dish.

Back home, I am feeling uncharacteristically lazy. I change into Ches' plaid bathrobe that he never wears, so it doesn't smell like him, and make a pot of tea. It's only one thirty in the afternoon and it feels like I've been up for days. I watch Drew Carey invite another contestant to bid on a set of golf clubs on *The Price is Right*. I try to play along with the games but I'm way off since a tin of soup is so much cheaper in California compared with what I have to pay at Hayward's. I think about what Ches would say if he were here. Most likely he would pass comment on the models, describing one as a fine piece of ass and the other as having a nice rack.

I overbid on a refrigerator and think about all the things I ought to be doing instead of sitting around watching game shows, so I go into the kitchen to tackle the sinkful of dirty dishes. There is cheese all over the kitchen floor and flour all over the countertop. I am about to crumple up the recipe, since I don't imagine wanting to make macaroni and cheese from scratch anymore, when I notice the article on the other side.

Spoil Yourself — Today!, it says in bold type. There's a photograph of a woman soaking in a tub, surrounded by softly lit candles. Her intimate parts are concealed by soapy bubbles and a washcloth is folded over her eyes. I roll my eyes at the picture since I can't imagine indulging in such extravagant, almost sinful, behaviour. I think of my own bathroom with the rust stains on the tub and the mildew that I can never get out of the grout no matter how hard I scrub.

I think about my sister who lives in Calgary with our parents and her husband. I've never been there but my mother tells me about my sister's Jacuzzi tub at almost every opportunity. My sister did all the right things in the right order: college, career, marriage, house and kids. I've done all the wrong things at all the wrong times so I can hardly blame my parents for moving in with my sister in Calgary instead of sticking around Paradise Bay. I don't blame my parents for leaving, but I miss them, or at least the idea of them, especially when I see pairs of mothers and daughters wandering around town together, shopping for groceries or stopping by Lawlor's for a sandwich and a cup of tea. In reality I know if my parents stayed in Paradise Bay, we'd be doing none of those things together. They have never forgiven me for getting pregnant and marrying Ches even as they pretend they did. In every hello there is judgement that floats from their breath like a feather escaping from the lining of a pillow.

It's almost four in the afternoon when the police knock on my door. The faces on the officers are grim and I know they are about to deliver bad news that will change my life forever. My ears are ringing and my mouth is dry and I have to hold the door to keep from falling. I feel the tears come before they can even tell me what's happened. When they tell me Ches is dead, I cry tears of relief that it isn't Marianne.

CHAPTER SEVEN

Georgia

I hate funerals, which makes me something of an anomaly as far as the population of Paradise Bay goes. Here, funerals are akin to great social events and family reunions. Long-lost relatives fly in, not to mourn, but as an excuse to catch up with everyone left behind. There are plenty of hugs and laughter and shared experiences recounted ad nauseum. I could never fully grasp the excitement of people as they poured over the pages of the obits searching for some connection, however tenuous, to the deceased, as if they were trying to get into an exclusive party rather than a funeral.

I know Ches' funeral is going to be very different than most because of the rare and tragic circumstances surrounding his death. A suicide is fodder for gossip, especially in a small close-knit community. There will be no laughter or reminiscing about Ches' playful youth, no lamenting the way times have changed; instead there will be only whispers and unanswered questions.

I can empathize just the tiniest bit with Ches since I know what it's like to want to die. I've thought about killing myself, although it's never more than a fleeting thought that pops into my mind from time to time, although less so of late. I used to wonder if I took the entire bottle of sleeping pills that Dr. Ferguson prescribed for me after Joseph died, would they kill me? How long would it take me to die, would I be aware I was dying, and would it really be painless, like falling asleep? I don't know why these thoughts aren't more serious to me. After all, I have far less to live for than Ches. I have no children, no family, and a dead husband waiting for me. But I prefer to wish for my death under less deliberate circumstances. I wish for things like ovarian cancer and accidental drowning the way other people wish to win the Lotto.

Everyone is talking about what a shame it is that a young man like Ches had to go off and kill himself, and while I feel sorry for whatever it was he was going through, my heart is overflowing with sympathy for Lottie and Marianne. I know the pain of being left behind so acutely that I wear it every day, spritz myself with it and bathe in it, the way other people wear their favourite fragrance.

As I make my way to St. Augustine's for Ches' funeral, I wonder what Joseph would say about Ches' untimely demise. I can picture him eating his Cheerios, shaking his head about what a shame it all was, and that would be that. He wouldn't try to speculate because Joseph never believed in what ifs. What's done is done, he'd say. I wish I could follow his creed, but my entire existence for the past five years has been a series of what ifs. I wonder if he could so easily accept the circumstances if it were me who died instead of him.

I look up at the spectacular spire of St. Augustine's and hold my breath. St. Augustine's is the only church in Paradise Bay and although it's beautiful, quaint and historic in its own right, for me it will forever be the place where I said my final goodbyes to Joseph. As I'm about to attend another funeral, I can't help but think about Joseph's. I remember following his casket up the centre aisle, my head bowed low to avoid the stares. I concentrated on counting the rows of pews to keep my mind from thinking the unthinkable. I felt Fred's eyes on me, and in them a plea to be forgiven, but I refused to meet his gaze and ease his burden. I remember the slow pace as I walked behind the pallbearers, but most of all I remember the significance of my own two feet. From that moment on I became painfully aware that I would walk alone; there would be no more running to catch up with Joseph's long-legged gait and no more hand to hold to keep him at a more leisurely pace. I wanted to cry right then and there, but I didn't. I just kept counting the pews, and when I emerged from the darkness of the church into the sunlight, I counted all the cars in the parking lot over and over again to stop from breaking down every time someone said they were so sorry or that Joseph was a good man or that he was in a better place, as if being in a casket were better than being out on his boat.

In fact, I never once cried during the whole funeral, not until after everyone had left my house after they put Joseph in the ground. It was only then that I screamed and cried and wailed and threw all the casserole dishes against the wall so I could hear something break besides my heart.

I don't know why St. Augustine's has to remind me of that day when I have so many happy memories there too, including my own wedding. I wonder why I can't look upon the church and see Joseph, so handsome, standing at the altar in his black suit, with a smile from ear to ear, waiting for me. I wonder why I can't picture myself in my simple white silk gown with my hair falling in black waves around my face, wondering if the fairy tale was real. I don't think about Christmas Eve services, when me and Joseph would share a songbook and sing carols before heading home to exchange gifts. Those memories are dreamlike, and yet every detail of the funeral is so vivid it seems to defy the laws of time. Nothing about it has faded.

I indulge, or torture, myself — I'm not certain which — with the day I met Joseph for the first time. I close my eyes and I'm there, on Route 80, hopelessly lost and waiting to be rescued.

Ten years earlier: I'm on the way to Heart's Content to photograph the famous lighthouse for a bank calendar. It's my first freelance job that doesn't involve corporate headshots or the clichéd handshakes and ribbon cutting, and I'm so excited to get started that I ignore the perilous snowstorm warnings. I think I'll beat its arrival, but it moves in quicker than predicted. By the time I figure I should probably stop somewhere to wait out the storm, I realize there is nowhere to stop. It's getting dark; I can not even see the road for all the snow blowing and swirling in front of me, and civilization seems to have stopped about ten kilometres back. I could pull over on the side of the road but the prospect of stopping is more frightening than forging ahead, even though I have no idea where I'm going.

I wonder if I'm still even on Route 80 when I feel the car skid into an embankment. I try to fight the panic rising in my chest and breathe deeply, telling myself to stay calm. The wheels spin hopelessly in the snowbank in both drive and reverse. I get out and try digging around the tires until my fingers are numb, but it's hopeless. I climb back in the car exhausted, near hysteria, and feeling like the last person on the planet. I think about getting buried alive, not being able to open the car door, and I even make a concerted effort to slow my breathing down in order to conserve oxygen. I don't know how long I sit there before I see the lights from a snowplough coming toward me. I jump out in front of the gigantic yellow beast, which comes to an abrupt stop before me.

"What the hell are you doing out here, missus?" Joseph yells over the howling wind and the swirling snow. "Don't ya know we're getting hammered by a nor'easter?"

I think it's a dumb question since it's quite obvious I am stranded in the middle of a snowstorm. I think about providing a sarcastic response but I'm too tired, cold, and, most of all, relieved to be anything less than thankful.

"I'm lost and I need a ride," I say and he hoists me up into the cab of the snowplough in one easy motion, as if he were used to saving stranded women on the highways. We drive about a kilometre before I realize that I haven't given him a specific destination, nor has he asked.

"I have reservations at a motel over in Heart's Content," I say, not remembering the specific name of the motel and realizing I've left my paperwork with all the reservations in the glove box. I don't imagine there are too many other motels in the vicinity to cause any confusion.

This seems to amuse him because I hear him chuckle. "Then you're pretty lost," he says. "The exit for Heart's Content is back about six kilometres. Welcome to Paradise Bay."

"Can you bring me back that way?"

"Does this look like a cab to you?"

"Look, I'll pay you," I plead.

"Save your money and your breath, missus," he says. "It's not my route. I'll have the union on my back if I tread over that way."

"Well what am I supposed to do?" I ask. I am beginning to think I've gone from a bad situation to a worse one. "Is there a hotel on your route?"

He laughs heartily, but I don't think I've said anything remotely funny. "No, my love, there is no hotel around here, but you can stay at my place."

I scoot over to the edge of the door and shoot him a look that says I have a black belt in karate or my father is the chief of police, although neither is true. I am staring at him, trying to think of the things I could say about him to police in the event he attempts to attack me, but he is wearing a snowsuit and a hat so things like build and hair colour are impossible to gauge.

"I don't bite," he says with a trace of amusement. "In fact, I'm not even going to be there. Late storm means overtime and I'm working the night shift. I can drop you off at my house and I'll dig out your car and get it back to you by morning and then you can be on your way." He glances at me, scrunched up alongside the door of the cab, and shoots me a smile that reaches all the way up to his eyes, which I notice are neither green nor blue, but a combination of both. "Relax, missus. I aint gonna hurt ya."

I nod reluctantly, not seeing much choice in the matter. "My name's Georgia," I say, feeling slightly old at being called missus.

He nods in acknowledgement, and smiles playfully at me. "That's a lovely name, missus. You can call me Joseph."

We drive the rest of the way in a comfortable silence. His house is small but cozy in a ski lodge sort of way and I feel instantly at home there. I listen to the crackle of a fire he's made hastily before venturing back out into the storm. I wrap a blanket around my shoulders, which smells of spruce with a hint of kerosene. I swear that I will stay awake until morning, but I drift off into a deep sleep within minutes.

I awake to the smell of coffee brewing and the sizzle of bacon on the stove. Judging from the sunshine streaming across my face, the storm has subsided. I glance out the window, a veritable winter wonderland of fresh snow blanketing the ground and tree branches buckling under its weight. My car is in the driveway, dwarfed by a tunnel of snow piled high, but it's not the most impressive sight that greets me. I catch sight of Joseph, heaving an axe above his golden head and effortlessly splitting firewood, his muscles rippling under the thin cotton shirt, his hot breath a soft cloud of smoke against the cold air. I stare at him, transfixed, and I feel like I have just been transported into a fairy tale. I am Cinderella, Sleeping Beauty and Snow White all rolled into one. I am aware of my heart beating faster, pumping blood vigorously through my body, and my only thought is that I could gaze upon this man for the rest of my life.

Joseph and I talk and eat and laugh and eat again, until the day slips away and the sun sets once more. I am no longer stranded but I don't want to leave. For the second time in as many nights I am sleeping peacefully amongst the soft blankets of his spare bedroom.

He accompanies me to Heart's Content the following morning and I suck in my breath, awed by the magnificent lighthouse, the rugged coastline and the crisp sea air that fills my lungs, making me feel more alive than I've ever felt. I take more than fifty photographs, but my favourite is one that captures Joseph's shadow, long and lean against the towering height of the lighthouse. He's the most beautiful man I've ever laid eyes on, and all day as we laugh and talk I wait for the other shoe to drop, wait for him to grow surly or violent, or bring up his wife, something, anything to remind me that he's simply too good to be true. When he finally kisses me under the stars I feel such warmth radiate throughout my body, I have a hard time believing the air temperature is near freezing.

"Don't leave," he whispers.

I nod because I'm too uncertain of my raging emotions to speak. There would be an entire lifetime to converse, I think. Instead, we would have a mere five years.

I am brought back to the present by the sound of the church bells urging all of the latecomers to hurry inside. I sit in my car in the church parking lot, willing myself to get out. My legs feel slightly numb and my breaths come in rapid succession, betraying the nervousness I'm trying to hide. I watch two mourners make their way around the scaffolding that was erected so long ago it's as much a part of the church now as the peeling white stucco it was commissioned to fix years earlier. I enter through the inviting red doors. With a shaking hand, I smooth my dark hair in place and follow the crowd, leaving the warm June sun behind for the cool, musty church.

I glance around the church, catching sight of Lottie and Marianne in their appropriate places in the front pew. Marianne is sobbing, big heaving gasps that leave her little shoulders shaking, but Lottie sits stone-faced, her dry eyes staring ahead at nothing in particular, seemingly oblivious to her daughter's distress. I wonder if it's sunk in for her yet, or if she's thinking that if she just went home, she'd find Ches sitting down to a plate of toast and a cup of tea.

I spot a blond head next to a white-haired one and I know that it is Prissy and her mother. It's only been three days since Clara called me asking if I could speak to her daughter but I haven't done anything of the sort. I tried to call several times but I hung up before I finished dialling the number, my mouth dry and my heart beating nervously like a teenage boy asking for a date. I have no idea what to say to her that might make her feel any better. The only wisdom I have to share with her is that it gets worse, especially once reality sets in. I don't want to tell her that one long unbearable day blends into the next, until one day you just can't get out of bed, knowing there's nothing but loneliness waiting for you.

I glance again at Lottie and then back at Prissy and I feel something stir inside my chest, and perhaps it is because I'm in a church, but it fills me completely, this feeling. Perhaps there is something to what Clara said. Maybe I am meant to help people like Prissy and Lottie, but more importantly, maybe they are meant to help me. I pray to God. It is the first time I have prayed since I asked to have Joseph back, but of course it was too late to offer up such a miracle. I should have prayed before that night, and every night, to keep Joseph safe but I didn't. I thought there was nothing left to pray for, but I was wrong. I bow my head low and I pray for healing, for Prissy and Quentin, Lottie and Marianne, but most of all for myself.

CHAPTER EIGHT

Lottie

*P*rissy comes over two days before Ches' funeral. The obituary is not even published yet, but everyone's already heard the news. It didn't say that he committed suicide in the obituary because the funeral home told me to use the phrase "passed away suddenly," which was more appropriate in situations like Ches'. Not that it makes any difference since everyone already knows what Ches did. You can't kill yourself at the rink and hope no one finds out.

Prissy knocks on my door with a Pyrex tray covered in foil. I think about taking the dish and turning her away in the same fashion that Clara did to me the previous day, but I invite her in anyway.

"It's lasagna," Prissy says, placing the dish on my countertop. I see the name Mildred Peach written on masking tape along the side and I know that Prissy did not make it for me, rather she is handing me off some of her own leftovers that people made for her after Howie died. I can't believe she has the audacity to do such a thing, but I picture Clara placing the dish in her daughter's arms. *There's no sense making something when we got so much food here we'll never be able to eat it all. Take some of this over. I don't like lasagna anyway,* and Prissy walking over in a daze. She always did everything her mother wanted — with the exception of moving away.

"Would you like me to heat some up for you?"

I shake my head no.

"How are you doing?" Prissy asks. I can tell she's thinking about hugging me, but it's been years since we've seen one another and things are awkward between us.

"Just waiting for it to sink in, I suppose," I respond. "How are you doing?"

"I'm okay." She looks around the house nervously, eyeing all of the things that indicate Ches' death was sudden and unexpected. There is a package of cigarettes on the end table, an undershirt lying inside out on the arm of the sofa and a pair of his shoes thrown haphazardly in different directions in the entryway. "Do you want me to help you clean up?" she asks, but I shake my head no. I'm not quite ready to start putting Ches' things away because I don't know whether to box them up and send them off to the Salvation Army, or to put them back in the closet where they belong.

"I'm sorry," Prissy whispers and I get the sense that she means more than just for my husband's death. I wonder if she means that she is sorry I was turned away, sorry for losing touch, or for something else entirely.

"Me too," I whisper back, surprised by the tears I feel on my face. I have not cried for Ches yet, and even now my tears stem from embarrassment. I wish he could have died under different circumstances — drowned, snowmobile accident, car wreck, illness. I wish he died the night he broke his back, wish he came down on his head instead. Prissy takes a step closer and wraps her arms around me and I cry some more into her grey sweatshirt. It doesn't matter anymore that I haven't seen her in years or that she brought me someone else's lasagna or that I was refused access to her own grief the day before. I am just thankful that she is here and that she doesn't ask me why my husband committed suicide.

I don't know myself. All I know is that Ches was not having an affair after all. He did not head into St. John's to meet a woman that day. He did not even go to St. John's, but rather headed across the harbour a few minutes away, to the storage shed behind the ice hockey rink where I first told him I was expecting his child. Knowing no one would be there at that time of day, Ches moved the Zamboni onto the ice and parked his truck in the small shed, where he proceeded to rig up his truck in such a way as to inhale enough carbon monoxide to end his life. I wonder if he picked that locale for practical reasons. It was small and enclosed and would do the job adequately enough. Then I wonder if he picked it because it was where I told him I was pregnant all those years ago. Did he think back on his life and decide it was at that moment that his life was really over? He left no note, and no explanation.

Ches' funeral is something of an out-of-body experience for me. I hear the service, see the coffin, know that I am at my husband's funeral, and yet I feel as if I'm watching it on television. I suspect the funeral guests feel much the same way as me because I hear them offer up various opinions and theories as if they too were watching a drama unfold on the screen. I overhear some people speculate that Ches might have been gay, an assertion that others find completely outrageous considering Ches was often heard making disparaging comments about gay people. All the more reason to suspect that it was indeed the case, some say.

I also hear that Ches was a pedophile, was sexually abused as a child, that he had terminal cancer, suffered from depression and dealt drugs for the Hell's Angels out of Montreal.

I knew that people were going to talk but I had no idea of the extent of their imaginations. I know for certain Ches' life was no-where near as interesting as everyone is making it out to be, but I don't know why he killed himself either.

Following the burial, Prissy and Georgia come home with me. They move about my house with efficiency and a sense of purpose that I don't feel but I think is important for me to be around. Georgia is working in my kitchen, grouping all the food people brought me by course — sandwiches, salads and sliced ham in the fridge. Fudge, brownies, rolls and rice krispie treats in the breadbox. I can't see her from my spot on the sofa, but I know that's what she's doing because I can hear the tinfoil crinkling, and I estimate my refrigerator is over-flowing with food that will probably spoil by the time I experience anything resembling a hunger pang. I am about to ask her to put a plate away for Ches, but I catch myself.

Prissy has found the vacuum but she is struggling with the switch. I am too embarrassed to tell her that she has to press the *on* switch for five seconds, let go and then press it again, but it's getting uncomfortable watching the confused look on her face so I give her the instructions anyway.

"That's the way Ches fixed it," I add. "He was good at fixing things, you know. He knows a lot about how things work. I think he knew just what to do to rig the truck up so he'd … you know." I hear a tiny measure of pride in my voice and I feel ridiculous paying my husband a compliment for his expertise in knowing exactly how to poison himself to death. Prissy is looking at me sympathetically, and I hate it because I don't feel like I deserve anyone's sympathy. If anything, I feel partly responsible and I feel the need to confess.

"I thought he was having an affair," I say and Prissy pales instantly, although I don't know why it should upset her so much. "I thought that's where he was going the other day, and I didn't try to stop him because I didn't care if he was screwing someone else."

Prissy is biting her bottom lip, unsure of what to say to me, but it doesn't phase me since no one knows what to say to me.

"I should have known though, because Ches spent all day in bed lately," I continue. "He wasn't interested in anything, not even going to the Legion for a drink, or watching the hockey game. I knew he wasn't right, but I didn't care. I don't care now either. Honestly, if I had to do it all over again, I don't know that I'd do anything different. I think I'd let him go right ahead and kill himself." I wonder if this is true or if I'm just angry and ashamed.

"You have every right to be mad at him," Prissy says hoarsely. "It's okay to be pissed off."

I wonder how she always knows exactly how I feel, even with all the years of absence that have passed. I don't know what Ches was going through. I don't know if any of the rumours are true or not, and none of it seems to matter.

I think about all of the things I'll have to do now that Ches is gone and I feel a fresh wave of anger overtake me. I wonder what will happen the next time my washing machine goes. I think about the way he would scoop spiders out of the bathtub in a wad of toilet paper. I think of how I could always rely on Ches to open a new jar of jelly with the lid screwed on too tightly. I don't know what I will do without him and this thought makes me feel selfish and whiny. My husband has just committed suicide and all I can think of is how it's going to inconvenience me.

I have not said a word and yet Prissy is looking at me as if she knows exactly what I'm thinking. Perhaps it's because we've shared a bond of friendship since childhood, or because she has just gone through the same loss as me. Regardless, she kneels on the carpet in front me so we are face to face now.

"I liked it when Howie did things for me too," Prissy whispers. "It's nothing to be ashamed about. It's the way people are made."

Before I go to bed, I check on Marianne. I can tell she's asleep now by the steady rise and fall of her chest. I tuck her hair behind her ears like I used to when she was little. This has been hard on Marianne, much harder than it's been on me. I pry a photo album out of her hands and begin to skim through it. Marianne compiled the album years earlier for a school project on the family. The first pictures are of Marianne, a tiny baby being held by me, by Ches and my parents. I come across a picture of Marianne and her once treasured but now forgotten Barbie house. I remember how it took Ches two full hours on Christmas Eve to put it together. There are pictures of Ches, walking along the beach with Marianne on his shoulders because she was too tired to walk the rest of the way. There are pictures of me too, but I am always doing something, hanging clothes out to dry, cooking dinner, ironing.

There is one more picture but it isn't in the protective sleeve because it's too big to fit. It's of me and Ches on our wedding day. We are standing on the steps of St. Augustine's just minutes after the ceremony. My brown hair looks almost red in the sun and is styled in soft curls that bounce off my shoulders. I am almost five months pregnant but you can barely tell in the dress. Ches is clean-shaven, his hair is combed neatly to the side, and he's wearing a black suit with a white shirt and a narrow black tie. He has an arm draped possessively around my shoulders and he's whispering something to me that I find amusing, judging by the smile on my face. I don't know whether to feel envious of our former selves, or to pity them for all that lies ahead.

CHAPTER NINE

Prissy

"*I*'m dying."

My mother casually makes this announcement at the dinner table as if she were announcing she was tired, hungry, or had to go to the bathroom. She offers no more details, puts out her cigarette and proceeds to start cleaning up the supper dishes.

I look to Charlie with my brow furrowed in confusion, hoping he might be able to enlighten me, but he sits there looking uncharacteristically sombre and as confused as I am. Quentin looks scared, and eyes his grandmother nervously, as if she might drop dead at any moment. It is in sharp contrast to the mood just a moment earlier when we had all been laughing, even me, which is astonishing under the circumstances.

Charlie is proving to be my tonic in the week and a half since I arrived back home. He somehow manages to be present for every meal despite the fact he no longer lives here. He swears, he drinks beer even with his breakfast, and he tells stories with so much colour that you feel as if you were a first-hand observer. I have the feeling sometimes that I am on vacation and that Howie is just working and will come once he gets the time off.

Today Charlie is telling the story of the time me and Lottie decided to hold a séance and resurrect the souls of the Irish princess, Sheila NaGeira, and her dashing pirate, Peter Easton. I remember sneaking into the cemetery of St. Augustine's with Lottie under the cover of darkness, but I have forgotten the details that Charlie remembers, like that we wore black nail polish and wrapped our hair up, gypsy-style, in our grandmothers' paisley scarves. He even remembers the exact words we chanted to call the spirits forward, or perhaps he is just embellishing. It is only when he mimics the look on our faces when a group of drunken teenage boys came running out from behind the church claiming to be ghosts, I realize he wasn't even there.

But my mother's announcement catapults us all to the present. I put down my teacup and gingerly lay my raisin square back in the plastic container, alongside a jelly donut and a coconut snowball. With a desperate look, I implore Charlie to say something, but he is preoccupied with wiping jelly and powdered sugar from his goatee. I don't know what to say so I stare at a tear in the vinyl tablecloth while I think of something appropriate. I am hoping that if I don't say anything, my mother will elaborate, provide more information, and then give me an opportunity to ask questions.

I don't want my mother to die, not now, not when everything else in my life is falling apart. I need her to help me through this mess, and then I realize how selfish I sound. I am so ashamed of myself it takes a tremendous effort just to look up at her right now because I'm afraid she can read my thoughts.

But my mother has her back to all of us. She's hunched over the sink, washing dinner plates with her swollen, arthritic hands in hot soapy water. I want to get up, urge her to sit down, rest, work on getting better, but I can only watch stupidly as my mother scrapes chicken bones off a plate into the garbage can. She wraps a bowl of leftover boiled potatoes in plastic wrap to fry up in bacon grease for breakfast the following morning. I've seen her do this at least once a week throughout my childhood and the normalness of it annoys me more than it appeals to my sympathies. Only Mom could drop such a bombshell and then go on about her business as if nothing out of the ordinary had happened. People don't just make such statements about their imminent death and then finish cleaning up. Maybe they cry, maybe they put on a brave front, but they certainly don't wash dishes.

My mother has always had a flair for drama, which she demonstrates, typically, by thrusting herself in the spotlight and then acting embarrassed by all the attention. I am partly convinced she lied about Howie's death not to protect me, but to garner more attention than would be the case if she told the truth about Howie's philandering. I know that she is annoyed that she had to postpone the memorial service after Ches killed himself. She says things like, "I don't know why that SOB had to wait until now to kill himself," and "I don't know why everyone wants to talk about Ches Crocker all of a sudden. You wouldn't know but there was nothing else to talk about." I think she's jealous people aren't talking about us anymore.

I know I should ask Mom what, exactly, is wrong with her, why, in fact, she believes she is dying, what the doctor specifically told her, and what treatment options are available for whatever illness she has, but the longer the silence goes on, the more annoyed I get. I wonder if this time my mother's illness is real or if it's simply a ploy to keep me in line about Howie's death. I know it sounds cruel, but my mother is not above such methods.

For as long as I can remember, my mother has been "dying" in one way or another. If Charlie and I fought, if I broke my curfew by five minutes, if I did not get good grades in school, Mom would place a hand across her chest and tell me I was going to put her in an early grave. I lived in fear that everything I did to disappoint her would result in me being orphaned. *I won't be around forever* was her mantra. My mother said this so many times, I was convinced that she would not be alive to witness my wedding or the birth of my child, much less my divorce. That she has been talking about her imminent demise for the past twenty-five years is tiresome, especially now that I am facing a genuine crisis.

"You're dying again then?" I ask, surprising myself with a detached, almost sarcastic tone. "You've been dying at least once a year for the past twenty-five years. In fact, I think you were dying around this time last year too. Maybe you should just get it over with already."

As soon as I say it I regret it. The words hang in the air like a cloud of smoke that has not yet settled and I long to sweep them away with the stroke of my hand. Charlie looks at me as if I've lost my mind, which I'm beginning to think I have, and I can't even look at Quentin since I imagine how hurt I'd be if he said something like that to me. Mom is clutching her dishrag and I can tell she's mad at me. I want to be anywhere else but here right now and I almost wish she would send me to my room for my smart mouth.

"I was sick last year, yes," she says quietly and deliberately. "And I don't think you have the right to pass judgment, when you didn't even bother to come see me."

I know I should just apologize and let it drop but I feel as if I've come this far I have to finish it, so I answer her with the same quiet, deliberate tone she just used on me. "You had a kidney stone removed. They didn't even cut you open." I take another sip of tea so I have something to do with my hands.

"Well I could have died now, couldn't I?" she asks calmly. I am about to tell her that I've never heard of anyone dying from a kidney stone, but she continues before I have the chance to speak. "Any time an old woman like me has to go into the hospital there's a risk of complications. Besides, it was one of them foreign doctors who did it and I don't have to tell you what they're like. Not to mention I felt like shit afterwards and it would have been nice for you to come and help me get back on my feet, but I guess you had more important things to do. The only reason you're here now is because you got nowhere else to go."

Mom is right but hearing it out loud makes it hurt more than I could have possibly imagined. My guilt moments earlier quickly escalates into anger.

"So is that what this is about, Mom?" I ask defensively, all pretence that we are having a benign conversation gone. "You're mad at me because I didn't come home for your procedure. I get it. Charlie told me you were going to be fine, didn't you, Charlie?" I turn to him for support but he looks so uncomfortable at being caught in the middle that I give up on him being my ally.

"I called you in the hospital. I sent flowers. It was a very difficult time of year to travel. Quentin was in the middle of finals and Howie had this big client thing going on at work and I—"

"Well I'm sorry, Prissy." My mother stops me in mid-sentence. "I'll try to die at a more convenient time for you. Why don't you tell me when's good and I'll see what I can do."

How about now, I want to say but I have enough sense to keep the words to myself. I let escape an exaggerated sigh and roll my eyes in dramatic fashion. I know I'm behaving inappropriately in front of my son, but in the presence of my mother, I can't help but act the child. I take a deep breath and resolve to put myself above it all and act more like a concerned daughter.

"All right, Mom," I begin, "let's start over. Now why don't you tell us about what the doctor said and we'll take it from there."

"Oh, I haven't seen a doctor," she says and I want to scream at her in frustration.

"Then how do you know you're dying?" I ask.

"I just know. I don't know exactly when I'm gonna go, but I just want you to know about it so if I don't come down for breakfast one morning, then it might be cause I passed in my sleep, God willing." Mom looks heavenward before continuing. "So if you don't have anything better going on that day, maybe you could call the funeral home and get things going."

I know I ought to humour her, maybe say something encouraging, or inspiring, but I'm too frustrated with having the same conversation about death I've been having with her for most of my adult life.

She takes a seat at the kitchen table with me and Charlie and Quentin. She looks serious now. "I don't think it's too early to start talking about the future. Now I don't want anything fancy. Funerals cost a lot of money these days. You're better off spending money on yourselves than on a fancy coffin for me to rot away in. I'd ask you to just double bag me and throw me out to the curb on garbage day, but I checked with the depot and they said it's against the law. So Charlie, this is where you come in."

I am anticipating my mother asking my brother to sneak her body over to the town dump under the cover of night but she goes in another direction entirely.

"Charlie," Mom says, "I want you to make me a coffin." I choke on my tea and I expect Charlie to object vociferously, but to my astonishment, he nods like an obedient child. "There's some spare lumber out in the yard. Your father was going to build a boat out of it before he died so I knows it's good wood. Use that, okay? You were always so good with your hands."

Charlie smiles at the compliment. "I'll build you the best fuckin coffin this side of the bay."

I stare first at my brother and then to my mother before daring a glance at my son. Quentin looks horrified and I can't blame him. This is the side of the family he's only been partially exposed to and this conversation sounds freakish even to me.

"Mom, this is the most ridiculous conversation I've ever had with anyone in my life, even you," I say, standing up. "You're not going to die, not for a very long time."

"You got to face facts, Prissy. You've been away for a long time and I'm not the same woman I was when you left."

This much is certainly true. My mother is most definitely older, whiter, more wrinkled, and often appears frail, particularly when she thinks no one is watching.

Mom lights a cigarette and inhales deeply, turning her attention from my brother to focus on me. "Now Charlie is doing just fine now. Got himself a decent job and a place of his own, but it's you I worry about, Prissy."

My stomach does a flop at hearing this, and I feel like I'm on an elevator that descends too suddenly and too fast. Charlie has always been the child that demanded worrying about, not me. Charlie got poor grades in school, hung with the wrong crowds, and got fired from his summer job at Dee's Takeout because all his friends loitered about in the dining room, turning off any would-be customers. I've always been the mature one, the one who never got into trouble, married a responsible man, kept a house and raised a child. That it's me, and not Charlie, who my mother worries about in her golden years, is enough to make me dizzy.

"You and Quentin are welcome to stay here as long as you want. But when I die, I want you to have the house." My mother's features have softened and I know she's serious. I am strangely touched by the gesture and briefly entertain the thought of living here with Quentin, a single mom navigating my son through the ups and downs of small town life.

"No friggin way," Quentin says. It's the first thing he's said since he called Charlie a tool for teasing him about his dyed hair at the beginning of dinner. Quentin stands up abruptly and turns to leave the room.

"Where do you think you're going?" I ask, my patience for dealing with another difficult family member gone.

"Nowhere," he mumbles, and then under his breath I hear him say, "unfortunately."

I feel a tinge of anger that I know is misdirected. None of this is Quentin's fault, but it's not my fault either. I blame Howie but I can't very well say so in front of Quentin. My mind swirls with the events of the past week, the pain of Howie's infidelity, my own humiliation, and the guilt at pretending I've been widowed, especially to my friend who actually has been widowed. And now my mother's apparent death looms before me. My head hurts and I have to pinch the tip of my nose to relieve some of the pressure. I get up and leave through the back door without providing an explanation since I don't know where I'm going myself.

The sky is darkening and a gentle mist permeates the air. I've forgotten my sweater and I hug my arms in the chilly evening. A bank of fog sits off in the distance, hovering over the bay. Typical capelin weather, my father would say, and he'd grab a bucket and head down to the beach to pluck the flitting fish from the rocky shore. I walk toward the beach, enjoying the feel of the mist on my face and the cool air in my lungs. I long for my father's quiet reassurance right now. He would have been able to talk my mother out of making up the obituary; he would have been so uncomfortable in bringing up my failed marriage that he wouldn't say anything at all. But as quickly as I wish he were alive, I'm thankful he's not around to witness my life in shambles. It would have broken his heart to know what's happened between me and Howie.

I pick up the pace, walking quickly and then running down the narrow, winding road that leads to the beach. My sneakers are wet and shiny with mist as I drag them through the tall grass. I pass houses painted green, yellow, blue, red, and even pink. People wave at me from their front steps and invite me inside for tea and biscuits. I wave back and politely decline the offers. I watch women in housedresses and rollers hurry to bring their clothes in from the line before the rain comes. Children ride bikes up and down the narrow streets, gawking curiously at me, a strange woman walking along their stomping grounds. I think of my house in Chestnut Circle, as nondescript as every other house on the block.

I break into a run, my feet expertly gliding across the damp pavement, through a narrow path and over slippery rocks until I am here, standing before the ocean. I listen to the rhythm of the waves and the sound instantly calms me. I sit on a rock and watch the rise and fall of the ocean until the sun sets and the mist turns into a steady rain. I have been gone for two hours and I wonder if my mother is worried.

By the time I make it back up the hill to the house I am soaking wet and so tired I just want to slip in the back door and climb the stairs to my bedroom to seek comfort under the soft quilts of my childhood. I don't feel like discussing Mom's health, and I certainly don't want to hear her talk about her own funeral arrangements. For the first time since I've arrived home, I just want to go to sleep.

But when I slip through the back door, I see Mom light one cigarette from the butt of another. Her expression is troubled and I feel guilty for having worried her. I am about to apologize for being gone so long but I don't get the chance.

"I have some bad news," she says.

"In addition to your imminent demise?" I ask sarcastically.

"It's Quentin," she whispers. "He's gone."

CHAPTER TEN

Georgia

In twenty-two minutes Joseph will have been dead for five years, which makes him dead for three months longer than the duration of our entire marriage. I ask myself, not for the first time, if four and a half years of happiness is worth an entire lifetime of grief. I always knew that something bad was looming over us, particularly in those moments of utter contentment, like falling asleep in the crook of Joseph's arm or propping my feet in his lap under the kitchen table after supper.

As the clock approaches the exact time of Joseph's death, I wait for a sign as I do every year. I wait for the room to get cold or to feel the bed sink under his ghostly weight, but he never comes, and I can't help feeling slighted, as if he's forgotten my birthday or our anniversary. I locate Joseph's death certificate, an official looking document, because I need proof right now that he really existed in the first place and that he is not a figment of my imagination. The little details about him are starting to recede from memory, and I can feel him getting further and further away from me. I concentrate on recalling the melodic inflection of his voice when he wanted a favour from me, but I can't quite get the tone right in my head. I feel my mind travel to the time and place that I know I will never forget.

Five years earlier: I'm too late. The doctors tell me Joseph probably died on impact, and I get the sense that I should somehow be relieved by this news. I don't scream, cry or burst into any other form of hysterics. I just want to see him one last time.

His lifeless body is caked in dried blood and his eyes and nose are black and swollen. I ask the nurses for an ice pack to bring down the swelling and they look at me with a mixture of pity and discomfort. I turn my attention to the smudges of grass and dirt on the knees of Joseph's sweatpants and I wonder how I'm going to get the stains out. I make a mental checklist of my laundry room. I have a full bottle of Shout and about half a container of Oxyclean, but I am almost out of bleach and I will definitely need more. These are Joseph's favourite sweats and I know he'll want them on Sunday.

An hour earlier Joseph had been playing baseball with Fred, along with most of the boys from the Paradise Bay municipal depot. Three hours earlier, I chastised him for swinging my rolling pin at a ball of pie dough, and he just grinned back at me sheepishly before I ushered him out the door, telling him to practice on a real ball.

I don't know how long I stand there fretting over grass stains before I realize that I haven't touched him yet. I'm afraid, I realize, that he will be cold, and Joseph is always warm. I am constantly warming my hands on his chest and my feet on his legs under the covers at night. When I finally reach out and feel his cool skin, Joseph's death hits me and that's when I display the reaction the doctor and nurses were expecting. I wail and sob and shake my head, and the nurses look visibly relieved that I am no longer asking for an ice pack.

Fred appears, seemingly out of nowhere, and he pulls me off Joseph and holds me by the shoulders. His pants are torn and blood seeps through a square of gauze taped to his left temple. His eyes are red with tears.

"I'm sorry, Georgia," he cries. "I killed him. I'm sorry, I'm sorry, I'm sorry." He keeps repeating the words over and over again, as if he's waiting for me to say it's okay. But it isn't. What are you supposed to say to the person who drives your husband into a tree? *Don't worry about it. Just be more careful with my next husband.*

"Let go of me," is the last thing I say before I scream for the nurses to remove him from the room.

———————————————

I'm standing in the cemetery in my pyjamas at midnight. I hadn't intended to be here, had specifically promised myself I would not come tonight, but I knew I couldn't sleep, knew I would simply look at the clock and relive the horror of that awful night over and over again. Perhaps it is the fog and drizzle, which make it seem like a scene from a horror movie, but I get the distinct feeling that I'm not alone. I can feel someone behind me and I think that this is finally the time that Joseph is going to show himself to me. But when I turn around it is not Joseph at all but a teenage boy. His hair is a horrific shade of yellow and he's wearing pants that are too big for him and a t-shirt that reveals scrawny arms.

I assume he's a vandal because I can't imagine what else a teenager is doing in a graveyard at this hour, unless it's to spray-paint vulgar messages on headstones or to drink beer or smoke drugs. I think about the possibility of anyone defacing my husband's grave and it makes me so angry I can feel my limbs shake.

"What the hell do you think you're doing here?" I say.

"Nothing," the boy mumbles, shoving his hands in his pockets and looking down at his slick canvas sneakers.

"Don't you have any respect for the dead? I mean, do you really think it's funny to go around defacing people's graves?"

"No," he answers defensively, shaking his head. "I'm not doing any of that shit."

"Then what are doing here at this hour?"

"I could ask you the same question. At least I'm dressed."

I have forgotten that I am wearing pyjamas until the boy brings it to my attention. "I'm visiting my husband's grave. It's an important anniversary for us." I realize how crazy I must appear, in the rain at a cemetery in my pyjamas to acknowledge a macabre anniversary.

His head shoots up and he looks at me. "Are you the lady whose husband just gassed himself at the rink?"

"No. My husband died a long time ago, in a car accident."

"That sucks ... I guess. Look ... do you think you could buy me some beer? I been to two stores already and I got the money, but I don't have ID on me." He says it as if he's plenty old enough to drink but just can't remember where he's put his driver's license. "I'll pay you an extra twenty," he adds when I don't answer right away.

"What do you want beer for?" I ask.

He regards me strangely. "Isn't it obvious?"

I can't help but smile at the boy, who I find amusing enough to distract me from dwelling on the reason I'm here in the first place. Throughout our brief exchange, there is something vaguely familiar about the boy, but it is not until I catch a glimpse of his blue eyes that I recognize what it is. "Are you Prissy's boy?"

"No," he answers, so quickly that I know for certain he is indeed Prissy's son.

"Well, does your mother know where you are?"

"Maybe," he mumbles again, his blue eyes now focusing on his sneakers. "Don't tell her I asked you to get me beer, okay? She'll like totally freak out."

"After all she's been through, why would you put her through all this extra stress by running off at this hour looking for trouble?" The boy casually shrugs his shoulders and I feel an outpouring of sympathy for him. He's been through so much and yet so much more lies ahead for him, and for Prissy. "I am so very sorry about your father," I say.

"My dad's a dickhead," he shouts. It is the only time in our conversation that he's made eye contact and spoken clearly.

"It's okay to be angry with him for dying. I know you must feel betrayed and hurt at losing him."

"My dad aint dead," he scoffs. "He's just off screwing around, that's all. The whole thing is bullshit. Now, are you gonna buy me some beer or not?"

I can feel my jaw drop and I'm aware that I'm staring stupidly ahead, but I'm still trying to grasp what he's just said. Prissy has accompanied me to the flea market twice this past week and she is pleasant company to be around, although she refuses to talk about Howie at all. She does not discuss his illness, the funeral, or her future, preferring instead to stick to the safety of conversations about the weather and about how much the flea market has grown over the past year. For a split second I wonder if the child's assertion is true, but I dismiss the notion almost as soon as I entertain it. I remember the conversation with Clara about how difficult this has all been on her grandson, how he still hasn't accepted the truth about his father. I remember I refused to talk about Joseph with anyone for months after, and that for weeks I convinced myself that Joseph was still alive out there somewhere. I know that the boy is just trying to cope with the fact that his father is never coming back.

"Okay," I say. "I'll get you your beer. Come on and get in the car."

He looks surprised at his good fortune but of course I don't stop at the twenty-four hour Irving for beer, and I can hear the boy curse silently under his breath at having been fooled. When I pull up in front of his grandmother's house and his mother comes running down the driveway in hysterics, screaming his name, he looks at me with wounded eyes that make my heart break.

CHAPTER ELEVEN

Prissy

$\mathcal{I}$am too nervous to pay attention to what's going on at Howie's memorial service because I'm too afraid that Howie will barge in on his own funeral. There will be gasps and finger-pointing followed by a public stoning for my mother and me. I haven't told Mom but when Quentin went off on his own the other night, I called Howie from the car. I had been driving all over town and even into several neighbouring towns. There was no sign of my son, because, I assumed, it was quite obvious he'd run away, not from home but back home. I was so convinced he was halfway to the St. John's airport that I called Howie. It was nearly midnight here but only ten thirty in Toronto and I was hoping Howie wouldn't make the connection.

"Have you heard from Quentin?" I asked immediately when he answered his cell.

"No." There was a pause, at which both of us began to sense panic in the other. "Prissy, is everything okay?"

"Yes," I replied, perhaps too quickly. "It's fine. He just wanted to call you and tell you that he saw a moose today. It wandered right up the backyard and we could see it plain as day from the kitchen window." I was channelling my mother with the lies but I didn't dare admit to losing our child, not yet anyway.

"Prissy ..." Howie sounded doubtful. "Put Quentin on."

"He's asleep," I said. "He'll call you later." I hung up the phone and let it go to voice mail four times when I saw Howie's cell number on my caller ID.

I was so relieved to see Georgia show up with Quentin safe and sound that I forgot to call Howie back and assure him everything was fine. Now I'm terrified that my husband is going to come looking for his son, only to end up witnessing his own funeral.

I keep my head bowed low from my place in the front pew and it looks as if I'm praying. St. Augustine's is nearly filled to capacity, and I feel almost every set of eyes on me. I want to slide underneath the pew and hide from them. I feel like a charlatan and I have to bite my tongue to stop myself from standing up and screaming the truth to everyone. I have been home in Paradise Bay for eleven days now and I don't think I can endure one more hug from someone who tells me how sorry they are for my loss.

Mom, on the other hand, seems to bask in the glow of all the attention. She smiles the appropriate smile at just the right moment, hugs well-wishers in just the right manner and, to my horror, even nods in agreement that I should attend the next singles night at the Legion. It doesn't seem to matter to her in the least that Howie is not dead, nor does she appear to even notice my angry glare each time she fabricates a new thread to the story. I can only stare in disbelief as she talks about Howie's doctors, how they tried to get him approved for an experimental treatment but by the time the bureaucrats in the hospital administration okayed it, the cancer had spread. The more details she makes up, the more I think she believes it.

Barb Donovan is singing "Amazing Grace," which means the service is nearly over. I look up for the first time throughout the entire memorial service because I feel like Barb is singing directly to me and it's probably impolite not to acknowledge her efforts, but then I see it. Atop the altar, just below the crucifix of Jesus Christ, is an easel with an oversized photo of Howie surrounded by pink and white carnations. Howie looks so much younger than I remember that I'm reminded for a moment of the man I first fell in love with.

I immediately recognize the picture because I took it myself on our first visit to Paradise Bay after Quentin was born. Quentin was little more than a few months old and so I was constantly armed with my camera, snapping pictures of my child with his grandmother, his grandfather, his Uncle Charlie and everyone else who pleaded with me to hold him. At the time the picture was taken Quentin was nuzzled into the crook of my mother's arm and I had taken so many photos of them that my mother shooed me away lest I wake the baby.

I ventured outside to where Howie and my dad were drinking beer and sitting on lawn chairs in the late afternoon sun. I don't know what they were talking about but Howie was laughing so hard that I couldn't help smiling at whatever private joke they shared as I snapped the picture and then joined them in the yard.

I shift uncomfortably against the hard wooden pew and wonder what my dad said to Howie to make him laugh that afternoon, and inexplicably and without warning, I burst into tears at the thought. They are loud heart-wrenching sobs that bounce off the stone walls of St. Augustine's and echo back into the air. At once, I am embarrassed and horrified and yet completely incapable of stopping. At first my mother shoots me a look of confusion and places a hand on my shoulder, although whether it is to quiet or encourage me, I don't know.

When the service is finally over, I am utterly exhausted and relieved to put it behind me. The only thing I want to do is go home and take Quentin in my arms and hold him the way I used to when he was little.

But by the time I arrive back at the house, the only thing I want to do is disappear. There is a black sedan parked in the driveway, with Howie sitting in the driver's seat. He gets out of the car when I pull up behind him and I can hear Mom asking for Jesus to help us.

"What the hell is he doing here?" she asks.

I clench my jaw and hold my stomach and I think I might retch right here in the front seat of my father's old Chrysler. This is all my fault and I confess my role in this disaster. "I called him."

"You invited him to the memorial service?" She is looking at me as if I were simple.

"Of course not. When Quentin ran off the other night, I thought he might have tried to go back home so I called Howie. I must have freaked him out."

Howie leans against the door of his rental car as if it were holding him up. He has a habit of leaning easily on everything — doorways, countertops, railings — throwing his weight around with a sense of entitlement. He waits for us to get out and acknowledge his presence, but neither my mother nor I make any move and I suspect Howie must be growing suspicious.

"Follow my lead," Mom says, and before I can say another word, she is out of the car and racing toward Howie.

"Howard, what a surprise. Come on inside," she says, placing a hand on his arm. "Sure, it's enough to freeze your arse off today." There is a slight chill in the air but my mother doesn't care about that; she only wants to make sure that Howie is not spotted by neighbours. There is no trace of my mother's weak hip as she ushers Howie quickly inside. I follow slowly behind, thanking God that we are not expecting any mourners to stop by.

"Clara," Howie says pleasantly when he walks into the kitchen. "It's nice to see you." I wonder why he feels he has to go through the motions when we all know he isn't pleased to see my mother under these circumstances at all. In fact, we're all painfully uncomfortable. Howie hasn't addressed me yet and I wonder if God has miraculously answered my prayer to be invisible, or if my husband has simply stopped speaking to me altogether. Finally I feel his eyes on me. The confusion on his face is obvious as he processes my formal black attire and swollen eyes.

"Is this a bad time?" he asks.

"As a matter of fact, yes," Mom answers. "We've just returned from a funeral actually."

"I'm sorry," Howie says. "Who died? Anyone I know?"

"No one important," she says with a casual shrug of her shoulders. "So did you bring your girlfriend with you?"

I am so embarrassed and caught off guard I can't even reprimand my mother for her insolence.

Howie sighs but does not respond to my mother's accusation, which makes me wonder if there is a woman waiting for him in a St. John's hotel. The thought makes me lightheaded and I have to grip the laminate countertop to steady my legs.

"I just want to see my son," Howie says, turning to face me. "Where is Quentin? Is he all right?"

Charlie has taken Quentin for the morning since I drew the line at allowing him to attend the service. "He's fine," I answer, finally finding my voice. "He's spending some time with Charlie right now, but he should be back soon. Please ..." I gesture to a chair at the kitchen table. "You can wait with me. I'll put on some coffee."

"Maybe I'll just go over to Lawlor's and wait there." Howie looks at his watch. "I'll come back in an hour."

"You will do no such thing," my mother insists. I can tell from the scowl on her face that she does not approve of entertaining Howie in her home, but it's better than the alternative, which is that someone will recognize him over fish and chips at Lawlor's. "They'll be back any second."

Thankfully, after a moment of indecision, Howie relents and takes a seat at the kitchen table.

"Don't go giving him any of the raisin squares, Prissy. I only got a couple left and they're my favourite." On that note my mother excuses herself and I purposefully dig the raisin squares out of the bread box and place them on the table in front of Howie. There are enough there that I predict at least one quarter of them will go stale or grow mould by the end of the week.

"You'll have to excuse Mom," I say, trying to control the tremor in my voice. "She's angry with you. I'm sure you understand, given the unfortunate circumstances." I can't remember ever speaking to my husband with such formality or such forced politeness.

Howie nods in understanding, giving me a half smile before taking the steaming cup of coffee from me. I've made it strong, just the way he likes it, and he takes several small sips. I know he's here for Quentin but I can't help but feel a glimmer of hope that he wants to see me too. As if reading my mind, Howie places a warm hand over mine and all I want is to stay like this forever.

"Are you okay?" he asks, stroking his thumb over my chewed cuticles. He's not wearing a wedding ring and I pull my hand away, his touch suddenly too uncomfortable to bear.

"Yeah, I'm doing great." I am trying my best to sound happy. "So what are you doing here, Howie?"

He sighs and rubs his forehead with his thumb and index finger and I already know I don't want to know the answer. "I spoke to Quentin on the phone yesterday and there seems to be a lot of things going on that I find particularly disturbing."

My heart is beating faster because I was unaware that Quentin spoke to his father and I have no idea what he might have told Howie. I don't think he would tell him about the obituary, but I can't imagine what else Howie might find disturbing enough to fly out here unannounced. "Like what?" I ask.

"He says you've been talking about moving back here, in this house. He's my son too, Prissy, and I won't let you up and move here with him. You're only supposed to be here two weeks." Howie looks agitated and I'm momentarily torn between a desire to calm him down and keep the peace and a desire to taunt him and further agitate him.

"I swear I don't know what you're talking about," I say. "Quentin is fourteen and he has a way of misinterpreting things. You should know that better than anyone. Mom simply said that she wanted me to have the house when she died, that's all. You know how she gets. She plans for her death every six months. Me and Quentin are not moving anywhere." Howie looks so visibly relieved that I can't help myself from blurting out, "At least not yet anyway." I can see the panic in his eyes and at first it makes me feel the slightest bit powerful, as if I've suddenly gained the upper hand. I feel like shouting that Quentin doesn't want to live in Toronto with him and that he wants to be here with me, but I am too ashamed that I've even thought it. "Well I'll need to live somewhere," I say rather petulantly.

"You can have the fucking house," Howie says. "I've told you a hundred times I will take care of you."

"Well that's very noble of you," I spit at him, "but I'm quite capable of taking care of myself." I expect him to disagree with my assertion; I figure he might even laugh at me, but he does something far worse. He smirks at me in the most patronizing way, and nods in agreement the way one might humour a child who claimed that he was going to be a superhero when he grew up.

"Fuck you," I shout at him so loudly that I don't even care that my mother can hear me from whatever room she's escaped to. "I don't need your money or your help or anything else to look after myself, or my son."

I watch a vein in Howie's neck grow thicker and purple under his skin. He doesn't say a word but the smug expression on his face incenses me more than anything he could say. I am overcome by such a desire to wipe the smirk off his face that I don't know what I'm doing until my hand makes contact with his cheek. My fingers tingle and my palm stings and we've both grown so silent I can hear the humming of the refrigerator. I can see the imprint of my hand on his face and I am just about to apologize when Charlie and Quentin enter the kitchen through the back door.

"You okay, Prissy?" Charlie asks and I love my brother more in this moment than I ever have in my entire life. He has a protective hand on Quentin's shoulder and I know that if I told Charlie to take Howie outside and beat the shit out of him, he'd do it willingly.

"I'm fine," I say.

"Hey Dad," Quentin says tentatively.

"Hey buddy," Howie answers back as if he were speaking to a younger version of Quentin. His tone is forced, exaggerated, and comes across as fake. Howie's eyes look darker than I remember, or maybe it is just that his skin is paler. He looks awkward and vulnerable sitting here in my mother's kitchen, unsure of how to talk to his own child, but it doesn't make me feel the slightest pang of empathy. If anything, I take perverse satisfaction in his discomfort and I'm not even ashamed.

"I came to see you," Howie says to Quentin. "Want to take a ride with me to Lawlor's? Grab some dinner? Sandwich?" His sentences get progressively smaller as he grows more uncertain.

And then Mom appears out of nowhere, swooping in once again to save the day. She's changed out of her funeral garb and is wearing a pink bathrobe over her housedress. "Lawlor's is infested, I tell ya," she says shrilly. "Vermin crawling all over the place. Sure, it's only a matter of time before the Department of Health closes 'em down."

My mother and I ate at Lawlor's three days ago and she failed to mention this so-called pest problem and I know it's because there's not a shred of truth to it. It's nearly four-thirty in the afternoon and Lawlor's will be filled with the supper crowd, many of them having come directly from the memorial service, and I know the last thing Mom wants is for Howie and Quentin to appear in public together.

"Now, we're having pork chops this evening and I have plenty to go around. There's no need for anyone to be eating out tonight, not when we got good food here. Howard, take off your coat and bring me up some potatoes and a couple of onions from down in the cellar." Howie stares blankly at her, chewing the corner of his lip like he always does when he's debating what to do about a particular problem. "Go on," she says, giving him a gentle shove. "You knows where they're to."

An hour later we are all sitting at the dining room table because the kitchen table only has four chairs. Aside from Charlie asking me to pass him the fuckin pepper, my mother is the only person who speaks. She talks about the flea market and how wonderful it is for tourism; she talks about the right time to pick blueberries as if it were the most exciting thing in the entire world. She chatters endlessly about boiling beets and the new scratch and win card from Atlantic Lotto. We all sit in silence, chewing our overcooked pork chops and waiting for the evening to end, when my mother brings up a more controversial topic.

"So," she says, moving her potatoes around her plate, "I was thinking Quentin would really love to stay here for the summer."

Howie is shaking his head but my mother won't let him speak.

"Now just hear me out," she interjects. "Quentin is half Newfoundlander and the poor child doesn't know the first thing about his culture. No one has taught him how to go jigging for cod, tie a good fishing net, track a moose, or sing the second verse of 'I'se the B'y.'"

"Sure, I don't know how to do any of that fuckin shit and I lived here all my life," Charlie snorts, and my mother shoots him a deadly look, but otherwise ignores him.

"I know that Artie always dreamed of taking his only grandson out fishing and camping and teaching him all the things he ought to know about where he came from, but he just never got that chance." She places a hand on her heart and looks upward. "I know his only regret in this life was that he never got to be the proper granddad he wanted so much to be cause Quentin was so far away. All he ever wanted was for Quentin to know where he came from. You know how much Artie loved that child."

My mother is doing what she does best — planting the seeds of guilt, and I can tell it's working because Howie has taken to chewing the corner of his lip again.

"It's just for the summer, Howard," Mom says, reeling in her catch. "In September, Quentin goes back to school in Toronto."

Howie turns to Quentin. "Is this what you want, bud?"

Quentin shrugs, which is as good a yes as any fourteen-year-old will allow. I want to jump up and down, clap my hands in triumph and hire Mom to be my attorney, but instead I retrieve the blueberry pie from the kitchen and divvy it up amongst the five of us.

It reminds me of another night some sixteen years earlier when Howie showed up completely unannounced, just like he'd done today, albeit for different reasons. He'd come to surprise me, having made dinner reservations in St. John's, and just like this evening, my mother wouldn't let him go. She insisted he needed a home-cooked meal and coaxed him into staying. That night, my mother made a feeble attempt to teach Howie the intricate rules of the beloved card game 120, but it was hopeless, and we all ended up laughing so hard at what a poor card player he turned out to be, forgetting the value of the ace of hearts while struggling to understand the rules of reneging. By the time Charlie showed up and we introduced the concept of calling for your partner, poor Howie threw his hands in the air in defeat but laughed at himself almost as hard as we all did.

I watch Howie now as he wipes the purple stain from the corner of his mouth and my triumphant feeling is gone.

CHAPTER TWELVE

Lottie

"Aren't you going to open it?"

Marianne is referring to the large brown paper bag sitting on the kitchen table. It contains everything that was found inside Ches' truck with the exception of Ches himself. The police told me it was mine now, and asked for my signature before handing it over to me, as if anyone else would want it. My inheritance is contained inside a paper sac just like the grab bags I used to beg my parents for at Hayward's. I have no idea what I will find, but I am nearly certain I will be just as disappointed as I was when I realized my grab bag contained no more than a plastic whistle that didn't work and a handful of cheap items that Mr. Hayward couldn't move off the shelves when they were out in the open. Still, there is an expectation in opening the bag, much like that of a child opening a present on Christmas morning. I suspect Marianne has that same expectation of finding something meaningful, but I know there's nothing more inside the bag than a few odds and ends that Ches left in the truck.

"Maybe later," I say and she looks crestfallen.

"Aren't you even curious? This is all we have left of him."

Even though I know the contents of the bag do not include a suicide note, I am the slightest bit nervous that there will be something mysterious that I can't make any sense out of, like a telephone number I don't recognize or a street address I don't know. I know it's unlikely since the police would have questioned me about such things. Still, I hesitate to open it in front of Marianne in case there's something revealing about her father that she might not be ready for. What if Ches was into something illegal or immoral?

"I think I know why Daddy did it the way he did," Marianne says.

I'm not sure if she's referring to the method of suicide or the reason he decided to kill himself in the first place so I simply ask, "Why?"

"Because he didn't want either one of us to find his body," Marianne says. "He knew neither one of us would ever go looking for him in the rink, whereas if he did it at home, one of us would have had to stumble across his body sooner or later. I think he was trying to protect us."

I can not believe that Marianne has rationalized her father's selfish actions into something downright heroic. "Yes, well, that was awfully considerate of your father now to go off and kill himself at the rink instead of in the bathroom or the bedroom now, wasn't it?" I can't help the sarcastic tone. "Was he trying to protect you when he left you fatherless? Is he protecting us by leaving a stack of bills we can't pay?" I am angry at Ches and I feel awful for taking it out on Marianne but I hate the way she defends him at every turn. "Would you really like to see what he's left us?" I take the bag and dump the entire contents out on the kitchen table.

There's a package of Dentyne Ice with three pieces missing, an empty package of cigarettes, a road map of Newfoundland and Labrador that has never even been unfolded, a receipt for a bottle of ginger ale and a bag of Doritos from the Irving convenience store, three dimes and two pennies, a newspaper, a stack of napkins bearing the McDonald's logo, an *Eagles Greatest Hits* CD, his wallet, a rubber hose and a half-used roll of duct tape.

It is the latter that commands our attention. I can feel my heart rate slow just looking at it, as if it might make me breathe the same poison gas that killed Ches. It looks like the hose Ches used to fix my washing machine last year, but it has the same effect on me as a bloody knife or a smoking gun. I don't know why the police have returned this to me since it feels as if it should be tagged as evidence and stored in a lab somewhere. It's certainly not something the family of the deceased would want hanging around, but I can't bring myself to pick it up and throw it away. Marianne is looking at me with a mixture of disappointment and horror. I know she was hoping for something else, because I was too. We both want a clearer idea not only about why Ches killed himself, but I think we also crave something more. We want to know that we mattered on some level, since it seems to me that in taking his own life, Ches didn't give a moment's thought to how that might make his wife and child feel. We also need a sign that it wasn't our fault, that we couldn't have known or done anything to prevent this. We get neither.

CHAPTER THIRTEEN

Prissy

*I*t's Charlie who informs me that Quentin was looking for alcohol and drugs the night he ran off. Since he offers me no proof other than the fact he's a teenager with only one preoccupied parent to dupe, I give Quentin the benefit of the doubt. I am almost angry with Charlie for making the assertion in the first place when Quentin could just have easily been carrying out some altruistic pursuit like performing CPR on an accident victim or trying to save a stray dog. I don't know why he has to believe the worst about my son, but he laughs at me when I ask this question and calls me gullible. "No wonder Howie got away with fuckin around on you as long as he did," he says.

This remark stings so much I feel my skin prickle with heat. I feel like telling him he doesn't have the first clue what he's talking about, neither with respect to my husband nor my child. I could simply go to Georgia and ask, but other than thanking her profusely for returning my son safe and sound, I haven't questioned her one way or the other on what transpired or how she happened to find him, since the truth is, I would just rather remain in the dark. I don't really want to know that my son is trying to get drunk any more than I wanted to know that my husband was having an affair. I think that whoever coined the phrase that not knowing is the worst had to be completely out of their mind. Not knowing is perfectly fine with me, since I'd much rather subscribe to the old adage that ignorance is bliss.

But Charlie is insistent and by the time Quentin makes it down-stairs for breakfast, Charlie is intent on proving his point.

"Hey shithead," he says, "were you drinking when you were out the other night?" Charlie rummages in the fridge and takes out a Molson as if to emphasize his point. He twists the cap and a small puff of smoke rises from the neck of the bottle as the cold liquid is exposed to the warm air. He drinks greedily from the brown glass bottle and I take another sip of my coffee. It is nine thirty in the morning and I look at my brother with disapproval mingled with disgust.

Quentin shakes his head. "I wish. Don't I look nineteen to you?"

"Not even close," Charlie answers. "Why don't you just get your mom to buy it for you? She used to buy it for me when I was around your age. She had a fake ID and she used to be able to go into Carbonear and get it for me."

"Charlie!" I say sharply.

"Be prepared to work for it though," Charlie continues, ignoring me. "Your mother used to make me do all her chores in exchange for getting it for me. I did so many fuckin dishes for her I had dishpan hands."

"Mom please," Quentin pleads. "I can do dishes."

"Are you out of your mind?" I look to both of them since the question could apply to either of them. I think that Charlie is wrong. I think that Quentin ran off that night for the same reason I ran off that night. Because our family is falling apart, because my mother can't stop talking about dying, because we are not where we are supposed to be, and because he is just a frightened little boy. When I look at Quentin at that moment, I don't see a teenager bursting forth with hormones. I don't see his pimpled forehead or the brown hairs sprouting from his forearms. I see my little boy, with smooth skin and wide trusting eyes, and my heart breaks that he's going through something I can't kiss away.

"Quentin honey, do you want to talk about it?"

"What?" He yawns loudly and rests his head on the kitchen table as if he were bored.

"About why you ran off on your own the other night?"

"No, not really," he answers into his chest.

My mother, who has ignored the discussion to this point, is cracking eggs into a mixing bowl and whisking vigorously. "How many eggs do you want, Charlie, er … Artie, er … Jesus … Quentin!" My mother shakes her head in frustration.

"Should I wear a nametag?"

I am less surprised by my son's sarcastic tone than my mother's failure to recall anyone's name of late. I am called Sade, Fran and Luce on a regular basis before she realizes her error, and Charlie is called Artie so much he doesn't bother to correct her anymore.

"Quentin, enough please," I say calmly. "Now, can you tell me where you were the other night?"

"St. Augustine's."

Charlie grins triumphantly, knowing it to be a typical hangout for Paradise Bay's drunken teens, but Quentin could not possibly know that.

"What were you doing there?"

"Praying," Quentin says flatly. "We orphans have a lot of unresolved issues with God. It's been tough dealing with my dad's sudden death."

"An orphan doesn't have *any* parents," I correct him, ignoring his derisive comment. I hesitate to ask but I know I have to now. "Quentin, were you trying to buy alcohol or drugs, or …" I don't know what else there is.

"No," Quentin says and I want to believe him. "I wasn't trying to buy drugs. I was just looking to trade sexual favours for a quick hit. You wouldn't believe what some perverts would pay for a fourteen-year-old boy."

Charlie has the audacity to laugh. "Is that why Georgia brought you home? Everyone knows that chick is lonely but she is way too old for you."

"Gross!" Quentin gags, but then laughs along with his uncle.

He doesn't look the least bit scared, nervous or fretful. I wonder if he's genuinely okay, or if he's just becoming as adept as I am at hiding his feelings.

That evening I sit out on the porch, sipping a cup of tea and listening to the distant rhythm of the ocean. I make a mental list of all the things I need to worry about as the single parent of a teenage boy and I am shocked at how long the list is. There are drugs, alcohol, gangs and tattoos. There are deadly diseases, crippling diseases and sexually transmitted diseases. There are drunk drivers; there are car accidents, motorcycle accidents, boating accidents. I even fret over things like e-coli and salmonella outbreaks.

I think that if Quentin and I stay right here in Paradise Bay, we can avoid some, but not all of these risk factors. Paradise Bay is still insular, subscribing to a traditional way of life that seems simple and uncomplicated compared with our lives in Toronto. I don't know why but even the thought of Quentin experimenting with alcohol and drugs seems far less dangerous here.

I always thought I might someday return to Paradise Bay to live, but never alone. I imagined an old house near the ocean that Howie and I would fix up. I imagined the two of us cooking meals together and sitting out on the porch on a night like this one to listen to the ocean's waves. I am so lost in thought that I don't even hear my mother take a seat in the vacant rocking chair next to me.

"He's gonna be all right," Mom says.

I am startled by the intrusion. "What?"

"Quentin. I said he's going to be all right," she says again. "Where were you just now, Priss?"

"Nowhere," I say, embarrassed at having been caught daydreaming.

"Thinking about him again, were you?"

"Who?"

"Howie. Who do you think I mean?"

"No, well, maybe a little," I concede. "I was just thinking about how nothing turns out the way you plan."

"You think I planned on having my daughter whisked halfway across the country to raise her family? I never imagined that you would up and leave us, but it was the only thing you ever really wanted, to be with him. You were so in love, you'd have followed him all over hell's half acre to be near him."

I smile sadly, knowing it was true. I didn't think about the consequences at the time. I was just smitten, eager to run away with Howie and start a family in a new and exciting place. I didn't think about how it might make my mother sad that there were leftovers at Sunday dinners all of a sudden, or that *Coronation Street* would no longer hold its appeal for her in my absence. I didn't think about the fact that Mom would grow old one day and need help getting to the store or doing laundry or climbing the stairs. I never thought she'd end up all alone in the house that was always bustling with activity.

"It just about killed your father," she says. "I never seen your father raise his voice to anyone in my life except to Howie the day he asked your dad's permission to get married."

I am shocked by her revelation. I thought Dad loved Howie, and I know for a fact that my husband loved him. I remember Howie's reaction to the news of my father's death. He had been stoic throughout it all, making the plans for us to travel on the next flight back home, taking the burden off my mother and making all the arrangements with the funeral home from his office in the den. He was efficient and orderly, clearly comfortable in the role, and yet when it was time to lower the casket into the freshly dug hole, my husband had looked to the wet ground, his eyes red and moist with tears for the first time throughout it all. I remember squeezing his hand to let him know that I was there for him without drawing attention to his grief.

Every year, during our sojourn here, Howie would get up at the crack of dawn to trek after Dad and Charlie in my father's boat. They would return hours later, my father's and my brother's buckets overflowing with fish, and Howie following sheepishly behind, toting an empty bucket that had been filled with bait. He good-naturedly endured a ribbing from all of us while he regaled us with stories of the one that got away. At the end of the day though, there was always enough fresh fish for everyone and we all sat together sharing a good meal and a few beers.

That my father harboured any sort of resentment toward my husband was nothing less than shocking. "What are you talking about?" I ask Mom accusingly. "Dad and Howie got on just fine. Better than fine." I am verging on annoyed. "You can't change the relationship between Dad and Howie just because you don't like him anymore." I think about the picture from Howie's memorial service and I remember the way the two of them laughed whenever they were together. "Howie and Dad loved one another," I add.

My mother nods in agreement. "Afterwards, yes," she says quietly, rocking back and forth. "But not in the beginning. Your father hated Howie. He used to wonder what on earth you saw in him since he didn't know anything about fishing, or how to pitch a tent, or drive a snowmobile."

I think that these are ridiculous reasons not to love someone, but I suppose to Dad, who lived and breathed the outdoors, Howie might have been a hard person to accept.

"But the truth is your father was jealous he wasn't the most important man in your life anymore, although he'd never admit it."

I feel a rush of warmth at the thought of my father. At this moment I feel exceptionally close to my mother and at the same time slightly uncomfortable since it's rare for us to speak so openly and honestly.

"So when did Dad come around?" My father was always so good-natured that I find it hard to picture him angry about anything or anyone.

"I told you. The day Howie asked us if he could marry you." The wrinkles around her eyes grow more pronounced as she bursts into spontaneous laughter, obviously remembering something of great amusement. "Don't tell me Howie never told you?" She chuckles softly. "No, I dare say he didn't."

I lean forward, eager to hear the story about the two men in my life that I thought I knew better than anyone else. "Tell me," I plead.

"Howie come up from Toronto all decked out in his Sunday best so he could formally ask for your hand. It was the week you spent over in Carbonear with Lottie while she had the baby. I guess Howard thought an old-fashioned gesture like that would win over a couple of old farts like us, but your dad wasn't falling for it. He tells Howie that out on the water is his thinking place and that they should talk about it there. Howie points out that he didn't bring a change of clothes since he's flying back later in the day, but your father doesn't say a word, he just stands in the doorway with his rubber boots on. 'Well, do you want to marry my daughter or not?' And so Howie follows your father down to the wharf with his fancy suit on. Your dad has him put gas in the motor, buy the bait and untie the boat from the pier, but he falls in the water trying to get aboard and your dad has to pull him up. By the time they got back, Howie was drenched, smelled of fish guts, his flight was after taking off without him, and his suit was ruined."

I hang on every word of the story, completely transfixed that I did not know of this pivotal event. Howie had simply told me that he spoke to my dad and had received his blessing.

Mom continues, "After they got back, your father got right down to business. 'I make no wonder you're smitten with my nineteen-year-old daughter. She's young and beautiful and innocent.'"

I place a hand to my mouth and wonder what Dad would have thought if he had known of our first meeting. Innocent I was not.

My mother smiles at me in such a way I wonder if she is thinking the same thing I am. "Then your dad shouted that Howie was nothing but a fucking pervert chasing after a young girl, and Howie responded by calling your father a God-damned sonofabitch and swore he was going to marry you whether we liked it or not."

I laugh out loud imagining this exchange, picturing my stubborn father and my irate husband, dripping wet and covered with mud and fish scales.

"Howie got all emotional then." Mom puts a gnarled hand on my knee. "He told us he couldn't imagine life without you in ten years, twenty years, or God willing, even fifty years. Said the thing he loved most about you was that you made him feel like the strongest, smartest man in the world. He told us he would always love the way you laughed at his jokes even if you didn't think they were all that funny, and that you were always thinking of ways to surprise him. But he said the thing that got him most was the way your face lit up when you saw him. He said no one had ever looked at him like that and it made him feel like he could do anything in the world.

"Then your father shook his head in defeat, like there was nothing going to stop you two from running off together, and he said, 'If you break her heart I'll kill you.' He meant it too. All's I can say now is that it's a good thing your father never lived to see this day, cause I wouldn't have to make up an obituary, if you catch my drift."

But I'm not listening anymore, because my thoughts are frozen in another time, back when we were courting, as my dad used to say. I remember the way I practically worshipped my future husband. I would constantly look for little gifts to surprise him with, even if they were small items meant only to bring a smile to his face — a coffee mug boasting World's Greatest Fisherman because he could never catch a thing, a comic strip I cut out from the newspaper because Howie had secretly nicknamed my father Hagar, or a beach rock because we skipped stones on one of our first dates and he told me it was the best date he ever had.

I remember saving up things to say throughout the day so I could be interesting when he telephoned. I would even rehearse how I should sound when relaying all the finer points of my day. And when he'd come to visit, I would sit by the window until I saw him pull into the driveway, and then I'd bound down the stairs, out to the yard and jump into his arms.

I think about the last ten, twelve, however many years. They are a blur of chores, errands and coexistence. We speak only when it's necessary. We've become strangers to one another, our conversations a string of stunted questions and one-word answers. Of course our marriage was ending, perhaps had been for years. I only wonder why I hadn't seen it coming.

CHAPTER FOURTEEN

Georgia

*I*nvite Lottie and Prissy to my house, although I don't tell them why since I'm convinced neither of them will come if they know my purpose is to start a support group for young widows. I think of me, Lottie and Prissy getting together to talk about what it's like to lose a husband, what we need to do to survive the loneliness, and how we can cope with such milestones as holidays and anniversaries. I imagine we will share stories; we will laugh, cry and emerge stronger than ever because we share a special bond. And then my exuberance diminishes as soon as I think about how neither Prissy nor Lottie seems interested in talking about her situation. I ask myself, What's the point of a support group if no one is willing to show their vulnerability in the first place?

I expect a certain level of apprehensiveness when I reveal my intentions. Prissy, I know, does not like to talk about Howie, so the idea of a group with a specific intention of doing the very thing she avoids is unlikely to go over well. Lottie does not talk very much about Ches either, except in disparaging terms. It seems me, who has been widowed the longest, is the only one interested in speaking about my dead husband. I'm disappointed by their reluctance to discuss such matters since I was so certain this was meant to be. I cling to the notion that Lottie and Prissy are meant to be my salvation with all the desperation of someone hanging precariously off a cliff with nothing but their fingernails buried in rocky gravel to prevent them from falling.

"I can't stay long," Lottie warns me almost as soon as she walks in the door just moments after Prissy's arrival.

It makes me feel rushed, and so instead of easing into the purpose of our gathering, I smile nervously and make my announcement. "Well … I invited you both here this evening because … well I thought that since the three of us were in the same boat, that maybe we could start a little support group for young widows. We could get together every few weeks and … talk about some of the things we're going through." I tuck a lock of hair behind my ear and then decide I prefer it to cover my cheek instead.

My announcement does not elicit the response I'd hoped, rather the response I'd feared. No one claps, embraces me or even smiles approvingly. Lottie wears such a look of confusion that I wonder if she heard me right, but then I steal a glance at Prissy, who looks pale and horrified, and I know at least that she's understood.

"Before you say no," I urge her, noticing that Prissy is already shaking her head and her hands are trembling, "we can take it as slow as you want. The most important thing is to be around people who know how you're feeling and what you're going through."

"You don't know what I'm going through," Prissy says defensively, biting cuticles that are already raw from being picked at.

I want to say that I do know what she's going through, but I don't, not really. Everyone's grief is different and I don't have a child to raise on my own.

Lottie, on the other hand, laughs outright, suggesting there ought to be a support group for married people instead of widowed folks. "I was far more miserable being married to Ches than I am now that he's dead," Lottie adds with conviction, but I don't necessarily believe her.

I look to my journal where I've written the five stages of grief in script, the agenda for my gathering. *Shock and Denial, Anger, Isolation, Bargaining and Healing.* I still don't know which stage I am at myself, since some days I am all five before lunch, and on other days I am still struck by the shock of it all.

"Prissy, how did you feel the day Howie told you about his diagnosis?" I figure it's time to push Prissy since the last thing I want is for her to repeat the same pattern I've gone through. I refused to speak to anyone about Joseph and my entire existence has been mired in unbearable grief for the past five years. "Were you in shock? Could you believe this was happening? Can you believe it now?"

I'm hoping that she'll crack under my line of questioning the way a person on trial might break down under a brutal cross-examination, and once she's confessed to feeling helpless or angry or alone, then I can help her begin the healing process, although whether it's for her or me, I'm not sure; maybe both.

"I told you I don't want to talk about it," Prissy snaps.

"But you need to," I implore. "You need to let it out. It's okay to be upset and angry and everything else you might be feeling right now."

"I gotta go." Prissy gets up to leave and I beg her to stay, promising I won't ask another question about Howie, until she eventually relents.

"I'm not joining this support group of yours," Prissy adds with steadfast determination.

"Of course you don't have to do anything you don't want to do, but I hope you'll reconsider. I just want to help you." I can't mask the hurt in my voice and Prissy looks guilty for snapping at me. "I would have wished for a group like this to help me out when Joseph died. There was nothing like this out there."

Prissy still looks uncomfortable, but a look of excitement crosses Lottie's face as if the most amazing idea has just come to her.

"Does this support group have a name?" Lottie asks.

"A name?" I repeat dumbly. It hasn't occurred to me to come up with a name. "What do we need a name for?"

Lottie looks at me as if I were lagging behind the conversation. "So we can get a government grant. If Fred Bishop can get a grant for the flea market, we can get one for a support group."

It hadn't occurred to me to apply for a government grant, nor do I want to. I only wanted to share a few thoughts and feelings with Lottie and Prissy so they can heal and I can heal and one day I can wake up without my limbs feeling as if there were 100-pound weights attached to them. I mull over the idea of a government grant to form a support group and I comfort myself with just the tiniest fraction of possibility that Joseph's death was not entirely frivolous, that some-one somewhere could actually benefit from a support group that I helped start. "Why don't we call ourselves the Young Widows of Paradise Bay?"

Lottie keeps repeating the phrase over and over, trying it on like a new sweater but then suddenly deciding the fabric scratched her skin.

"Young Widows of Paradise Bay," Lottie says again with a face. "That would be YWPB," she says, shaking her head. "No, that won't do. The letters should spell out something so people will remember us. What's that called again, when the letters that stand for something spell out something else, like MADD or NOW?"

"An acronym," says Prissy.

"Right, we need something catchy to grab everyone's attention. Something that's easy for the reporters on the CBC to say. The government is never going to give money to a group that calls themselves the Young Widows of Paradise Bay. Not only is it a mouthful, but you can't have Paradise Bay in the name because you need to think bigger."

I'm surprised that Lottie seems to know so much about strategies for procuring government funds, but, more so, I am having serious reservations about obtaining such a grant in the first place. It seems premature to me. We haven't accomplished anything amongst ourselves; we can't even talk about why we're here in the first place, and I feel as if we ought to have some sort of breakthrough before we go about seeking a government grant. I am about to make this point when Lottie begins to offer additional suggestions for a proper name.

"Widows In Need, or WIN," Lottie says, "might be good, but, then again I don't know. I don't like the word need because it makes us look helpless, which defeats the purpose of a self-help group. What do you think?" she asks, looking around.

Truthfully, I think it's a fitting name since I feel helpless most of the time, but I understand what she's trying to say. "How about Widows in Need of Support, or WINS?" I counter, thinking that Lottie couldn't possibly take exception to that, but I'm wrong.

"Widows in Need of Support is actually WINOS," Lottie points out doubtfully, but it makes Prissy laugh. It's the first time I've heard her laugh since she landed back in Paradise Bay and the sound is melodic and uplifting, and I think even if we didn't get to talk about our grief, it's wonderful to hear Prissy's laugh and to see her smile.

"Everyone will be thinking we're all just a bunch of drunks." Prissy is giggling so hard now that her eyes are tearing up and she waves a hand over her mouth to try to gain her composure. The sound is contagious and it isn't long before Lottie and I are laughing too.

"I got it," Lottie shouts, snapping her fingers, and Prissy and I smile in anticipation of what could possibly be better than WINOS. "Widows Helping Other Widows, or WHOW! What do you think?" Prissy and I both nod our approval and Lottie smiles excitedly and clasps her hands together. "We'll have to come up with a mission statement and develop some membership guidelines. If we're serious about this, we have a lot of things to think about."

"We certainly do," I add, thinking of such things as strained relationships with in-laws that eventually buckle and cave in, anger at a dead spouse for not being able to mow the lawn in the summertime, and the kind of loneliness that you grow to tolerate until it defines who you are. These are clearly not the same things Lottie is thinking of.

"For starters," Lottie says. "How old is a young widow? Forty, fifty? I mean, you have to draw the line somewhere or else we'll have the crowd at the nursing home with their feeding tubes signing up tomorrow. And then there's the question of men. Men usually die first but there are occasions when the women go early. So are we a widows' group or a women's group? And then, what if you get married again? Are you banned for life until your next husband dies?"

I am starting to feel the beginnings of a headache. "I just wanted to get together and talk about what we're all going through as widows," I say apologetically. "I didn't mean for it to be such a project."

Lottie stands and puts on her coat. "Georgia honey, I think this is a fantastic idea." I believe her when she says this because Lottie's eyes are animated and she looks more excited than I remember seeing her ever before. "Like you said, there's nothing else out there like it. I could talk about this all day, but I can't talk about Ches, not yet."

Maybe I'm rushing it, pushing too hard with my formal agenda and my meeting. Maybe if we just get together to talk about nothing in particular, then other topics will come naturally. Lottie apologizes to me as if she's hurt my feelings, and then she turns to leave, having promised Marianne she'd be home by nine.

"She gets scared sometimes being alone at night," Lottie says and I nod in understanding.

Once Lottie leaves, Prissy and I look uncertainly at one another. I can tell she's readying her defences, waiting for me to bring Howie up again, but I won't.

"I meant to thank you for bringing Quentin home the other night," Prissy says. "I was just so relieved to see him that I never did get the chance to thank you properly." Prissy smiles shyly and then takes a sip of her tea.

I think Prissy has a long road ahead of her with regard to her son. It is such a vulnerable age. He is on the verge of manhood himself and has lost his role model of what it means to be a man. I wish Joseph could be here to help the boy. "How is Quentin doing?" I ask. "I'm concerned for him," I say, before Prissy has a chance to answer me. "I think he's experiencing denial hard and fast. He told me his father was still alive and that he was just off screwing around somewhere. I mean it's not uncommon for a child—"

I stop in mid-sentence because all the blood is gone from Prissy's face and she covers her shocked expression with trembling hands. She is shaking her head and muttering that she is so sorry, and it takes me a while to understand what she's talking about, but when I do comprehend, everything hits me like a train. Prissy does not like to talk about Howie's illness because there is no illness. She cringes when people ask her how she's coping with her husband's death because there is no death. I'm confused and angry and I have the sensation of falling from the sky. I've let the gravel and dirt go from my fingernails and now I'm falling off the cliff I've clung to so foolishly and so steadfastly. "How could you?" I gasp.

"It wasn't my idea, I swear," Prissy says defensively. "I came home to get away from things and the next thing I know, Mom is waving this obit at me. She thought it'd be easier for me that way. I knew it was stupid but I went along with it anyway. And truthfully, it was easier to pretend Howie was dead instead of with someone else."

I can hardly think straight. I recall the bogus memorial service and picture Prissy sitting before the statue of Christ with tears in her eyes. I remember the way she sobbed from her place at the front pew, putting on a show unlike any I'd ever seen before.

"What were you thinking, Prissy? If you only knew what it was like to lose a husband, you wouldn't go around pretending, getting people to feel sorry for you and trying to help you." This time it is me whose hands are trembling, but with anger.

Prissy stands up to put her coat on, but her shaking hands fumble so much with her zipper that she gives up trying and looks me in the eye. "I did lose a husband," Prissy says quietly and I see a momentary flash of her own anger reflected in her eyes. "You're lucky Joseph died when he did. Because he died when he was still the great love of your life and your marriage will forever be paused on this idyllic setting when you were happy and in love. You'll always be the grieving widow whose husband was taken in the prime of his life."

No one has ever dared say such things to me, and all I can do is stare stupidly at her while she tells me how lucky I am that my husband died one night five years ago.

"If Howie died a few years ago, I'd be the same as you, all beside myself with grief. But then that would be before Howie decided to warm someone else's bed, before he decided he didn't love me anymore, before he decided I wasn't a good enough wife for him, before he decided to cast me aside. It's so easy for you. You didn't fail at anything. Joseph never came home from work one night and told you your marriage was over. How do you know what would have happened if Joseph didn't die that night? How do you know that in ten years he wouldn't have screwed around with someone else? You don't know. You'll never know, and for that I am so completely envious of you."

And then Prissy is gone too, and I am alone with a book on grief and three empty journals.

Later that night, I toss and turn in bed for hours thinking about all the things Prissy said. How was I to know that if Joseph lived, we'd always be happy? I imagine Joseph telling me he didn't want to be married to me anymore, and I have to sit up and open my eyes until the image is gone. I don't understand Prissy's pain but I do know it's as raw as my own and I decide not to tell anyone her secret, not yet. For the first time in a long time, I fall asleep feeling sorry for someone other than myself.

CHAPTER FIFTEEN

Prissy

I don't feel as bad as I probably should for saying such awful things to Georgia because I was only telling the truth, which is something of a rarity for me these days. I keep waiting for the fallout, but it doesn't come. No one gives me the evil eye or sneers at me when I'm out about town or just taking a walk along the beach. To the contrary, people continue to send sympathetic looks my way, and I'm almost disappointed to know that I haven't been found out yet. I'm surprised, since I fully expected Georgia to call me out on my horrible secret, but instead she has become a reluctant participant in keeping it, which makes her kind of the same as me.

I'm tempted to ask Quentin what possessed him to reveal such things, but it feels wrong to confront my child for telling the truth. Quentin, it seems, has forgotten about the entire incident anyway. He spends so much time with Charlie I can't help but feel jealous. I try to coax him into spending more time together, but he avoids my efforts, or snubs them outright. I invite him to come peruse the flea market with me. "The market's boring," he mutters, without even so much as looking in my direction, which in retrospect it probably is for a fourteen-year-old boy. I invite him to go hiking with me, horseback riding, take a boat ride around the icebergs in the harbour, camping, whale watching, fishing, and an endless list of activities, each one he deems gayer than the last. When he tells me that sea kayaking is for losers, I get the message that it isn't the activity he objects to, so much as it is the company.

His uncle, on the other hand, says things like, "Come on, shithead, I'll take you for a ride," and Quentin positively beams. He adores Charlie and I think Charlie delights in having someone follow him around with such blind devotion. I can only imagine what Howie might say if he knew Quentin was riding around town on the back of Charlie's motorcycle, because it makes me slightly nervous too. But I trust my brother to be cautious and I could never say no when I know how much pleasure my son derives from these excursions. They go out for fish and chips; they spend the day in the woods driving ATVs on rustic trails. They ride up and down the coast on Charlie's motorcycle and have even gone as far as St. John's to the top Signal Hill and to the ruins at Fort Amherst. Today, though, they have spent the past four hours in my father's workshop, doing God knows what.

I am cooking dinner tonight because Quentin asked me specifically if I could make him spaghetti. To be asked was akin to being physically embraced by my child. To have something I alone can do for him makes me feel needed in a way that I haven't felt since he was a toddler and needed me to clear the room of monsters before he could go to sleep.

I don't understand why it hasn't occurred to me earlier to cook supper for him, other than the fact I can't really remember the last time I was hungry. Mom is eager to serve me up a variety of childhood favourites, including fried potatoes doused in malt vinegar, fried bologna with ketchup, and pea soup, so thick and salty I'm parched by evening. I have no interest in eating any of it, but I don't want to insult my mother so I eat enough to satisfy her. Quentin, on the other hand, has no such qualms about insulting his grandmother. He plugs his nose whenever he meanders into the kitchen around suppertime, asks who farted when his grandmother is boiling cabbage, and makes all sorts of gagging noises when she is shaping meat and potato pies.

I think that Mom will be happy to have the night off and let someone else cook but she is immediately suspicious. "What is that?" she asks warily when I place items such as capers and basil in my shopping cart. When I add a bulb of garlic, she asks me if we are warding off vampires or cooking supper. She asks why I have to make sauce when it comes in a jar in aisle seven at Sobey's. I want to counter that gravy comes in a jar too, although she'd never think of purchasing it in a million years. She stands over me as I chop, dice and stir, saying nothing except for the occasional ewww. It's as if my mother is channelling my son. I don't understand how someone who eats fish from a tin can be disgusted by something as benign as tomato sauce.

I can hardly blame my mother. Meat and potatoes and salt and pepper are all she's ever known, so it's perfectly understandable that she might resist the taste of something garlicky or balk at the pungent aroma of freshly grated parmesan cheese.

I lower the sauce to a simmer when Charlie and Quentin finally come in from the shed. They smell like freshly cut wood and leave a trail of sawdust along the floor.

"Jesus, I'm half starved to fuckin death," Charlie says. "What's for supper?" He picks up a stale biscuit that's been left out on the vinyl tablecloth since early afternoon and pops it into his mouth.

"Ask your sister," Mom says, blowing a cloud of smoke across the room. "She's feeding you this evening, although I doubt a bit of tomatoes and spaghetti is going to put any meat on them bones of yours."

"Sure, I'm after beefing up the summer." For emphasis, he flexes his biceps and my mother and I both laugh.

"What the fuck are you two laughing at?"

"Go on, Charlie, I seen more meat on Good Friday," Mom says, stubbing her cigarette in the ashtray.

"I can't help it if I'm skinny," Charlie counters, as if being slim were a character flaw like being weak or simple-minded. "Sure, I eats like a horse," he adds.

"You'll be eating more like a rabbit tonight," my mother says. I bite my tongue, because I don't want to start an argument and ruin Quentin's supper. "You know I never been one for ethnic food," Mom continues, apparently not content with her previous litany of complaints. "Always gives me the shits."

I roll my eyes in frustration. I don't know what's more annoying, that my mother refers to spaghetti as an ethnic food or that she suggests my cooking is likely to cause her a severe case of the runs. "Would you rather I just pick up some fish and chips?" I snap, throwing the wooden spoon into the sink. A path of tomato sauce appears on the linoleum floor from the oven to the sink, and I promptly bend down to wipe it clean with a paper towel.

"Calm down, Prissy," Mom says. "My God, you always were sensitive to a fault. Could never say boo to you and you'd be off to your room crying."

I am hurt by the comment and want to say something to that effect before I realize that only an overly sensitive person would be hurt by such a comment in the first place.

"How long before dinner, Priss?" Charlie asks. "It smells fuckin great in here, really."

"Bout a half hour," I answer.

Charlie sighs as if I'd told him it would be another three days before he could eat. "But I'm fuckin starving," he says, as if that could speed up the cooking process. "Jesus, Prissy, it's almost five o'clock already. Mom usually has supper ready by four thirty. Sure, by now the dishes would be done."

Mom is beaming under the praise from her son. "Yes, well, maybe we won't all be hungry again by eight o'clock," I say, which is really a dig at my mother for having supper ready sometimes as early as four o'clock, but she is quick to fire back.

"With what you're feeding us, we're all likely to be starved to death again by six thirty."

I'm losing patience with the pot of water that seems to be taking forever to boil under the small electric burner. "So," I say, changing the subject, "whatcha guys been doing in the shed?"

"We're making Nan's coffin," says Quentin.

I stop what I'm doing and turn to glare at my brother. "Excuse me? You're doing what?" I am so angry right now there are a million things I want to say and yet I'm rendered speechless. I flex my hands by my sides to stop from hitting my brother square across his face.

Charlie looks away and squirms uncomfortably in his seat. He knows he should not have involved my child in this ridiculous project. "Quentin's got a lot of potential for woodworking, and he has good ideas. He's a real artist."

I wonder what sort of good ideas my fourteen-year-old son could possibly offer up in the way of coffin making. "Then make a table," I say evenly.

"Well, you can't bury me on a table," Mom pipes in. "I think it's wonderful that Quentin is helping." She is smiling contentedly for the first time all day, frustrating me to no end. You'd think sitting down with a glass of wine while I cook supper might make her happy, but the one thing that puts a smile on her face is that her son and grandson are building her a coffin.

"You would," I say, sneering. "You ... you ... do you have any idea what you're saying?" I am on the verge of losing it with my mother, but Charlie raises his hands, signalling for our attention. He is trying to broker a peace deal between Mom and me, yet it was Charlie who I was mad at in the first place.

By the time the pasta is ready I don't have much of an appetite anymore. Quentin and Charlie finish their plates though, so it makes me feel a little better — that is, until Charlie tries to coax my mother into having some. "It's not really that bad," I hear him say as if he'd eaten something past the expiration date. In the end, my mother eats toast and drinks tea for supper like a disagreeable child.

CHAPTER SIXTEEN

Lottie

After another unsuccessful day of job hunting, I meet Georgia at Lawlor's for lunch. It is busy and we have to wait a long time for the waitress to take our order. I order a coffee since all I have in my purse is a loonie and a few dimes and nickels. Georgia orders pea soup, a garden salad, and a slice of coconut cream pie, which she asks to be brought out along with her soup. I think it's an odd request but she explains that she can hardly taste things anymore unless she has something sweet first since she's always baking and has gotten accustomed to eating dessert first.

"Aren't you going to have anything?" Georgia asks.

"I had an early lunch," I lie. The smells are making my stomach grumble and I am thankful the dining room is loud enough to hide the noise. I don't know why I agreed to meet her for lunch in the first place, other than she sounded so lonely on the phone.

"You okay?" I ask, because she looks as forlorn as she sounded on the phone earlier this morning. She is rolling and unrolling her utensils in the paper napkin, her mind clearly not here with me, but someplace else.

"I wanted to ask you something," Georgia says. She looks nervous and I feel my own stomach knot in anticipation. "If Joseph didn't die that night, do you think we'd still be happy?" Georgia looks away, embarrassed, and rightly so. It's a ridiculous question since it doesn't matter one way or the other.

I know that something must have happened to bring this particular question up since Georgia has never once uttered anything that could be interpreted as uncertainty about her marriage. She talks about how she and Joseph were meant for one another and how the fates conspired to bring them together that stormy night. She talks about how right it felt walking down the aisle, how safe she always felt with him. Never has she ever questioned the future that might have been.

"Why are you asking me that?"

"The other night when we got together for our support group … After you left, Prissy and I talked, and she suggested that if Joseph hadn't died, maybe we wouldn't be as happy as I like to think we'd be. It got me thinking that maybe I'm just idealizing everything about Joseph and our lives together. That maybe we weren't that perfect for each other after all. What if she's right? I've never doubted our relationship until now."

I don't know what on earth could have gotten into Prissy to suggest such a thing, to Georgia of all people, who looks like she's about to burst into tears at any moment. It hardly seems like something Prissy would say. "Maybe you just misunderstood," I suggest, but Georgia shakes her head.

"No, I didn't misunderstand anything."

"Georgia," I say, "it doesn't matter anyway since Joseph is dead. Why bother worrying about what might have been or might not have been?" I am trying to be patient but I'm having difficulty summoning any sympathy for Georgia. I think about my empty bank account, the stack of bills with *Final Notice* stamped on the inside in bold lettering, and my dwindling pantry, and while I would like to sit here and entertain all the possibilities with Georgia, I can't imagine what a luxury it must be to spend all day moping about after a dead man. Perhaps if I didn't have to worry so much about money, I might spend more time thinking about Ches and why he killed himself, but I think it might drive me crazy to think about nothing other than why my husband took his own life.

"But what if he didn't love me anymore?" Georgia's voice is shaky at the possibility.

I do think Georgia has a tendency to idealize her marriage. I can't imagine a man who doesn't have his share of annoying habits, but Georgia doesn't talk about them at all. I'm sure Joseph left his dirty clothes on the floor and shed his body hair all over the bathroom sink like every other man, but she's forgotten, or doesn't care. There are no guarantees that they would still love one another, but I don't have the heart to tell her. "Of course you'd still be happy," I say. "Joseph and you were meant for one another."

I have told Georgia everything she wants to hear and she looks instantly relieved. My coffee arrives along with a packet of sugar and a plastic container of creamer. I'm not accustomed to the bitter taste and Georgia looks oddly at me, noticing that I am not drinking my usual cup of tea. I explain that I am mired in a job search and am hoping the caffeine might give me a jolt of much-needed energy.

"How's that going?"

"Lousy. There aren't that many jobs around here and I have no experience." Job hunting is proving not only to be humbling, but embarrassing. I spend day after day travelling from store to store in Carbonear, Bay Roberts, and every place in between, filling out applications, but I feel defeated almost as soon as I am handed the paper. I can feel my face burn with embarrassment as I hand the application back to a clerk half my age, with nothing filled out save for my name and address and telephone number. I don't have an education, experience, volunteer activities, or even an e-mail address to report.

I think about calling my parents in Calgary to ask for a loan when it occurs to me that not a single relative came to Ches' funeral. *Mom and Dad just aren't up to travelling that far.* At least that's the excuse my sister gave. Her excuse was that she had to stay behind to look after them since they couldn't manage on their own for more than a few hours. At the time, it didn't bother me a whole lot since I was mostly in a daze and I knew Ches wouldn't be thrilled with having them there in the first place.

The last time I asked my parents for money, Marianne was but a few months old and Ches and I were completely taken aback by the price of diapers and formula. I bought generic brands to save money but Marianne went through everything almost as soon as I bought it. I was so exhausted in those first weeks that I could barely think beyond the next feeding or changing, but when I found myself diluting a bottle of formula with water so I would have a bottle for Marianne's nighttime feeding, I began to panic. It wasn't like Ches was drinking away the money, not way back then anyway. We just didn't have any since it was the height of summer and Ches only worked in the fall and winter, and sometimes into the spring, when the ice was down on the rink. "I can go to my parents," I said. "They won't let their own granddaughter starve." But Ches became so incensed he put his fist through the bedroom wall, telling me my parents could go fuck themselves. I couldn't blame him. My parents hated Ches. Not for getting me pregnant. That, they could forgive. It was the getting married part they objected to.

I fed Marianne cow's milk for the next three feedings and watched in heart-wrenching guilt as my infant daughter writhed in pain before spitting up almost half of the milk. My breaking point came when Marianne woke up from her morning nap and I let her sit there in her wet diaper for two hours because there were only two clean ones left. I cried when I thought of Marianne's baby-soft skin chafing against the urine-soaked diaper. I debated which would be easier for Ches to take, going to my parents for help or going to the welfare office. Both were an affront to his pride but my daughter's welfare was more important. In the end I asked my father for help, but I begged him not to let Ches know. He tried to convince me to leave Ches, but I was too full of idealistic hope that we would be okay. In the end my father relented, giving me two hundred dollars.

Ches found out about it. He had to, because all of a sudden I wasn't complaining about money anymore. If I'd have kept after him, he might never have known the difference, but I didn't have the energy to keep fighting with him. He was predictably angry with me and he took the money and went to the Legion with it. He got so drunk he passed out on the side of the road on the way home and had to be carried through the front door by three of his drinking buddies. I left him the next day when he was sleeping it off. Marianne and I stayed at my parents for more than a month, and while I promised my mother that I wouldn't go back to Ches, somehow I knew that eventually I would.

When Ches came back for us, he looked awful, like he'd been wasting away without us. He was pale, unshaven and had lost weight. He begged me to let him hold Marianne, which struck me as odd since he couldn't be bothered holding her when I asked him to, especially if she was crying or fussy or needed her diaper changed.

"I'm going to take a course," he told me. "Flagman. So I can pick up some work during the summer. They're always doing construction in the summer and I figure I can pick up a few hours here and there. We'll get by," he promised and I watched his adam's apple go up and down his whiskered neck as he swallowed nervously waiting for my answer. Of course he never enrolled in any course, never applied for work in construction or anything else, but in that moment I sensed that he needed me even as he assured me he was the one who would take care of us. I packed up my things while my parents shouted at me that I was going to regret this decision. Of course they were right, but I think in the end they were more concerned with being right than anything else.

I think that Ches has always needed me because I made him feel as if he was worth something when no one else did. But that was a long time ago and I hadn't felt like Ches was worth much of anything lately. I didn't kill my husband, but I feel partly responsible all the same. I think about the money I owe, my inability to get work, and last night the light bulb went out on the back porch and I haven't the slightest clue how to change it. I think of Ches in heaven or hell, laughing at me. *Who's better off now?*

It takes a half hour for Georgia's soup and her pie to arrive, a ridiculous amount of time considering the soup was probably made several hours earlier. The waitress is harried and apologetic, claiming they are short-handed.

"My friend Lottie here is looking for a job," Georgia tells the waitress as she opens a package of crackers to put in her soup, and I immediately feel embarrassed. "Maybe she can speak to the manager."

"He's in back, but I'll let him know," the waitress says, rushing off to the sympathetic stares of a dining room full of hungry yet patient people.

Once Georgia is done with her soup, I put on my jacket, eager to get home and make myself some toast.

"You can't go yet," Georgia insists. "You haven't seen the manager."

"He's not going to hire me anyway," I say, my voice full of defeat. "I don't have any experience waiting tables and nobody wants to hire someone they have to train." I have heard it all before, thirteen times today alone.

"Of course you have experience," Georgia says, and I look at her like she's delusional. "You were married, what, sixteen years? You have a teenage daughter. That's not experience?"

I close my eyes and for a second I can hear Ches' voice. *Lottie, these God-damn eggs are too runny. Lottie, go get me ice for my soda, will ya? Why is there no lemon in my tea? Put the mayo on only one slice of bread and butter on the other.* I can hear Marianne too. *More lemonade please. Mom, the syrup is making my pancakes all soggy. I only want gravy on the potatoes. I dropped my fork. Can you cut the crusts off my bread?* Waiting on other people just may be the only thing I know how to do. It takes nearly two hours before the crowd thins and the manager has the time to speak to me. I'm hired just five minutes later.

CHAPTER SEVENTEEN

Georgia

I leave the flea market early because I can see the fog beginning to roll in and in half an hour I probably won't be able to see the person at the next table anyway. I can scarcely believe that in a few short weeks it will be over for another season and I will return to another long and lonely winter. It is funny to think that it is exactly the ferocious snowstorms and frigid temperatures that I loved to experience with Joseph, but hate the most now. Paradise Bay can be the most desolate and lonely of places in the winter. I used to love the feeling that Joseph and I were the only people in the world, and now I hate feeling like I'm the only one left.

I watch the tents and the people from the flea market disappear from my rear-view mirror and berate myself for dwelling on another long winter when it is only the end of August and there are still plenty more beautiful days to savour. I turn on my radio program, a talk show hosted by recently ousted politician Gerald Gosse, whose callers consistently mangle his name into one syllable by calling him Jerld. I enjoy listening to people call up and offer opinions on whatever strikes their fancy on a given day, be it politics, economics, education or something else entirely. I suppose I like listening to the program because I imagine the callers are a little bit like me, lonely souls who don't have the luxury of sharing their thoughts with anyone else.

After a carpet commercial, Gerald's booming voice comes through the speakers once again. "Welcome back to the show. We have a caller on line two. Go ahead, caller." There's a pause followed by an uncertain, "Jerld? Hello?"

"Go ahead, you're on the air," he says encouragingly.

"Is that you, Jerld?"

"Yes, caller, now what is your name and where are you calling from?"

"My name is Lottie and I'm calling from Paradise Bay."

My mouth drops open at the sound of Lottie's familiar voice broadcasting province-wide, and I turn up the volume in anticipation tinged with trepidation.

"What's on your mind today, Lottie? Did you want to comment on the upcoming visit of the prime minister?" Gerald asks. "Or perhaps you'd like to comment on the Brigus Blueberry Festival going on right now."

"Oh no," Lottie answers. "I wants to talk about widows."

I can't understand why Lottie, who remains tight-lipped around me, thinks nothing of calling up a radio program to broadcast her situation across the entire province.

"Widows? Okay, what about them? Are you a widow yourself?" Gerald asks.

"I am," Lottie's voice says with a certain measure of pride. "Thirty-seven days since my husband committed suicide."

There aren't too many things that leave Gerald Gosse speechless, but silence fills the air for almost a full five seconds before he recovers enough to convey his condolences.

"It's all right," Lottie answers. "I joined this support group for young widows called Widows Helping Other Widows. That's wHOW, for short. It was started right here in Paradise Bay by my friend, Georgia Reid, after she found out the hard way there wasn't anything like it out there. Her husband died five years ago and she's still an awful mess."

I don't hear anything else Lottie says because I stop breathing and stare at the radio as if my glare could shush her from saying any more to publicly humiliate me. She's revealed my first and last name and exposed my grief to a provincial audience. I can feel the soulful eyes of every listener stare at me, their faces filled with pity. I am so consumed by this image that I forget for a moment where I am and I don't see the bend in the road that I've been navigating with ease for years. I feel my tires skid along the shoulder of the road, toward a steep cliff that ends with a 300-foot drop into the ocean. There's a guardrail, but I am travelling fast and I don't think it's going to stop my car. My heart jumps into my throat and I close my eyes while I wait for the sensation of free-fall to overtake me. I feel a nervous excitement grip my entire body, and in a split second so many different things enter my mind. I think it's a little ironic that both Joseph and I die in fatal car wrecks. I wonder if Joseph will be the one to bring me to the other side and I wonder how I'll know it's him. I wonder if I'll be able to see him and reach out to him or if I'll simply sense his presence and know that he's there. I wonder if there really is a light and a tunnel, but most of all I wonder if I will finally be rid of the gaping wound in my heart that refuses to heal. I am not afraid at all.

But my car misses the guardrail altogether and skims a jutting boulder on the edge of the embankment instead. I come to an abrupt stop and am thrown forward only slightly before being forced back into my seat by my seatbelt. My heart still pumps blood through my body and carries oxygen to my brain, which is reeling now, trying to determine what went so horribly wrong. There is no tunnel, no white light and not a sign of Joseph anywhere. I'm certain that nothing is broken or bruised or bleeding. Even the air bag didn't deploy, although the car has skidded off the road and is now shrouded in fog on an embankment.

I am unable to move, paralyzed not by injury, but by disappointment. I grip the steering wheel until my knuckles are white. I sob, I curse God and all the saints, and in my anger I even curse Joseph for not coming to take me with him, but I remain rooted to the driver's seat. I know I ought to get out and inspect the damage and flag someone down for help, but I just don't have any desire to do so. I can hear cars passing above me but I know they don't see me in all the fog.

I'm not sure how long I stay that way but I know it's a long time because it's nearly dark by the time I see Fred's panicked face in the car window. He opens the door, unfastens my seatbelt, pries my fingers from the steering wheel and pulls me out of the car. As his eyes inspect every inch of me, his hands massage my flesh in search of broken bones, cuts and bruises. I laugh under his examination, a hollow sound that's scarier than any gruesome physical wound.

"There's nothing there," I tell him flatly. "Not even a scratch. I guess

I'm just lucky." For some reason the irony of the entire situation strikes me as hysterically funny and I resume my laughter, giggling and hiccupping until I'm spent. I can feel Fred's eyes on me, his expression filled with concern, and it makes me hate him even more than I already do. Silence hangs between us, broken up only by the sound of the ocean waves. It all sounds like a peaceful meditation CD and I am nowhere near at peace with anything in my life.

From somewhere deep inside I release a wail that travels all the way down to the ocean and bounces off every jagged rock below until it echoes back to me. It is a horrible, frightening sound.

I don't protest when Fred holds my elbow and guides me into his truck. I'm not sure where we're going, nor do I care, but when he pulls into my driveway, I realize I don't want to go inside and feel the weight of the silence that greets me every evening.

Fred seems to sense this because he walks me inside and tells me to sit on the sofa while he makes me tea. I don't even realize I'm shivering until he drapes a quilt from my linen closet over my shoulders. I can hear him put the kettle on and rummage around my cupboards in search of teabags, cups and sugar. He hasn't set foot inside Joseph's house in more than five years and he still seems to remember where everything is kept, navigating the cupboards as if he's lived here all his life. I can hear his voice but he isn't speaking to me. He's on the phone.

"It's up on the back road, bout three kilometres from Powers' Field. Ya can't see it from the road, Al, ya got to follow the tire tracks. Tow it back to the shop and see if it can be fixed. Looks like it's just the bumper and the left headlight. Thanks, b'y." I hear the phone being placed back on the base, followed by the whistle of the tea kettle.

He hands me a steaming cup of tea and then sits next to me on the sofa.

"Can I call anyone for you?" he asks.

I shake my head. "I have nobody, not anymore anyway." I think this hurts Fred but I really didn't mean anything accusatory by it. I was merely stating a fact. "I might be dead a very long time before anyone would even notice." This too is a fact not worth disputing.

"Don't be talking such nonsense," he says, shaking his head. "You're in shock is all. It's normal to feel a little numb."

Numb is the very thing I am not. People who are numb don't feel anything and that is most certainly not a word you could ever use to describe me. I feel everything — pain, loneliness, grief, loss — so intently that it's like a knife constantly slicing through my flesh. "Do you know what I would give to feel numb, just for one day? Not to feel anything would be the most treasured gift in the world."

Fred's face is shadowed under the brim of his baseball cap, but I know he's uncomfortable. I've never opened up to Fred about anything, even when Joseph was alive, and he's unsure what to do now that I'm baring my soul. I study his hands, folded together in his lap, tanned and with a layer of dirt from working on his farm. He has big hands, I notice, and my gaze travels upward from his lap to his neck, until my eyes rest on the stubble, grown quickly back from a morning shave.

Much to my own surprise I become acutely aware of his maleness. I wonder what it would be like to feel the stubble against my skin and to feel his large hands stroke my back. It's been so long since anyone touched me and I ache so badly to feel someone hold me the way Joseph used to that my skin feels hot and my belly tingles in anticipation of something. Before I can change my mind I bring my lips to rest on his, but he jumps away from me as if I'd burned him.

"Have you gone cracked, altogether?" he sputters.

"I'm sorry," I stammer, embarrassed. I don't know why I'm being so honest other than I sense the same pain in Fred as I do in myself. "I just want to feel something else for a change, something that doesn't hurt so much inside all the time. I think you do too."

With that admission, Fred obliges me, awkwardly taking my head in his big hands and kissing me. I feel a need stir deep within me and I gently encourage Fred to continue his boyish exploration of my body. I am surprised by the heat that radiates through my centre, and even more surprised by the way my body responds to Fred's touch. I can feel him harden against me and I hear a moan that I vaguely recognize as my own voice. I never thought I'd ever feel sexual pleasure again, but I am hot and panting and naked under him, whispering encouraging words in his ear. But when Fred collapses on me, sweaty and spent, I recoil from him in shame.

I hadn't thought of Joseph once during our lovemaking, and that realization leaves me terrified. Had I pretended to be making love to Joseph, pictured him when I closed my eyes, then my actions could almost be forgivable. As it was, I had been completely caught in the moment and Joseph hadn't even entered my mind. Now, naked underneath the quilt that Fred had covered me with earlier, I become keenly aware of Joseph's presence in the room. He's here in our wedding picture on the end table; he's here in the barometer that he hung by the front door years earlier so he could predict when a good nor'easter was coming. I don't even know how it works but I could never bring myself to take it down. His copy of *The Farmer's Almanac* is still in its proper place in the bookshelf, sections still dog-eared by Joseph's own thumb. The guilt is smothering and it's getting harder for me to breathe.

Fred is pulling on his jeans now, but his hairy chest remains bare. I am filled with such remorse for cheating on my husband that I begin to sob into the soft folds of the quilt. Fred kneels down to offer a comforting hand but I scoot away from his touch, repulsed almost as much by myself as I am by him. I want him to leave but he stands there with his hands in his pockets like he doesn't quite know what to do.

"I don't think I ever made anyone cry after making love to them, but I have to think it's a bad thing," he says lightly, but I'm in no mood for humour.

"You need to go," I whisper. "Please, just go."

He still stands there and I think I might have to forcibly throw him out myself. "Are you okay?" he asks uncertainly. "I could run out and get us some supper or something and we could talk about it," he says, putting his t-shirt on. "Dee makes a fine fish and chips. The batter is nice and crispy and the fries is homemade too, made from locally grown potatoes and I ought to know cause Dee buys 'em right off my truck every Wednesday."

"I thought I told you to go away," I say, more forcefully this time, wondering if he really thinks a feed of fish and chips is all we need to make things right. "I just want to be alone right now."

"Look, I know this is weird but Joseph, he would—"

"Don't," I say, choking back a sob. "Don't say his name. Don't dare tell me what Joseph would want, because I know what he would want. He would want to be here with me. Don't for one second pretend that this is what he would want."

But it is Fred's turn to look angry and self-righteous. "I'm not the one pretending," he says quietly, and I am all alone once again.

CHAPTER EIGHTEEN

Prissy

I fully expect my son to be drunk because the police used the word intoxicated several times, but I am still taken aback by his appearance when I arrive at the police station in Carbonear. He has the look of a teenage runaway about him and he smells faintly of vomit and Doritos. His friend is also at the police station, although I only know him as Boner. I feel foolish for having allowed my child to venture out in the first place with a child I know nothing about. These are the things Howie would know. Names, parents' names, addresses, phone numbers, emergency contacts, and the like. I was just so happy that Quentin was making friends, aside from his uncle, that I didn't think I needed to be in possession of so much personal information. He seemed like a nice enough kid, and they were only going to get a bite to eat and walk around town for a little bit.

The police officer reads me a list of the charges that have been laid against my son. They include public intoxication, underage drinking, and theft. Quentin has the decency to look chagrined, even in his drunken state.

"Do you have any questions, ma'am?" the police officer asks.

Questions, I think. Of course I have questions. I have a million questions, beginning with what Boner's real name might be and ending with how my son managed to sneak onto a delivery truck parked in front of the Irving and steal a dozen beer and a box of Doritos. I want to find out what's going to happen to him now. I want to know what the fine is for all of these charges and if my son will have to go to court.

I have so many questions I can barely sort through them all but I also have no desire to find out the answers right now.

"No," I say, because I just want to take my child and leave the police station as quickly as I possibly can. I sign a paper that acknowledges they are releasing my child into my custody, and another paper where I promise to return him for a hearing to be scheduled later. I get up to leave just as Boner's father arrives and we eye one another warily because we're both certain the other child is the bad influence on our little angel. I can tell he thinks Quentin is the bad seed because he's a kid from Ontario with dyed hair and no father.

"One more thing," the police officer says before I go. "Your son here says his father is deceased."

I nod affirmatively out of habit, but then I realize this has gone way too far. Lying to the people of the community is reprehensible, although it is not illegal. But I'm afraid that lying to the police about Howie being deceased, especially after my son has been arrested, might either net myself time in jail, but more likely, will have me proven as an unfit parent.

"Actually, no. We're … we're getting a divorce," I say. "His father is in Ontario at the moment."

The police officer looks suspiciously at me and I'm fearful that he's going to run my name or license or detain me. "I'm going to have to alert the boy's father," he explains, and I nod in resignation, jotting down Howie's number on a slip of paper.

At home, I put Quentin on the sofa and cover him with a blanket while I make myself a cup of tea and wait for Howie to call me up and ask me a series of questions that I have no answers to. I am so mad at Quentin I just want to shake him and ask him what the hell he was thinking about when he did something so stupid, but my mother is doing her best to downplay the whole incident.

"It's just the way young people experiment," she says. "We've all done foolish things. Even you."

I shoot her a look that conveys my annoyance. "I've never been arrested," I remind her.

"No, you just got married."

I am about to ask what that's supposed to mean but my cell phone rings. "That's Howie," I say.

"You told him?" Mom is incredulous.

"I didn't tell him anything. The police did."

My mother looks physically ill and starts shaking her head as if I've told her the world was coming to an end. She is taking the news that Howie has been informed of Quentin's antics more seriously than her grandson's arrest in the first place.

"Hello," I say.

"What happened, Prissy?" Howie's voice is calmer than I expect, although I shouldn't be surprised. He's always been even-tempered and if this doesn't make him start screaming, nothing will.

"Quentin got into a little bit of trouble," I respond, wondering what I might describe as a lot of trouble.

"So I gathered from the police," he says sarcastically.

"Quentin is sleeping right now." Passed out, more like it. "I'm going to talk to him in the morning. Maybe we should wait and talk about it then." I'm tired and defeated and I'm not in the mood to carry on a conversation like this with my son's father.

"Prissy?" Howie's voice is hesitant. "It's almost time anyway."

"Time for what?"

"It's nearly the end of August. Summer's over, Prissy. Quentin starts school in another couple of weeks. He needs to come back home."

I don't say anything because I'm still trying to process what he's just said. Summer seems like it just started. I'm not ready for Quentin to go back. I'm not ready to go back myself and deal with the fallout. I don't think I ever want to go back there.

"I'm coming day after tomorrow to get him," Howie says with such authority I don't question him. It was, after all, the understanding we had back in June when my mother swayed Howie into letting Quentin stay with me for a few months.

"It's best for him right now," Howie continues, as if I had objected and he is trying to persuade me otherwise. "He should be with his old friends, in his old school."

I nod warily and I hear Howie sigh in relief as if he could see my gesture. I look at Quentin, asleep and trashed on the sofa, and my anger at him instantly dissipates. I kiss his cheek and I miss him already.

CHAPTER NINETEEN

Lottie

The dining room is filled mostly with regulars, which makes the man who walks in and takes a quiet booth in the back stand out all the more. There's something familiar about him although I can't quite figure out what it is. I grab my pen and notepad and make my way over to him, ready to recite the breakfast special, which hasn't changed in the entire month I've been working here.

I can hardly believe I've survived an entire month here at Lawlor's when I thought for sure I would be fired after the first week, assuming I didn't quit first. My uniform fit too tightly, restricting my movements, but I was too embarrassed to ask for a larger size. My feet ached at the end of every shift and I sprouted blisters on the backs of my heels. But it wasn't so much the physical discomforts that bothered me. It was the litany of mistakes that caused me so much distress. I confused skim milk with whole milk, regular coffee and decaf. I served a chocolate éclair to a diabetic and I put a surf and turf platter in front of a vegetarian.

The register gave me all sorts of problems too. On my second day a man gave me eleven dollars after I rang up his order for $5.78. I gave him the loonie back since ten dollars was plenty to cover the check, but he kept insisting I take it. Assuming it was a tip, I placed it in my apron pocket and thanked him. He laughed at me and told me he just wanted a five-dollar bill back. I could feel my face get red as he counted out the change for me and asked me if I was new, as if new was synonymous with incompetent.

But when I was handed my first paycheque, I held the envelope in my hands with as much wonder and amazement as someone holding a million dollar lotto ticket. I worked my entire shift with renewed determination, and once I balanced my cash to the penny and punched out, I headed to the bank and set up a chequing account entirely in my name. When my cheque book came in the mail wrapped up in brown paper like a parcel at Christmas, I ripped open the paper and traced my fingers over my name, printed in bold block lettering.

I approach the solitary man at the back booth. He is reading a booklet called *Understanding the Young Offenders Act*, which he flips over when he hears my approach, making an attempt to conceal it in the folds of his shirt as if I'd caught him flipping through a dirty magazine. I think he might be a television reporter from the CBC because he has that serious look about him. He's wearing a pair of khaki shorts that fall just below the knee, and a navy t-shirt that fits well enough to reveal that he's in reasonable shape. His hair is cut short, revealing flecks of grey that are more pronounced around the sides. He's wearing sunglasses and I wonder how he can read at all in the dark-panelled dining room. The air of familiarity is stronger now and I'm racking my brains trying to figure out how I might know him.

"Good morning," I say. "Would you like to hear the breakfast special?"

"Just coffee," he says, signalling to the place behind the counter where the fresh pots of coffee sit.

"Come on now, you looks hungry," I say, trying to coax him into staying a while, thinking that if I could observe him a little bit longer then his identity might come to me. "The special is two eggs, any style. That means scrambled or fried because we don't poach here. The crowd from St. John's comes in looking for eggs benedict all the time but we don't do anything that fancy. So it's two eggs, fried or scrambled, your choice of bacon or sausage, and toast with jam or butter. If you want cheese whiz or peanut butter, it's ten cents more. The special is served with juice and your choice of coffee or tea."

"I'll take coffee."

"How do you like your eggs then, scrambled or fried?"

"I don't want any eggs. Just coffee."

"Oh." I'm a little disappointed and more than confused since I thought he had indicated he wanted coffee with his breakfast special instead of tea. "So you don't want the breakfast special then, or you do?"

"No breakfast special. Just coffee please." I sense the irritation in his voice and I feel slightly offended by his tone.

"I can ask the cook to start the grill if you're more in the mood for lunch. He can probably make you a hamburger or a turkey sandwich. It's served with fries or mashed potato, and we got the best fries here cause we buy them local from Fred. He's sitting over at the counter right there," I say, pointing to Fred with my pen. "It's kinda funny he pays to eat his own potatoes, don't you think?"

"Please, can I just get a cup of coffee?" The hint of annoyance to his tone is more pronounced now.

"Fine then, just coffee," I say pleasantly, although I don't appreciate the tone and it makes me want to irk him further. "How do you take it? We have whole milk, two percent, one percent, skim, light cream, heavy cream, evaporated milk and non-dairy creamer. We also have sugar, Equal, Sweet 'n Low, Splenda, and honey." My voice is as sweet as all the aforementioned items.

"I'll have it black, please."

I retrieve the coffee pot and study him from behind the counter. Everything about him is familiar to me — his face, his voice, his mannerisms — and yet I can't place him for the life of me. I pour the coffee and smile at him. "Sure you don't want anything to eat? Muffin? Coffee cake? Turnover?" He gives me a half smile and shakes his head no and returns to his booklet.

"So whatcha reading?" I ask.

"Nothing," he mumbles, protectively covering the book with his forearm. "Thank you," he says dismissively and I leave him alone before he complains about me. I still haven't figured out who he is by the time he approaches the register with his wallet in hand.

"How was everything today?" I ask him.

"It was fine, thank you."

"That'll be a dollar twenty-five."

He hands me a crisp twenty-dollar bill from his wallet, which gives me a fantastic idea. "Can I see some ID with that?"

He looks at me like I'm some kind of idiot and I can tell he's probably reached his breaking point and social pleasantries are about to be dismissed.

"ID for what?"

"There's been some counterfeit twenty-dollar bills going around and we just have to protect ourselves is all. If I goes taking bad money, it gets docked out of my pay." I smile pleasantly and commend myself for my quick thinking.

The man looks at me in bewilderment and sighs in annoyance, but complies all the same, reaching into his wallet and handing me an Ontario driver's license with the name Howard John Montgomery. I read the name and look at the picture and furrow my brow in confusion as I struggle to grasp what's happening.

I try not to faint and have to hold the counter tightly to keep from stumbling. I can no longer grasp the laminate card and it floats softly to the counter. I put a hand over my mouth, eyeing Howie from head to toe and wondering how it was that I did not recognize him instantly — other than the fact that I didn't expect to run into a dead person on my breakfast shift. He's older and greyer than I remember but mostly he looks the same.

"Excuse me?" he asks. "Is everything okay? I probably have smaller change if the twenty is no good."

For some reason all I can think about is macaroni and cheese. I made it from scratch. I shredded cheese against the dull blade of the grater until my knuckles bled; I stood over the stove, stirring the milk carefully so as not to burn; I browned the top evenly and placed tinfoil over the dish and carried it to Prissy's house only to be turned away by Clara. I can feel my cheeks get hot as I realize the extent of Prissy's lies. She lied about her husband's death, took out an obituary, and arranged a memorial service. It was little wonder she couldn't look anyone in the eye whenever Howie's death was mentioned.

But it isn't the lies that bother me so much, it's the fact that I wasn't in on them. Prissy was my best friend, my only friend for as long as I can remember. She could have trusted me with whatever secret she was harbouring but she chose instead to dupe me also, and that stings most of all.

"You don't remember me, do you?" I say quietly, although it's little wonder. I don't look much like the person I once was. I am larger, rounder, and there's a weariness about me that never used to be there but practically defines me now.

The poor man looks thoroughly confused and I feel bad for him. "No, I'm sorry," he says. "Should I?"

"I didn't recognize you at first either. I'm Lottie," I say, smiling at him and extending a hand. "Lottie Crocker. I was the matron of honour at your wedding."

A flicker of recognition crosses his face. "Oh, yes, of course," he says, looking visibly relieved. "How have you been?" he asks politely.

"My husband killed himself earlier this summer, but other than that, I've been good."

Howie shifts uncomfortably, and I can't blame him. No one really knows what to say about death in general, but when someone kills themself it makes all the usual lines about being in a better place or your time being up or God having a plan for you completely obsolete. He rocks back and forth on the balls of his feet with his arms folded while I count out his change.

"So what exactly happened between you and Prissy?"

"I'm sure Prissy has already told you everything," he says, putting his hands in his pockets.

"Actually, she told me you were dead."

Howie looks like the type of person who isn't easily ruffled, but I suppose if your estranged wife fakes your death, it can be kind of hard to keep it in. His eyes grow large and he raises his left eyebrow. "I'm sorry, what did you say?"

"She told me you were dead. The whole town thinks you're dead," I continue, unable to stop now even if I wanted to. "Prissy even took out a death notice in the paper saying you died of cancer, and Clara's after telling a bunch of people you had testicular cancer. There was even a memorial service for you. It was lovely, not too flashy or anything, but Prissy's always had good taste. I'm sure you know that better than anyone."

Gone is the look of surprise and in its place is a simmering anger.

"I don't know what you did, but you must have really pissed her off."

He swallows hard and turns to leave, forgetting that I have his change in my hand, or just not caring. I sure as hell wouldn't want to be Prissy right now.

CHAPTER TWENTY

Prissy

I have a knot in my stomach that started the instant Howie announced he was coming to bring Quentin back home with him. I know I should be spending the final hours of our summer together just savouring the time we have left. I ought to be holding him, laughing with him, telling him how much I love him, and how proud I am of him, but that seems like a foolish thing to say in light of his arrest the day before yesterday. I can no more enjoy our breakfast together than I suspect a death row inmate can truly enjoy his last meal without thinking of how he's going to die in the next few hours.

Howie telephoned last night to let me know he was in St. John's and would be driving over in the morning, following an appointment with a defence attorney to discuss Quentin's case. It's nearly 11:00 am now and in any minute I expect Howie to come and pluck Quentin from my embrace. My stomach twists painfully at the thought. I try not to look at Quentin's backpack all packed and ready to go by the back door.

Charlie gets up to leave, claiming he has to be at work, but Charlie has never rushed off to work a day in his life. I know he just doesn't want to stick around for a sad goodbye.

"Be good, shithead," he says, ruffling his nephew's hair, and he is gone.

Even Mom is uncharacteristically quiet and I wonder if she felt the same way I do now when I moved away with Howie.

"Did you pack your toothbrush?" I ask.

Quentin shrugs and I don't know if that means yes or no and I know it isn't important anyway. I just feel like I need to say something because the silence is making the air stale.

"You should probably get some gum at the airport," I say. "It helps when you have to land."

He yawns.

"So are you looking forward to seeing your friends again? I'll bet they can't wait to see you." I smile pleasantly but he shrugs once again and I'm tired of talking to myself.

"God-damnit, Quentin, come on! Answer me for once."

"Leave him alone, will ya, Prissy," my mother scolds. "No one wants to talk right now except you."

I don't particularly feel like talking either but it's preferable to sitting around a table and waiting for the end of the world.

"I just want to know that he's going to be okay," I say to my mother as if Quentin weren't present.

"What do you care?" Quentin asks, and I'm shocked that he's actually spoken something that might give me the smallest inkling as to how he's feeling.

"Of course I care," I say gently. "Why would you think I don't care?"

"Because nobody even bothered to ask me what I want."

This is true. I didn't ask Quentin if he wanted to come here in the first place. I didn't ask him if he wanted to spend the summer with me and I didn't ask if he was ready to go back to Toronto with his father. I made all of those decisions for him, me and Howie both. There is a good explanation for this and I wonder how I can explain it without sounding patronizing, and in a way that's respectful of his feelings. I want to explain that it's unfair to put him in the position where he has to decide between two parents who both love him. It's too much of a burden to place on the shoulders of a fourteen-year-old child so we're just trying to do what's best.

"Quentin, everything I've done has been because I love you and I want to protect you." It still comes out patronizing but before I have a chance to expand on my explanation, Quentin has already weighed in.

"That's bullshit."

"It is not bullshit," I say. "Everything I have done has been in your best interests whether you can see that right now or not."

"I've been telling you the same thing since you got home, but you don't want to hear it either," Mom says to me.

I know she's referring to the obituary and the memorial service, but I fail to see how either is in my best interest. "And what exactly are you protecting me from?" I ask her in my most confrontational tone, but as if on cue, Howie is here, and looking enraged.

"Prissy!" he shouts. "Open up this fucking door and let me in!" He continues to bang on the door blindly. "Open up, Prissy, God-dam-nit!" He is pounding on the glass now in complete rage and I'm afraid he's going to kick it down if I don't open it right away.

"Save your breath, you old blowhard," Mom shouts. "Door's un-locked." Howie steps inside, practically foaming at the mouth, and I look at him in confusion. He was nowhere near this angry when he found out about Quentin's arrest in the first place so I don't under-stand why he's so upset now.

He looks like he doesn't know what to do with himself. Howie is never angry, not even the time I forgot he was bringing a senior partner over for dinner and I met him at the door in sweatpants and with a half-eaten pizza. He's practically panting, and a trickle of sweat runs down the side of his face. Even his stance is combative, with his feet spread wide apart and his hands in fists hanging by his sides. He looks like he's struggling to gain control over his own raging emotions, something that I can at least identify with.

Quentin swallows hard and I feel momentarily fearful for him. I know Howie follows more of a tough love philosophy than I ascribe to, but there's nothing loving about him at the moment, tough or other-wise. In fact, he looks downright violent, and I have second thoughts about letting Quentin go anywhere with his father in such a state.

"What's the matter, Prissy? Seen a ghost?" He smiles at me but his face is humourless.

"What do you mean?" Unfortunately I know exactly what he's talking about and it dawns on me that I am the target of his wrath, not Quentin. I can't look at him and I concentrate on the floor instead, hoping it might swallow me up. My heart is beating so loudly, I feel it echo in my head.

"Did you enjoy telling everyone I was dead?" Howie's voice is dangerously calm.

"It was a misunderstanding, that's all," I whisper.

"More like wishful thinking," my mother chimes in, but Howie motions her quiet with a wave and I am surprised by my mother's compliance. The only other person who could shush my mother was my father, and even that was only on rare occasions.

"If you don't mind, Clara, I'd rather hear from the grieving widow," Howie says.

"Mom, Quentin, could you please excuse us for a few moments?" I say, whisking Howie out the back door. A gust of wind swirls my hair around my face and I shiver, although not from the cold. We stand facing one another but neither of us speaks. Howie looks like he's trying to gain some semblance of control, and I can't stop staring at my feet.

"I'm sorry," I whisper. "It wasn't my idea, I swear."

"Don't give me your fucking bullshit, Prissy, cause I'm tired of it," he yells, pointing a finger in my face. "You can't just move my son to the middle of fucking nowhere and pretend I'm dead."

A look of understanding followed by one of fury crosses his face. "That day I came here. That was my so-called memorial service." He rubs his fingers through his hair and laughs cruelly at me. "Did you all have a good laugh at me after I left? Maybe have a few beers and share a joke about what an asshole I am?"

"It wasn't like that, Howie. It was nice, tasteful. People said nice things about you. William Harnum even made a point of telling me about how you helped him load firewood into the back of his truck one time. He said you were very ... pleasant for a mainlander." I can tell by the look of incredulity on his face that it didn't come out the way it was intended. I must sound like a complete lunatic.

"Does Quentin know?"

My silence is answer enough but he wants me to say it.

"I asked you, does he know?"

I shift my weight nervously. "Yes."

Howie clenches his fists at his sides and shakes his head in disbelief. "You are a piece of work, Prissy, and a pathetic excuse for a mother."

He's right. I have lied to an entire town about Quentin's father. Under my care and supervision, Quentin has run away, he answers to the name shithead, and he's been arrested. The most constructive thing he's done has been to help in making his grandmother's coffin. I am a lousy parent. I blink back tears, but it doesn't soften Howie's face at all.

"Tell my son I'll be waiting for him in the car," he seethes at me. "And don't be too long with your goodbyes."

I watch his retreating back a few moments before turning back to the house to retrieve Quentin, who is standing outside, having just witnessed the ugly exchange between his parents.

"Looks like I'm not the only one who's just been busted," he says. He smiles conspiratorially at me before flinging his backpack over his shoulder. He kisses me on the cheek and walks slowly to his father's rental car. "I liked you a lot better when you were dead," he says to Howie when he opens the car door, and it makes me want to smile, but I can't. It's the nicest my son has been to me since we both arrived in Paradise Bay at the beginning of the summer.

I stand stupidly with a hand in the air, waving until my arm aches. I watch until the car disappears before giving way to the tears.

CHAPTER TWENTY-ONE

Georgia

I have not left my house in the four days since I slept with Fred. In fact, I've barely left my bed. I am so plagued by guilt and shame for betraying my husband's memory that I have gone down in the basement and retrieved a number of Joseph's belongings out of boxes because I need his things around me right now. I hang his overcoat in the front closet and place his favourite sneakers on the doormat. I put his coffee mug back on the shelf next to mine and place his wallet, complete with his expired driver's license and his health card, on the end table like he's forgotten it and will come back any minute to retrieve it. I put on Joseph's favourite sweatshirt. It's huge on me and the sleeves hang all the way down to my knees, but if I wrap up in it and really concentrate, I can detect the faintest whiff of him mingled with the musty odour of the basement. I ask Joseph for his forgiveness over and over again, telling him how sorry I am and that it was an awful mistake. Even while I'm doing it, I know there's something off about my actions. Part of me feels as if I'm watching myself lose my mind, and the other part can't help it.

There is a loud banging on the door and I'm afraid it might be Fred. He stopped by twice the previous day, but I hid in my bed with the covers over my head until I heard his truck speed away so quickly I imagined his muddy boot stepping on the accelerator as if he were angry with it. When I hear a woman's muffled voice, I open the door to see Prissy standing on my front step. She looks angry and desperate and doesn't seem to notice my swollen, red eyes or my unwashed hair, or even that I'm wearing a man's clothing.

"How could you?" she accuses me, disgust dripping from every syllable as she pushes past me and stands next to Joseph's recliner.

I wonder how she found out about me and Fred, and I assume he's off telling everyone who will listen. He's probably bragging about his conquest and I feel one hundred times worse than I did five minutes earlier, if that's even possible.

"I don't know," I whisper. "I didn't mean to. It just happened and I feel terrible about it. I'm so ashamed," I say and cry into my hands.

Now that I have corroborated her accusation, Prissy doesn't seem to know what to do. She sits down on my sofa, looking as sad and forlorn as I've seen her, and I am admittedly confused by her reaction to news of my encounter with Fred. The only explanation I can come up with is that Prissy has her sights set on Fred. It seems an unlikely union, but I have no other theory.

"I'm sorry, it won't happen again. I didn't know you liked him, I swear."

"I don't like him, I hate him," Prissy groans. "Now Quentin is gone and Howie will probably use it all against me in the divorce. I'll be lucky to see my son on Christmas from now on. I hope you're happy."

Of course I'm not happy, but what I am is thoroughly confused. "Prissy, what in God's name are you talking about?" I ask, but Prissy doesn't get a chance to answer because Lottie knocks on the door and enters.

"Hey Georgia," Lottie says. "Are you okay? Fred stopped by Lawlor's this morning to tell me you haven't been at the flea market in a few days. He insisted I come over here to check on you as soon as my shift was over, although God knows why." When Lottie notices Prissy on the sofa her demeanour changes instantly.

"Well, if it isn't my best friend, the pathological liar," Lottie says. "What are you scheming up now?"

Prissy's features squint in confusion and then she looks at Lottie like she's just recognizing who she is. "So it was you," Prissy says calmly and deliberately. "You told Howie about the death notice."

Lottie corroborates Prissy's accusation with an evil smile. "You should have seen the look on your husband's face when I told him all about the memorial service."

"I can not believe you would do that to me," Prissy says, shaking her head in disbelief. "You've just ruined my life."

"You ruined your own life," Lottie snaps back.

I am finally beginning to understand what's happened, even if I don't know all the details.

"Why would you betray me?" Prissy asks with all the drama of how Jesus himself might confront Judas Iscariot. "I thought we were friends."

"Why would you lie to me, Prissy? I made you macaroni and cheese … from scratch," she adds for emphasis.

"And I made you lasagna."

"Mildred Peach made that lasagna, for Christ sake!" Lottie screeches and Prissy quiets instantly.

"Mom told me she made it," Prissy says defensively.

"Yes, cause your mother makes lasagna all the time," Lottie says sarcastically. "To think I actually felt bad for you. I was completely broke and I even made a donation to the Canadian Cancer Society! You ought to be ashamed of yourself, Prissy. I hope you get cancer for all the lies you told!"

Prissy, who most often holds the look of a wounded deer, takes on an expression I have never seen in her before. Her eyes turn into slits and her lips pucker into an angry glare and she is suddenly the hunter, ready to go at Lottie with an equal measure of meanness that unnerves me. "At least my husband didn't kill himself because he couldn't stand to be married to me!"

Before this spat gets out of hand, I diffuse it the only way I know how — by blurting out my awful secret. "I slept with Fred Bishop four days ago."

My confession silences Prissy and Lottie. They turn to me as if they are only noticing now that another person is in the room.

"What? Why?" Lottie asks. "I thought you hated him."

"I do."

"So why did you have sex with him then?"

"It was your fault," I say to Lottie.

"Mine?" she asks. "How is it my fault?"

"Because I was listening to that radio program and you were shooting off your mouth about widows, and I was so shocked to hear you talk about me on the radio that I skidded off the road until Fred came by and drove me home."

I can tell by the look on Prissy's face that she has no idea what I'm talking about, but Lottie actually looks amused. "What is it with you? You only have sex with men who pluck you up off the side of the road?"

The similarity between my encounter with Fred and my first meeting with Joseph hadn't occurred to me before. For some reason this fact upsets me all the more and I burst into tears. Prissy and Lottie look around the room, taking note of all the things they overlooked in their anger at one another. They take in the worn leather wallet on the coffee table, the hockey stick leaning by the front door next to Joseph's sneakers, and my sweatshirt with the Paradise Bay Municipal Depot logo on the front.

"Georgia, this is just creepy," Lottie says. "Joseph is gone, and you have to move on. He's gone and he's never coming back. Ches is gone and he's never coming back either."

Prissy doesn't say anything since we all know now that Howie has not suffered the same fate as Ches and Joseph. In some ways, I think it's even sadder.

Lottie begins to take Joseph's things and box them up, while Prissy runs the bath for me. I don't want them touching Joseph's things, but I stand quietly by anyway while Lottie moves about my house, expertly snuffing out everything left of my husband. She's so efficient I wonder if she's done the same thing at her own house. If I were to go into her house now, I wonder if anything is left of poor Ches or if Lottie has erased all traces that he ever existed.

CHAPTER TWENTY-TWO

Prissy

"Howie had an affair?" There is just the slightest inflection to Lottie's voice that makes it a question, although it could just as easily be a statement. I nod, confirming it to be true. We are at my mother's house, sitting down at the kitchen table. I wasn't expecting Lottie to visit anytime soon, especially after our heated exchange, and yet here we are together, sipping tea and eating jam jams like we've done one thousand times before. When she showed up at my mother's house with a box of Kraft dinner as a peace offering, I couldn't help but laugh. I thought she might never speak to me again after I deceived her about Howie and then blamed her for Ches' suicide. I am so relieved to see her again that I don't even mind her line of questioning about my marriage.

When she asks, "Who did he sleep with?" I realize that I don't know the answer. I have a picture in my mind of what she might look like, but I don't really know anything about her. She could be younger or older than me, with long or short hair. She could be fat or thin, short or tall, white or something else. I shrug my shoulders.

"You don't know?" Lottie is incredulous. "Didn't you think to ask?"

"Of course I asked," I snap. "He was vague. He just said it was someone he met at work." It could be anyone really. Howie rents space to all sorts of companies, architects, lawyers, mortgage lenders, accountants and so on. It could be any one of a thousand women employed by the companies that occupy space in one of his firm's properties, or it could be the secretary who gets him coffee every morning.

"Like the secretary?" Lottie asks as if she read my mind. It's such a cliché and my life was never supposed to be a cliché. It was supposed to be a fairy tale. I feel foolish thinking about how I turned out to be such a lame stereotype.

"So what's the deal?" Lottie asks. "You're hanging out here, making him sweat for a little bit, punishing him until you decide to take him back?"

"He doesn't want me back," I mumble. Lottie is surprised to hear me say this because she stops chewing for a few seconds and pretends to be interested in reading the label on the back of the cookie package.

"Then he's an idiot and you're better off without him," she says. I appreciate the sentiment even as I don't believe it. "I gotta go to work. I have the evening shift today." Lottie stands and puts her empty cup in the sink. "Things will work out for you, Priss. They always do," Lottie says, and I manage a half smile before she leaves.

Lottie is not gone five minutes when there is a knock at the door. I assume Lottie must have forgotten something and I open the back door fully expecting it be to her, but instead there is a young man standing outside my mother's front door, dressed in a suit and tie. I can hear my mother moan from the living room that it's probably the Jehovah Witnesses, and she urges me to slam the door in the young man's face. But I note that he is not carrying a Bible, just a large brown envelope.

"Priscilla Montgomery?" he asks. My heart beats nervously at the mention of my full name on this stranger's lips. My mouth is suddenly dry and I can't speak so I nod affirmatively. He hands me the envelope and tells me I've been served and then he turns to leave.

I can feel my mother's inquisitive eyes on me. "It's from Howie," I say, shutting the door. "From Howie's lawyer, anyway. They're divorce papers, Mom," I explain because her face is clouded in confusion. I am overtaken by the urge to rip the documents into shreds and throw them in the garbage without even opening them, because if I can't see them then they don't exist. Instead I toss the envelope on the kitchen table and sit forlornly, staring at it.

"Are you going to open it?" Mom asks and I shrug uncertainly.

"I'm scared to," I admit. "What if he wants sole custody of Quentin? I can't bear to lose him," I say, my voice quivering.

I carefully remove the papers from the envelope and lay them on the table in front of me. I read the first two lines and determine that I am referred to as the defendant, a title that seems apt under the circumstances.

"I can't read it," I say, pushing the papers away. I place one of my mother's cigarettes between my lips and struggle with lighting a match before my mother slaps the cigarette away.

"What the hell are you doing? I only got three smokes left until I get to the store and I don't need to be wasting them on people who don't appreciate it."

I'll need a lawyer but I don't have the first clue how to go about hiring one. I flip through the yellow pages with all the enthusiasm that one might look up oncology, abortion, funeral home or bankruptcy attorneys. It doesn't matter who I hire to represent me, I already know that Howie will get whatever arrangements he wants. Howie is smart and knows people from all walks of life. I'm certain he's already hired the best lawyer in Toronto, and a feeling of doom overtakes me when I imagine a lawyer putting me on the stand, asking me questions about Howie's fake funeral.

I reach for the phone. My mother thinks I am calling a lawyer but I call Quentin instead, because right now I still can. I am fearful that one day I will be ordered by a judge not to contact Quentin at all even as I know it's a ridiculous thought. Even crack mothers get to contact their kids. I've called Quentin every day, grateful for cell phones, which allow me to bypass Howie altogether. We never say more than a few words to one another, but sometimes all I need is to hear his voice.

"Hey honey, it's Mom," I say. "I just wanted to say hi."

"Hey," he answers.

"How was school today?"

"It sucked. Mr. McFadden is a total dick."

Mr. McFadden is Quentin's homeroom teacher and I smile, thinking how my son sounds more and more like my brother.

"I miss you," I say. "Your nan, she misses you a lot too. And Uncle Charlie says he can't wait to take you fishing again." I am remembering the day Quentin caught his first fish as an eager five-year-old boy, his chubby cheeks flush with excitement and wonder as my father smiled on proudly when he told me all about how he hooked it. Quentin's face is miles away from me and the distance between us is like a huge impassable abyss.

"I'm going to see you soon, okay? Be good."

I hang up the telephone and my mother, who has been watching me the whole time, looks upset. "What are you going to do?"

It's so out of character for Mom to ask me rather than to tell me what I'm going to do that I am momentarily bewildered why she has not thought up a plan for me. My mother's ideas are usually out of whack and completely crazy, but she always has one. I feel as if I'm careening out of control without Mom to tell me what to do, because I have no idea. Ever since Howie blindsided me with his announcement on that early June evening, I haven't known what do to. I second guess everything these days and avoid making decisions on anything of consequence. I question every day of the past sixteen years of my life, recalling countless conversations with my husband, wondering whether I've been wrong about him all along, or if he's simply morphed into another person overnight.

The only decision I have ever been certain of in my life was Howie, and if that was wrong, then nothing makes sense to me. I had chosen to define myself as Howard Montgomery's wife, and in losing him, I'd lost myself. The only thing left that matters is Quentin and I am determined not to lose him too. In a rare moment of clarity, I know exactly what I need to do.

"My marriage is over, Mom," I say, hearing the faint catch in my throat. "Howie is not coming back for me and it's time I stop pretending. I have to go back to Toronto." I surprise myself with the sense of purpose and determination in my voice. "Tomorrow." I know I have to deal with this head on. I don't want a long drawn-out fight with Howie about who gets what. I just want it to be over and I can't exactly get on with it if I'm sitting at my mother's kitchen table hiding from reality. "I have to settle this thing, Mom, the sooner the better. It's not going away no matter how much I wish it."

My mother looks at me as if I've completely lost my mind. All day long, I ignore her pleas to stay in Paradise Bay, and by the evening I am packed and I have a 6:30 am flight booked. I can be there in time to take Quentin to lunch. I lie down in bed by ten o'clock, too excited thinking about seeing Quentin again to sleep.

Eventually I settle into a light slumber that is interrupted by an unfamiliar thump, followed by the whistle of the kettle on the stove. The whistle gets increasingly loud until it threatens to explode with the force of the steam. Warily, I peel back the covers and then run down the stairs with my heart in my throat.

"Mom?" I call, racing to the kitchen, where my mother is lying on the floor in a twisted heap with shards of a broken teacup and sugar crystals littered all around her. "Mom!" I am screaming and crying and shaking her, but she is motionless, and the kettle continues to whistle so loudly I think my eardrums might burst.

CHAPTER TWENTY-THREE

Lottie

$\mathcal{M}$y knees and ankles are throbbing under the strain of being on them for the past thirteen hours, and all I want to do is soak my feet and sleep until I start my next shift in just six hours. But I can hear the telephone ring before I'm in the door and I know it has to be bad news because it's nearly eleven o'clock at night.

"Hello," I answer tentatively.

"Lottie!" Prissy shouts my name as if she spies me in the distance and needs to tell me to wait up. I sense the adrenaline in her voice and my heart begins to beat faster.

"What's the matter?"

"You need to get Charlie for me. I think he's at the rink playing hockey. That's why he's not answering his phone. I'm at the hospital in Carbonear. I think Mom is dying."

"Okay," I say authoritatively, although I can feel my stomach quiver and the pressure in my bowels at the mere thought of going to the rink. "I'll go get him and meet you there."

In moments I am standing outside the hockey rink, filled with trepidation. Everything about it reminds me of Ches. For months, I hung out here like a shameless groupie, watching him drive the Zamboni the way other girls watched their boyfriends score goals or check players into the boards. While everyone else went to the bathroom between periods or went out for a smoke break or to get a snack, I sat on the edge of my seat watching Ches expertly maneuver the Zamboni around the rink, starting with broad circles around the boards and moving inwards until only the smallest patch at centre ice was left. When he finished, the ice was slick and shiny, like something brand new. I thought it must be awfully satisfying to be able to make a clean slate out of something that had been scratched and gouged moments earlier.

The blast of cool air hits me immediately when I open the main door and it feels as if I've opened the door to a time machine. I will meet Ches at the snack bar at the start of the third period and we'll order fries and gravy, which will come in a yellow cardboard tray with a handful of vinegar packets. I'll grab two cans of Pepsi from the cooler and Ches will drink his from the opening in the tin, but I will sip mine from a thin white straw that I will chew until it's dented and bent from my bite marks. Ches will pay and it will make me feel so giddy I'll wear a ridiculous smile while Ches asks me what's so God-damned funny. We'll sit at a rickety table with a smear of hardened ketchup and sprinkles of salt and eat in silence. We'll listen to the muffled roar of the crowd to find out in whose favour the game has turned, and we'll watch as dads come in to order burnt coffee in styrofoam cups. They'll stir extra sugar and Coffee-mate around with a popsicle stick to conceal the bitterness and blow on their hands to warm them. We're invisible to them though and they won't notice that I'm six months pregnant or that Ches crushes his empty tin of Pepsi in his fists until there are tiny nicks on his fingertips from the jagged edges.

There is a lively crowd in the rink tonight, many of them standing along the boards, banging on the glass and screaming things like, "Put on your fucking glasses, ref!" and "Nail the sonofabitch!" My gaze is drawn automatically to the place behind the goal where the Zamboni is parked. My heart beats wildly and I wonder who is driving the machine now, and whether he is as good as Ches was. I take several steps toward the back of the rink before I stop abruptly, reminding myself that I am not here to make peace with my past, but to grab Charlie.

All the players look the same in their team jerseys and helmets, and I realize I don't know whether Charlie is on the red team or the green team, much less what number he is. I pound on the glass and shout his name, but either no one hears me or I just look like another irate fan. I push past the throng and run out onto the ice screaming his name before he skates over to me.

"What the fuck are you doing?" Even though the mask from his helmet obscures his face, I can tell he's petrified to see me here calling out to him, that I must be bearing tragic news.

He rides with me in silence to Carbonear. He is still wearing most of his hockey equipment, and the smell of sweat is so overwhelming, I have to crack the window to breathe.

"What the fuck happened?" Charlie asks for the fourth time, but I don't think he expects me to answer because I've already told him everything I know. I suspect he's just talking to himself now because he has to say something to break the silence.

Prissy is standing in the middle of the corridor when we get to Intensive Care. She looks childlike in her red flannel pyjama pants and ponytail. Her face is streaked with tears and she runs to Charlie to embrace him.

I sit with Prissy and Charlie in the waiting room for a long time while we wait for more news of her mother. It's a stroke, we know that much, but they are still trying to determine if Clara will pull through, and if so, how much damage has already been done. We look ridiculous, the three of us. Charlie is still wearing most of his hockey equipment, Prissy is in pyjamas, and I am dressed in my waitress uniform. I think we look like characters in a play rather than ourselves.

When it's nearly four in the morning, Prissy tells me I should go home, and I'm prone to agree with her, based solely on the fact that I have to be back at work in another three hours, but there's something so vulnerable about her that makes me reluctant to leave. There's a quiet desperation that reminds me of the morning Ches killed himself, and I'm afraid that if I leave Prissy, something bad will happen to her too. It seems like days ago I was at her house telling her that everything would work out, even though it was only the day before.

"I'm supposed to be getting ready to go to the airport now," Prissy says. "He served me with divorce papers today," she says by way of explanation. I can't tell whether she's upset about those circumstances or not because her face is completely devoid of expression.

"I could call him for you," I offer. "Let him know what's going on."

"No," Prissy says adamantly. I don't blame her if she doesn't want me to speak to Howie ever again after what happened the last time I spoke to him.

"What about Quentin?" I ask. "He should know if something happens to his grandmother."

"Nothing's happened yet," is all she says. Then her eyes get a far-away look, and although she's staring at an exit sign, I wonder if she actually sees it. "Do you think it's possible to have a stroke out of spite? Because if anyone could do it, it would be my mother."

I study Prissy, my friend since childhood, and I hardly recognize her. Prissy has always had a luminous quality to her. Her features were striking, her yellow hair was thick and glorious, and her blue eyes sparkled like the ocean's waves in the afternoon sun. No one would blame her for looking down on the rest of us, but she never did. Prissy was more beautiful than me and people seemed to like her instantly. She was effortless, but I never felt anything less than her equal because that was how she saw me. It was Prissy who chose to be my friend; it was she who gave me confidence to get through some of the roughest times in my life, especially when I was young and pregnant and terrified.

Now, under the harsh glare of the hospital's fluorescent lights, it's Prissy who looks terrified, almost ravaged by all that she's endured of late. She's lost so much weight, even in the brief time she's been back home, that her bones seem to jut out under the surface of her taut skin. Her face is hollow with dark circles that lend her a near ghostly quality. Even her hair seems to have lost its lustre and turned a dull shade of yellow. Her fingers, chewed and bloody, fumble with the zipper of her sweatjacket, zipping it up and down, over and over again, as she stares vacantly ahead. Even her shoulders are hunched, buckling under the weight of all that's happened. Looking at her now, I can't blame Clara for doing what she did. If someone snuffed the light out of Marianne, I suppose I might pretend they were dead too.

"I'm sorry," I say, "about telling Howie." I feel the remorse seeping out of my pores and it feels uncomfortably familiar. Regret, it seems, is the story of my life.

Prissy looks at me blankly. "I wish he really was dead."

I want to say, *Be careful what you wish for*, but instead I just tell her I have to go home and get ready for work.

CHAPTER TWENTY-FOUR

Prissy

My stomach grumbles in response to a tray of meatloaf, untouched by my mother for so long that the fat has congealed in tiny specks along the surface. I try to send it back since my mother isn't supposed to eat solid foods yet, but I can't find the orderly who brought it in and I don't want to bother the nurses. I can't remember when I've eaten last, although I remember munching on a package of crackers from the vending machine the previous day, and I don't remember if I ate anything since then. I am tempted to eat the offending meatloaf, frozen peas and mashed potatoes myself, but I'm afraid if I eat it they'll think my mother ate it and then they won't send her another more appropriate meal.

My mother has been transferred to a rehabilitative unit in the Miller Centre in St. John's to undergo various therapies. She has to learn how to do a number of things all over again. Things like walking, talking, even chewing and swallowing her food, are all things she'll have to work on, although I have no idea how much since she's made no effort to do either.

"I'm going to try and get you some Jello," I announce with more enthusiasm than I feel. She doesn't answer me, so I offer a few other suggestions. Soup, oatmeal, cream of wheat. I even try to tempt her with ice cream like I might a sick child who's just had their tonsils out.

The entire ordeal seems surreal to me. It's only been a week since she had a stroke so it's hard not to think that she'll be the way she used to be any minute now. Every time a nurse comes in to draw blood or take her temperature or check her IV, I expect her to sit up and curse the doctors and nurses for all the pinpricking and medicine they have her on. I can't help but imagine she'll get up and ask me for a cigarette at any moment. I can't believe she will stay this way forever.

When the physical therapists come in, I leave, mostly because my mother refuses to cooperate while I'm still in the room. Sometimes I steal glances through the window, trying not to be seen, in the same way I did when Quentin was having trouble separating at nursery school. They try to make my mother do things like sit up on her own, bend her legs, put on a sweater, or squeeze toothpaste out of a tube, but after watching her struggle with these simple exercises, it pained me so much I had to look away. She still hasn't spoken yet and I think she's afraid of the sound she'll make.

While my mother is in physical therapy I take the time to shop for things I never imagined I'd need, things like a special seat for the shower with suction cups that adhere to the bathtub, bars to hold onto in the shower, a seat that sits on top of the toilet, incontinence pads, a wheelchair, although not a motorized one because I think my mother would object to using something she felt was unnecessary. In a splurge of optimism, I also purchase a walker.

I wonder how I am going to get through the next four to six weeks here with her. That is how long the doctors and therapists say they will need to work with her, establish an exercise regimen and teach me how to properly care for her.

I'm uncertain of my ability to be a full-time caregiver to my mother. I will have to do things like bathe her, cut up her food into tiny pieces and feed them to her, bring her to the toilet, wipe her, change her when she has an accident, keep track of her medication, get her dressed on a daily basis, and be her personal cheerleader all at the same time. It is like having an infant, except an infant gradually progresses and, if anything, my mother's condition will only deteriorate further.

That evening I ask her about her therapy sessions, as I do every day, and like every day since the stroke, she refuses to answer me. I chat happily along, telling her that Charlie is building a ramp for her wheelchair to the back door of the house so it won't be apparent from the front. This is an important consideration since I imagine my mother would be mortified to come home to a wheelchair ramp at the front door. I tell her that Charlie is moving her things into the back bedroom so she won't have to deal with stairs anymore. I tell her that Quentin is playing left wing in hockey this year and that he scored two goals in the season opener, although he hasn't played for the past two years. I show her the new nightgowns I purchased for her at Wal-Mart earlier in the day and I hold them up for her inspection and approval. I flip through the pages of a *Star Magazine* and an *Us Weekly*, being sure to fill her in on who is dating, who has broken up, who had a baby. She still doesn't speak or respond in any way, and it makes me feel as if I'm talking to a comatose patient.

I am half asleep in the chair next to her bed when she finally opens her mouth to speak. "Where's Howie?" she asks me, and it sounds like someone who's drunk at four in the morning looking for a taxi home. I think she's just asked me about Howie but I'm not certain and I don't have the heart to ask her to repeat herself, especially given the effort it must have taken her to utter anything at all. The doctors told me a certain degree of memory loss was possible, but in a million years I never expected this would be the first thing on her mind deemed important enough to break her silence.

"Howie?" I repeat uncertainly and she nods expectantly. Because I can't bear to tell her again that he's left me, especially now that she has so much else to deal with, and because I can't even fathom that this is the same woman who concocted an elaborate scheme to convince everyone that he was dead, I simply smile and assure her, "Howie's coming. He'll be here soon."

CHAPTER TWENTY-FIVE

Georgia

I'm pregnant, and scared. Having a child means having another person to love, and for me that blessing is tempered only by the fact that there is another person for me to lose. I feel vulnerable in a way I haven't felt since losing Joseph, and yet at the same time I am in complete awe of my own body and its ability to grow another life.

I close my eyes and imagine the slightest swell of my belly and the glow of my skin. I imagine myself large and awkward with my hands caressing my belly, and I can visualize myself in the hospital, sweat dripping from my forehead, timing my breaths and pushing the infant from my body, and then I see Joseph by my side, his face full of joy and wonder as he tells me we have a healthy baby girl. Whether it is morning sickness or the image in my head that sends me into the bathroom to heave up the contents of my breakfast, I don't know. I do know that I am left with one very cruel irony. I am not carrying Joseph's child, I am carrying Fred's. The realization sends me back into the bathroom.

I'd long ago relinquished any dreams of one day becoming a mother. After Joseph died, I had hoped I might be pregnant, that we had made one small miscalculation that might miraculously result in the continuation of Joseph's life. I even missed a period, and it brought me a great deal of comfort to hope that if Joseph was dead, he would live on in all of the wonderful features he would pass on to our child. His own unique genetic code would be manifested in our daughter's blue-green eyes or in our son's athletic build. And then one day, a circle of bright red blood appeared on my underwear. When I showed up at the emergency room claiming to be miscarrying, the doctor examined me and then looked me sadly in the eye and told me I was never pregnant to begin with. I had just skipped a period from the stress and trauma I had undergone in losing my husband.

That I am pregnant now is nothing short of astonishing. I have taken the test three times, all at different times during the day, and the positive result is always the same. A wave of exhaustion overtakes me and I crawl into bed and sleep for the better part of the morning.

When I awake in the early afternoon, my senses are suddenly clearer than they've ever been. I can hear the roar of the ocean from inside my bedroom and the room comes slowly into focus. I can see the variation of colours in my patchwork quilt, feel the soft carpet fibres rub against the soles of my feet, and I know what it signifies and I know exactly what I have to do.

I go to the top shelf in my closet and reach around the extra blankets and pillows to retrieve an old wooden jewellery box. It no longer closes properly now, so filled with papers, cards and letters, almost all of them written in my own precise script. It began the first Christmas after Joseph died. I was at the drugstore looking for deodorant when I passed the aisle filled with greeting cards. I stopped when I saw one addressed *To my loving husband at Christmas* ... and I picked it up, read the beautiful sentiment inside, and I placed it in my shopping basket alongside my shampoo, a razor and a bar of soap. When I got home, I signed the card as if Joseph was still alive, sealed it shut with my saliva and wrote his name on the envelope and then put it away in my old jewellery box.

I did the same thing for Valentine's Day, his birthday, Easter, our anniversary, and then Christmas again. The following year I added Father's Day cards to the mix since I was convinced we would have had children by now. Sometimes I addressed him as if he was still alive and we were carrying on with our lives as if that day never occurred. Other times, I addressed him as if he were a ghost, or a figment of my imagination.

Sometimes I wrote him sweet love notes, complete with X's and O's for hugs and kisses, and other times I simply told him that I was angry with him for leaving me. I wrote to him about how hard it was to get through the holidays alone, and sometimes I even asked him if he was ever real in the first place.

Without them, I don't know how I might have gotten through those days. When no one was there to talk to, I imagined Joseph reading through the greeting cards, sometimes laughing at what I had to tell him, but mostly shaking his head sadly. I wonder what he will think of my last letter — sad perhaps, but relieved too.

I grab a sheet of stationery and begin writing to Joseph for the final time. When I finish, I place the paper inside the box, along with all of the cards and letters I have written over the years. Tucking the box under my arm, I grab my coat to ward off the chill and make my way to the cemetery. It's just turned November and the temperature has dropped to frigid seemingly overnight. The sky is overcast and the air holds the faint scent of an impending snowfall. My feet rustle up the leaves on the ground, announcing my approach, but there is no one else here but me. I take out the letter I've just written and read it.

Dear Joseph,

I'm ready to say goodbye to you now. I know it's taken me a long time but you're a hard person to let go. This morning I lay awake in bed thinking of you, as I often do, but this time I couldn't remember what you looked like. I closed my eyes and tried to picture you but the image was fuzzy and distorted, and then you faded away, peacefully. After that happened, I saw and felt everything around me clearly for the first time, like the fog had finally lifted. I realize now that it's okay if I don't remember things exactly as they were, so long as I remember the way it felt to be with you, that I will have with me forever no matter what happens. I'll always love you. Goodbye Joseph.

Love Always,

Georgia

I place the paper back in the box and lay it at the foot of Joseph's grave. I light a match and the box ignites quickly, the flames consuming the contents until there's nothing left but a few grey ashes. A light snow begins to fall and the wind picks up, swirling the ashes around the graveyard. I turn to leave, inhaling the scent of spruce and burning wood.

CHAPTER TWENTY-SIX

Prissy

I am feeding my mother cream of wheat from my bedside chair in the rehab unit at the Miller Centre. It is not her favourite food in the world but it is the right consistency for someone who is learning how to eat, chew and swallow all over again. Her tongue pushes the gritty substance around her mouth, before pushing it back out. It is not so much that she has spit it back out that causes my stomach to turn, but the way the creamy liquid settles into the cracks of her wrinkled skin.

It has the same effect on me as the time Gerald Cochrane had two rivers of greenish-yellow snot running down his nose and trickling on his lips during recess in the fourth grade. It was only when he sucked it all back into his nose that I felt my stomach turn, and without warning I vomited in the schoolyard and was sent home sick.

Years later, Charlie and his friends asked me to judge a spitting contest. I should have known better but I agreed since Charlie promised he'd wash the dishes for me that night if I did it. I had to judge based on velocity, distance and size. When a wad of spit fell about an inch from my foot, the outside rim bubbly and transparent, with a yellow mucous centre, it reminded me of a raw egg. Of course I vomited, sending Charlie and his friends into fits of laughter and causing them to spit with renewed enthusiasm until my stomach turned again.

When I witness the cream of wheat sliding down my mother's chin, I feel the familiar numbness in the back of my throat and I know that I am powerless to stop. I make it to the bathroom in time, but not before I gag horrifically in front of her.

In the bathroom of my mother's hospital room, I stare critically at my reflection in the mirror. I don't recognize myself. My cheeks look mottled under the fluorescent lights and dark circles mar my eyes, which are framed by fine lines I hadn't noticed before. My lips are dry and cracked and look thinner than I remember.

The bathroom smells of vomit and I reprimand myself for being so insensitive. I should have excused myself at the first sign, feigned an illness, anything but let my mother see how the simple act of feeding her made me retch. I am so overwhelmed that I just stay there for a while, sobbing and berating myself for being an awful daughter, an awful wife, an awful mother. I weep silently into the palm of my hand until it's wet with tears and spit and snot.

When I finally emerge from the bathroom I tell my mother that I must have eaten something that didn't agree with me, but I know she doesn't believe me if for no other reason than I haven't eaten anything substantial in several days.

The following day my mother finally starts talking to me. I should be overcome with relief at this breakthrough, but I'm not. It's not so much the quality of her speech that gets to me, it's the content. She expresses her displeasure with me, not for vomiting during her feeding, but for calling 911 when she collapsed on the kitchen floor.

"Why didn't you let me die?" she asks, and I don't know how to answer that kind of question.

"Because I didn't want you to die."

"I'd rather die than live like this."

I want to tell her that I didn't know she'd end up this way, but I'm afraid that if I say such a thing, it's the same as admitting she'd be better off dead. An image comes to mind of my mother when I was a child. She is carrying me on her back, along with two huge buckets of capelin, all the way from the beach to our house. Today in physical therapy they will be working on getting her to sit up by herself, and I wonder if maybe she isn't right.

"You're getting stronger every day," I tell her. I stop short of saying that she will be good as new since the doctors have already told me she will never be like she was.

"I don't want to be a burden. Just go on home and send me to a nursing home."

"You're not a burden, Mom," I insist, and I mean it even though it's the thing people say all the time whether the person is a burden or not. I want to continue to discuss this with her, assure her that things are getting better, but I can tell she is exhausted from uttering those few muffled sentences.

"Where is your husband?" she asks, and I wish I knew what was going on inside her head. Her speech still has a drunken quality to it, will probably always have the same slow, slurred pronunciation.

"He'll be here soon," I say quietly, but she looks at me with such confusion that I think she's already forgotten what she asked in the first place. I see Lottie and Georgia in the doorway. They come all the way to St. John's to visit once a week. They are here for me, mostly, although they do fuss over my mother as much as she allows them to. Georgia is carrying her customary bag of fudge, although my mother is unable to eat it and we give it to the nurses to take home and give to their families. Lottie brings in newspapers that her customers leave behind, which I read to my mother in the evenings, even though I don't think she's listening.

Lottie kisses my mother's cheek. "How are ya, maid?" she asks and Georgia smiles and grips my mother's cool hands. We talk in a nondescript manner until the physical therapist comes to take my mother for her exercise session.

Lottie and Georgia encourage me to leave the hospital for a little while and we end up at Tim Hortons sipping coffee and enjoying a donut. I feel almost guilty at being outside enjoying simple things like coffee and donuts when my mother sits in her hospital bed being fed a diet of Jello and mashed vegetables with no salt added.

"How's your mother doing now?" Georgia asks me. It's the same question she asks me each time I see her.

"She's started to talk a little bit," I say and I see the excitement in their faces.

"That's great," Lottie says, but I have to disagree.

"She talks about dying. She wants me to send her to a home and she's mad at me for calling an ambulance in the first place. Sometimes she just talks nonsense. But that's not the worst thing." I watch as

Lottie and Georgia exchange wary glances. "She keeps asking me about Howie."

"What about him?" Lottie and Georgia ask in unison.

"When he's coming to visit her. When he's coming to help me out." They stare at me in confusion. "I don't think she remembers," I say for clarification. "Anything."

"She can't remember killing him?" Lottie asks in disbelief. "Taking out the obituary? Arranging the memorial service? Nothing?"

I shake my head. "Not even that he left me."

Georgia places a warm hand on mine. "The mind is the strangest thing," she says. "Your mom just wants to believe that you're okay so she's blocked out all the bad things. For a long time, I honest to goodness sat at the kitchen with a big supper all cooked for Joseph and I waited and waited for him to come home to eat with me until it was dark. Then I wrapped his plate in foil because for a time, I really forgot he was dead. Your mother is just worried about you, that's all."

"A nursing home might not be all that bad, Prissy," Lottie says, and I look at her with disapproval, as if she'd just said something off colour. "They're not all bad places," Lottie insists. "At some point you're going to have to, Prissy, especially now that her mind is going. Losing your mental faculties is not necessarily a bad thing, especially if your body is already deteriorating. I mean, it's a lot better to lie in your own shit if you think you're seventeen and out at the Legion for a dance than to lie in your own shit and be fully aware of it."

Lottie has always had a way of seeing the world differently than anyone else and I love that about her, but on this I want to agree with Georgia's assessment of my mother. She's just blocking out some of the bad things, but I'm afraid that if she blocks out all the bad things, there won't be anything left.

CHAPTER TWENTY-SEVEN

Lottie

*F*red Bishop, it turns out, is one of my best customers, and a pretty decent tipper. Now that the flea market has ended and the weather is turning cold, he comes by Lawlor's with greater frequency. He sits at the counter every day and orders the exact same thing: two fried eggs with runny yolks, sausages, two slices of bacon done extra crispy, two slices of toast with butter, and one and a half cups of tea with evaporated milk and two packets of sugar. On Wednesday evenings he stops by for supper and orders either fish and chips with dressing and gravy or the hot turkey sandwich plate.

I know why Georgia harbours a certain level of resentment towards him, but he seems so harmless to me that I wonder if Georgia isn't just misdirecting all her negative feelings. Georgia has vilified Fred to the point where she thinks he might be the devil himself. As I watch him take his customary seat, I don't see anything sinister looking about him, nothing that might make me feel uneasy or uncomfortable. He is of average height, weight and build. He's lost most of his hair, which he hides under a baseball cap in the summer and a wool cap in the colder months. It seems to be his only expression of vanity. He wears checked flannel shirts over white t-shirts and worn jeans. He greets me pleasantly enough with a "Hey Lottie" and keeps pretty much to himself. Ironically, it is these exact same characteristics that have me scratching my head why Georgia slept with him in the first place.

I remember the day he came into the restaurant looking harried and nervously asking me all sorts of questions about Georgia. Had I seen her? Why not? Had I spoken to her since Thursday? Could I please check in on her? No reason why, he kept insisting.

"Want to hear the specials?" I ask Fred, although I already know his order. He nods and listens politely while I recite them because he's too polite to say no. I imagine that I could mess up his order entirely and he would eat it anyway without complaint. Similarly, I could short-change him and he'd still tip me the same amount as if I fell over backwards to accommodate him.

"How was your season at the flea market?" I ask and he looks at me in surprise. Aside from that one conversation several weeks earlier when he inquired after Georgia, I've never really asked him anything other than what he wants to eat and if he has anything smaller than a twenty. But Fred, for all the quiet solitude he exudes, has turned an obscure flea market into a boon for Paradise Bay. He's been its strongest advocate, securing funding first to have signage erected, then to have it included in the tourism guide, and this year he secured the grant to buy the tents for all the vendors. He's my best shot at getting a grant of my own to start up the widows' club.

"It was good," he says and goes back to reading his newspaper.

"Can I ask you a question?"

"What's up, Lottie?" he says, putting the paper down because he knows I am up to something if he's been here for ten minutes and I still haven't gotten him his tea.

"I need your help. I want to get a government grant and I have no idea how to apply for one."

"A grant for what?"

I want to be insulted by the tone of disbelief to his question, as if someone like me couldn't possibly want to do anything other than wait on people all day, but I admit it's an odd request coming from the woman who pours your tea every morning.

"Me and Georgia wanted to start up a support group. For young widows," I add, as if it weren't already apparent, but Fred is already shaking his head doubtfully. "Come on," I plead. "Don't tell me you don't want to do something to help Georgia after all you two have been through." I feel guilty for using Georgia in this way since obtaining a government grant was never really Georgia's intention in the first place, but I still believe it'll be good for her in the end.

Fred's face turns red even though I haven't made any specific mention of their encounter. I can hear him swallow amidst the clang of dishes and low conversation from nearby customers. "What did she tell you?" he asks me, although he's still staring at his paper.

I detect just the slightest measure of hopefulness in his question and I feel awkward for him. "She did mention something about a private moment, but that's all," I lie. I don't tell him that she couldn't get out of bed for the next five days because she was sick with regret.

"Look," I say, shifting attention away from their encounter to more important things, "we both know that Georgia has been devastated by Joseph dying. This support group is the only thing she's talked about with any real interest in five years. She really wants to help other people like her. So can you help us get a grant?"

Fred looks like he's contemplating my words, but then he scowls, as if remembering something that must have left a bad taste in his mouth. "Georgia doesn't want my help," he says, his expression darkening. I am about to say otherwise when he says loudly and firmly, "I'd like my tea now, please."

He's told me in not so subtle terms that I've overstepped my boundaries. I turn to get his tea and to place his order. Fred eats only half his breakfast, and I can't help but feel partly responsible for ruining his appetite. Still, he leaves me the same tip as he always does.

I don't have much time to reflect on it since it's one of the busiest days since I've started working. The cold weather must have everyone hankering for something warm to fill their bellies. It is almost three thirty in the afternoon before it calms down enough for me to break for lunch. I take a seat in a back booth and get ready to eat a bowl of pea soup when Fred walks in again. For a moment I think he is back for lunch since he left almost half of his breakfast, but he slides across from me at the back booth like we've arranged to meet all along.

"Do you really think this support group is going to help her?"

I nod vigorously, my eyes wide with hope. I think about all the phone calls I received after I gave out my phone number on the radio. Gerald Gosse was good enough to repeat the number several times throughout the broadcast, and my telephone rang for two days straight, all from young women across the province who were mourning the death of their own husbands. There were two cancers, one motorcycle accident, one hunting accident, a drowning, three heart attacks, two car wrecks and a brain aneurism. I haven't told Georgia any of this yet, and I don't know why, other than she seems so preoccupied of late.

"It's a long shot," Fred says. "I made some calls to a few friends over at Confederation Building, but it's not exactly a big percentage of the population clamouring for services. As far as they're concerned, they provide services to widows under Community Health."

"Oh come on, you know that's not true," I interrupt, wondering what the Department of Health would say if I called them up because I needed to change a fuse and my husband was dead.

"I'm not arguing with you. I'm just telling you the way it is." Fred reaches into his pocket and pulls out a piece of lined paper where he's scribbled notes, apparently from his telephone conversations with his friends at Confederation Building. I am surprised by the neatness of his handwriting. I'd never met a man who could write legibly. Fred, who is unpolished and whose fingernails always have dirt under them, writes in such beautiful script with perfect loops and curves, as if he spent all day writing in a journal instead of hauling carrots from the ground.

"You'll have to say some of these things about your support group." He reads slowly and without emotion from a list written on the paper. "Let's see ... establishing adequate support systems in rural areas, promoting mental health and wellness, fostering independence for women ... All that nonsense." He tosses the paper towards me, as if he were disgusted by what just came out of his mouth. He hands me a separate sheet of paper with a name and phone number: Dr. Dorothy Dunn and a St. John's exchange. I have no idea who this person is and I bite my lip in confusion, wondering why Fred is handing me the name of a doctor since I'm not sick.

"Who's Dr. Dunn?"

"She's a professor into the university. Women's studies or sociology, maybe both. She said she'll help you write the grant and make sure you say everything right so long as she gets to write a paper on you guys a year from now for some academic journal that she's been wanting to get into."

I go to thank him but he is already up and moving quickly towards the exit.

CHAPTER TWENTY-EIGHT

Prissy

The first night back home with my mother I am as nervous as the day I first brought Quentin home from the hospital. I am terrified that, without the competent nurses patrolling the corridors of the rehab facility, something terrible will happen, and there won't be anyone to call out to who will know exactly what to do.

My mother's rehabilitation stint is complete, but I don't know how the doctors can make such a conclusion since my mother still does not walk, not even with the help of a walker, and although her speech is often understandable, there are many occasions when I either have no idea what she's saying or she's saying something that makes no sense whatsoever. She has some control of her bodily functions but has enough accidents to warrant the use of an adult diaper most of the time. It's hard for me to accept that my mother has been discharged when she's nothing like the person who was admitted nearly two months earlier.

Charlie, at least, has built the ramp with access to the rear of the house. I walk up the ramp first, testing its sturdiness before attempting to wheel my mother up. The house is cool, having been vacant for almost two months now. I walk slowly through the house, checking to make sure that Charlie has moved her things into the back bedroom and installed all the proper fixtures into the downstairs bathroom. The medicine cabinet is stocked with the supplies I requested and the fridge and cabinets are filled with healthy fruits and vegetables and whole grains.

Part of me thinks, Thank God for Charlie, since I would have no idea how to go about building a ramp or drilling into bathroom tile, much less moving her dresser down a flight of stairs. And yet the other part of me wants to take him to task for otherwise abandoning us during my mother's illness. I can count on one hand the number of times Charlie has visited our mother in the hospital and at the rehab centre. The few visits he did manage were so strained they lasted less than fifteen minutes. He did not ask about her progress, her care, or what he could do to help with her transition.

On the other hand, I have not slept in a proper bed in weeks, choosing instead to sleep in the two chairs in my mother's hospital room. It's fallen on me to listen to the doctors and nurses describe her condition and her follow-up care. It's been up to me to read all the pamphlets about stroke, incontinence, feeding and nutrition, medication, and depression.

It feels strange seeing my mother back at home in her kitchen in her current state. I don't know why, since I've had two months to get used to the idea, but for some reason it pains me more than I thought it would. I could handle seeing my mother suffer the after-effects of her stroke so long as she was in the hospital surrounded by doctors and nurses, but I think I expected that once she returned home, she would return to normal, but she hasn't. She stares vacantly ahead, and when I follow her gaze there is nothing there for her to focus on save for a handle on one of the kitchen cabinets. I don't think she's really seeing anything at all and I wonder what or where she is in her mind.

"Would you like a snack?" I ask her.

"Smoke," she answers. Since her stroke, my mother speaks as little as possible, using mostly one-word requests.

"Mom, please," I plead. I would do anything for her, but I can not allow her to start smoking again. "You know you can't smoke."

She scowls as much as she can with her limited control of her facial muscles and I feel bad enough to reconsider.

"It's for your own good," I add, trying to reason with her, but it comes across as patronizing and I know she must hate me for it.

It takes Charlie more than a week to stop by. During that time, I have become adept at my new role as a caregiver. I change diapers with ease and efficiency, talking all the while to distract both of us from the task at hand. I no longer wince or feel my stomach turn during feeding, and I help my mother get showered and changed, although mostly she wears nightgowns all day and all night. I think about taking her for a walk to get some fresh air but it's gotten colder and several centimetres of snow has accumulated on the ground. I am afraid that either the wheelchair will get stuck or else it might skid on the ice.

When Charlie drops off groceries and my mother's prescription refills, I feel as if I've been banished from the outside world, like I'm depending on him to deliver another six months of supplies. I long to be the one who gets to run the errands, but I am afraid to leave my mother alone, and Charlie seems afraid to be alone with her.

For someone who showed up every day for breakfast, and again for supper, often with his laundry in tow, Charlie's absence is particularly pronounced. When he turns to leave after just ten minutes, I erupt. "Where do you think you're going? Mom needs you right now and you've turned your back on her."

It is a harsh statement and his look says so. "What the fuck do you want me to do, Prissy? Change her fuckin diaper? Wipe her ass? Shave her fuckin legs? I can't even stand to look at her like this."

"I don't like it any more than you do, Charlie, but I do it anyway," I say self-righteously. "Christ, Charlie, she's your mother too and I'm the one doing everything for her." I am speaking in a loud whisper since I don't want my mother to hear this conversation regarding the division of labour in her care. I know she already feels like a burden and the last thing I want to do is lend credence to the argument that I spend 90 per cent of my day disputing.

"Why don't you get off your fuckin high horse and tell me where the fuck you've been for the past fifteen years." Charlie is about as angry with me as I am with him, and I can tell we are going to have at it in a way we haven't since we were kids.

"What's that supposed to mean?"

"You know what the fuck it means."

"If you have something to say to me, I suggest you say it," I say, egging him on because I am itching to fight and unleash my own frustrations.

"You don't know shit," he spits at me. "Who the fuck do you think has been looking after Mom and Dad ever since you ran off? Me, that's fuckin who."

I laugh, an exaggerated fake laugh. "You? And how exactly does eating two meals a day here, and dropping off your laundry, I might add, qualify as looking after your parents? They're the ones who've been looking after you."

"You're such a bitch, I make no wonder your husband screwed around."

I can think of no other reason Charlie would say this other than to hurt me. The state of my marriage has nothing to do with the current conversation and I try to fire back with something equally cruel and misdirected. "At least I got married in the first place," I say. "You couldn't get a girl to marry you because you're … ugly and stupid."

I sound fifteen and he knows it because the corners of his mouth are twitching upwards like he's trying not to laugh at me, which makes me mimic his expression. I fight the laughter since it seems inappropriate to laugh in the middle of a heated verbal exchange, in the same way it's not appropriate to laugh in the library or during a lesson at school, which of course, makes it all the more tempting. Soon we are both smiling shamefully at one another, all forgiven for the moment.

"Look, Priss," Charlie says in all seriousness. "You haven't been here so you haven't known. Dad might not have been sick like Mom is, but Jesus, he got old fast. I had to do everything for the both of them. Do you remember when we were little?" he asks, but doesn't wait for a response. "All Dad wanted to do was sit down and watch the hockey game or read the newspaper or listen to the news, and Mom was always in the kitchen cooking and yelling at him to do something."

I remember my mother's uncanny ability to tell just when my father had closed his eyes, because it was at that very moment that she insisted the driveway needed to be shovelled, the grass mowed, the leaves raked, or the shopping done.

Charlie continues, "As soon as Dad retires he decides he actually wants to mow the lawn, paint the shutters and patch up the leak in the roof. I guess because he wanted to prove he could still do it, even though he couldn't, not really. He got winded every time he went up the stairs and that's when he decided to go up on the roof. Then all Mom wanted was for him to lie down. I used to get the same calls every day for two years: 'Charlie, your dad is up on the roof trying to clean out the gutters. Charlie, your dad is lifting something heavy again. Your father is out shovelling snow again and I'm afraid he's going to slip on the ice and crack his head open.' Are you getting the picture?"

"Yes." I nod, feeling a pang of guilt, but Charlie is not done.

"Since Dad died, I have been sent on every possible errand you can imagine. I am sent for Metamucil, dollar bills because she doesn't like loonies, Ben-Gay, Tylenol for arthritis but not the capsules, tea leaves, a 50-watt light bulb for Christ's sake because 40 is too low and 60 is too high. She wants me to run to Marks and Spencer and pick up meat pies, but Marks and Spencer closed twenty years ago and still she insists it's at the Village Mall. My whole fuckin life since Dad died has been one big scavenger hunt."

I laugh inappropriately since he's making me uncomfortable.

"It's like she haven't been right in the head for a long time. When was the last time she called you by your name, or acted halfway normal? You don't think the obituary was a sign Mom was losing it? This stroke, or what have you, this is just the beginning of the end."

I realize for the first time that I have left Charlie alone to tend to our aging parents. I didn't mean to. They were both fully functional when I left home. That's the way I remembered them and that's the way I always thought of them.

Charlie looks at me with a measure of contempt. "And then you comes home for one fuckin week out of the year and Mom and Dad act like you're the Queen of fuckin England, come for a royal visit. Everything is about having fun and seeing Prissy and the family, and then you're gone and I'm doing all the shit for them again."

"I'm sorry," I say. "I guess I didn't realize."

"It's okay. It's just this thing with Mom now. I can't do the kind of things that you do for her. I can't ..."

"I'll do it. I don't mind." And I mean it.

After Charlie leaves and I have settled my mother into bed, my cell phone rings. It's Howie's number so I ignore it, as I've done the last two times he's called today. The last time he called me was a week after my mother had the stroke. I was in a health supply store debating whether to purchase the cushioned toilet seat, which was more expensive, or the plastic one. He asked me if I received his package, and I asked him what package, even though I knew it was the divorce papers. I wanted him to come out and say it without sugar-coating it by referring to it as a package, as if it were a present he was sending. Besides, it was a foolish question since he had me served. It wasn't as if it could have gotten lost in the mail. At the time I thought it was cruel and insensitive to call me with that specific question, especially after what I'd just been through, but then I remembered he had no idea my mother had just suffered a stroke. For a split second I contemplated telling him, but then I thought better of it. I acknowledged that I had received it and then I hung up. When the girl working at the health supply store saw me wipe a tear away while I was holding two toilet seats and a cell phone in my hand, she smiled warmly as if it were a sight she sees every day, and the sad thing is, it probably is.

I don't want to call Howie back now so I call Quentin, just to make sure everything it okay. Until now, I've never been apart from him for more than two days. I miss him so much it's like a constant ache in my chest. I find myself constantly looking at my watch, reminding myself of where Quentin is and what he's doing at any given time during the day. I wonder if he's angry with me for not coming back to Toronto to settle things, and to visit him, but he's shows no animosity towards me when I call to say hi every day after school.

"Hey Mom," he answers now, pleasantly enough. "What's up?"

"Everything okay?"

"Yup."

"How's school?"

"It sucks."

I smile at his response. "I miss you," I say.

"Yeah, whatever. How's Uncle Charlie and Nan?"

"They're good," I say. I still haven't told him anything about his grandmother. "How's it going with your dad?" I figure Quentin might be able to give me a heads up as to why Howie is calling me.

"It sucks."

For some reason I am glad to hear this, although I'm sure I'm not held in any higher esteem. "Well, I was just checking in to see if you're all right."

"I'm fine," he sighs. "See you soon," he says, and I don't think anything of it until I've hung up.

CHAPTER TWENTY-NINE

Georgia

I keep my pregnancy a carefully guarded secret for a couple of reasons. For one, there's a certain degree of shame to my condition — real or imagined — despite the fact I am a grown woman. I don't have a husband, or even a boyfriend, for that matter, and when people find out it's Fred's child I'm carrying I'm certain to be the main topic of conversation. More importantly, though, I'm still trying to grasp the enormity of my condition, which I want to keep to myself for as long as I can. I have tried to tell both Lottie and Prissy but I can't seem to get up the nerve, which is odd since they both know of my encounter with Fred, and I can rest assured that neither of them will pass any judgment. I have also thought about telling Fred. He has a right to know, certainly, but things ended so awkwardly between us that I don't even know where to begin.

When Lottie invites me to breakfast before her shift starts at Lawlor's, I think about telling her everything. But when I arrive, I catch sight of Lottie in a back booth seated across from a woman with short greying hair and plump lips. She is introduced as Dr. Dunn and I think for certain that Lottie knows of my condition, for why else would she be inviting me to breakfast with a woman doctor?

"Dr. Dunn is a professor of sociology and women's studies into the university and she's going to help us get a grant for our widow support group," Lottie says.

I let out a sigh of relief that Dr. Dunn is a professor of women and not a doctor of female anatomy. Joseph would probably joke that she's a man-hater since she teaches women's studies and wears her hair short, although she is wearing wine-coloured lipstick and brown eyeliner. "It's nice to meet you," I say quietly, wondering how Lottie managed to find her in the first place.

"I think," Dr. Dunn says, "that your organization would make a fine study into the socioeconomic effects of a spouse's death on women under forty in rural communities." I notice that Dr. Dunn drinks coffee instead of tea and has ordered a fresh fruit platter with cottage cheese on the side. The chunky white cheese glistens and shakes in its bowl, seemingly taking on a life of its own. The sight of the cheese, combined with the smells of eggs and fried meat, is starting to make me nauseated and I concentrate on not throwing up.

Dr. Dunn roots around in her canvas knapsack and produces a stack of papers. "Historically," she says authoritatively, "Newfoundlanders have their roots in very dangerous occupations, chief among them fishing, mining, and more recently, oil and gas exploration. All of which pose a higher incidence of mortality amongst our male population. Add our climate and environment, and culture, to the mix and we have an even greater incidence of male mortality."

Since neither of our husbands' deaths can be attributed to those factors, I wonder if Dr. Dunn will be disappointed.

"Given those factors I don't think we have much of a problem establishing a need for an organization," Dr. Dunn continues. She blows on her coffee before taking a sip and then rummages in her bag for a pair of tortoise-shell reading glasses and a spiral-bound notebook. She flips the pages until she lands on the one with Lottie's name written on the top. I notice there are several scribbles written on the page and I squint to see them clearly, but the only thing I can make out is the word WHOW, which is written in all capital letters, the acronym Lottie lobbied so hard for.

Dr. Dunn lets her glasses slide down to the tip of her nose before continuing. "Lottie, I understand you have expressions of interest from ten additional women?"

"Eleven," Lottie corrects and Dr. Dunn makes the appropriate change in her notes. I look at Lottie in confusion, wondering where and how she has managed to locate another eleven young widows. Dr. Dunn looks happy to receive this piece of information, as if every time a young man loses his life, it bodes better for getting a slab of government money. I'm beginning to hate the entire concept of a support group and secretly wish I hadn't thought of it at all.

"I'd like to start with you, Lottie. How did your husband die?" Dr. Dunn asks the question while stirring her coffee.

I see the shame creep into Lottie's cheeks. She looks embarrassed by the question, as if suicide is a less honourable way of dying compared with Dr. Dunn's aforementioned occupational hazards. "He committed suicide," Lottie says softly, smoothing the hair on the back of her head with a shaking hand. "I don't know why for sure since he didn't leave a note, but Ches was never good at leaving notes. I might have been at Hayward's picking up a few things and if Ches was gone by the time I got home, he never left me a note to say where he was. He could have been down to the rink, to the Legion, anywhere. I'd have to wait till he got home so I could ask him, but by then it didn't matter anyway. A couple years ago, Ches broke his back. He could get around but he was in a lot of pain and he had to go on disability. He drank a lot, he slept a lot, and that's really all I remember."

This is the first time Lottie has spoken about Ches without making a disparaging comment, and I smile encouragingly at her. Lottie's enthusiasm for getting a government grant is something that's confounded me from the moment she first brought it up. She is not like me at all. She doesn't pine for Ches; she doesn't act as if her world is falling apart; she claims she didn't even like Ches all that much to begin with. I am possessed by a sudden desire to know why this is so important to Lottie.

"Why do you want this so much, Lottie?" I ask her just as Dr. Dunn looks as if she is about to pose a follow-up question of her own.

Lottie takes a deep breath, intertwining her fingers and placing them on the brown-speckled laminate table in front of her. "Because I have to do something. I knew Ches was in a bad place and I didn't do anything about it. I never told him I was worried about him because I wasn't. I never called the doctor to ask if I should do something. I was just annoyed with him for sleeping and drinking all the time. There were all the warning signs in the world and I missed every single one. I spend half my time feeling guilty because I didn't do anything, because I didn't care, and the other half I'm just angry with him for doing such a stupid thing in the first place. At least if I can get this support group off the ground then I might feel something else, something good."

This is the most emotional I've ever seen Lottie, whose cheeks, I notice, are unevenly flushed, and whose knuckles and fingernails are white now from her tight grasp.

I am surprised to realize that Lottie is the one who needs this support group, perhaps more than I ever did, and she needs it to make a difference on a grand scale. I put aside my reservations about chasing down government funds and becoming something bigger than I wanted, or even envisioned. I tell Dr. Dunn everything about Joseph, his death and its aftermath. I tell her why I wanted to start a support group for young widows in the first place, careful to stress that it was not for altruistic reasons, but for selfish ones. I tell her that I was happy to find out Lottie was a widow because it meant I wasn't the only one alone anymore. I tell her what I think a support group should do, what it should be and what it should feel like. By the time we are done, Lottie is assuring me that it's all going to work out and that we're going to accomplish something. For her sake, I hope she's right.

CHAPTER THIRTY

Prissy

I am waiting for my mother to finish her cigarette before I can go to bed, at least that's what I think she's doing in the bathroom. It usually isn't too hard to tell since the bathroom is freezing because my mother opens the window to let the smoke escape, and despite her last-minute spray of Glade, I can still smell the smoke. That, and the fact that I found a book of matches hidden under the bathmat when I went to clean the bathroom, pretty much gave me all the evidence I needed to nail her. But instead I let it go. I can not condone it, but I can ignore it.

Charlie argued with me about it one day. "Just let her have a smoke, will ya, for fuck sakes. It's the only thing left she can enjoy."

"If she starts smoking again, she'll die," I say. "All the doctors said so," I add for emphasis.

"So what," he says. "She's more than halfway there now."

I was angry with Charlie for saying so since it sounded like he'd given up, but I realize he's at least partly right. I feel bad for having her sneak around like an adolescent, but if I let her light up in my presence then I feel as if I'm doing something to physically harm her. I find it strangely encouraging that she, who does not possess the dexterity to cut meat or button a shirt, manages to open a window, light a match and inhale a deadly carcinogen into her body. It makes me think that half of her helplessness is but an act, or at least a state of mind.

I am about to check on Mom when a knock at the door startles me.

When I see Quentin standing there in the doorway, I hold my breath and place a hand over my mouth in gleeful surprise, bringing him into the folds of my bathrobe with shaking hands and hugging him until tears prick at the corners of my eyes. It's been nearly three months since I've seen him, but the ache of missing him heals almost instantly with his appearance. That Quentin does not hug me back is unimportant. He tolerates my affections for as long I dole them out, not pushing me away or sighing with annoyance. It is perhaps the most loving gesture a fourteen-year-old is capable of.

Howie follows Quentin inside and waits patiently for me to finish fussing over our son. He leans back against the kitchen countertop with all the comfort of someone who'd grown up here. Howie has always seemed to fit in my world better than I ever fit in his. I used to love that about him, but now it fills me with resentment.

He rubs his hands vigorously together, and then blows on them. My eyes fall to Howie's neck, freed from his customary dress shirt and tie and exposed now by a casual tan crew-neck sweater. I am overcome by a desire to bury my face there, breathe in his scent, feel the stubble on my cheek, and unburden myself. I want to tell him all about how horrible these past few months have been. I want to tell him about how I slept in a chair for eight weeks while my mother lay in a hospital bed recovering. I long to tell him every detail, from the number of pills my mother takes on a daily basis to the consistency of the food I have to prepare for her. I want to tell him that I have to help my mother on the toilet, and then help her off, assuming she makes it in the first place. I want to tell him that my mother's skin is paper thin and I can see every vein inside, and that it reminds me of the steamed dumplings we ordered from the restaurant in Chinatown. I want to tell him that mysterious bruises appear all over her shins now even though she doesn't walk and can't bump into anything, and that it takes all my strength just to clip her yellow toenails. Above all I want to tell him about the guilt I feel for agreeing just the slightest with my mother's assertion that she should have died the night she had a stroke. I want to tell him all of this, but I keep myself in check.

I think of how Georgia and Lottie must feel. I think about how they will never see their husbands again, but I don't feel like the lucky one at all. Surely it must be easier to imagine your husband's presence than to have him standing before you in the flesh, and still not be able to go to him.

The compulsion to confess everything is so powerful that I have to consciously remind myself of Howie's betrayal until the wound is fresh and festering and the familiar feel of loathing pushes aside the sudden longing.

"What are you doing here?" I ask.

Howie sighs, signalling his impatience with my question already. "If you would bother to open your mail or answer your phone then you'd know exactly why I'm here."

I have ignored all of Howie's phone calls to my cell, deleting messages without listening to them. I recall three envelopes postmarked from Toronto. The return address was a law office so I threw them amongst the divorce papers he sent the day of my mother's stroke. I wasn't up to looking at them, not yet.

"I've been busy," I lie. "What is it?" My mouth is dry wondering what might be in those letters I failed to open.

Howie clears his throat. "Quentin has a court date in Carbonear tomorrow to settle the charges from the night he got drunk and decided to rob a delivery truck of beer and chips. He's going to throw himself at the mercy of the judge and plead guilty on the grounds of being an incredibly stupid teenager."

Quentin shoots his father a look filled with animosity. "I hope I do go to jail," he mutters. "Can't be any worse than living with you. At least prisoners get out once a day."

I have completely forgotten his court date and I feel like the inadequate parent I am. If it was up to me to bring Quentin to court, an arrest warrant would probably be issued tomorrow afternoon for my child.

"I'm sorry, I must have forgotten," I say.

I can feel Howie's eyes on me, and I become self-conscious about how I must look to him. My bathrobe is in desperate need of washing. I haven't worn makeup in weeks, maybe months. I am wearing my eyeglasses instead of my contact lenses and the wire frames are old and outdated and bent on the right side. I'm not sure if I've taken a shower today or not and my hand unconsciously fingers my scalp, the greasy residue proof that I didn't get around to showering today after all. What a sight I must look to him.

It's not like he hasn't seen me this way before. Throughout our marriage Howie has seen me at my worst more often than I care to admit. I think of the time I got the flu and couldn't get out of bed for four days. And the time I got the stomach virus so bad I threw up for two days straight, and still Howie let me rest my head on his chest despite smelling of vomit. But that was different. I'm exposed now in a way that makes me feel vulnerable and I notch my bathrobe tighter in a nervous gesture that serves only to emphasize my shrinking waist.

Howie stares at me as if noticing my state for the first time. "Jesus, Prissy, you look awful. Are you all right?"

I feel like spitting at him. *No, I'm not all right, you selfish bastard.* "I'm fine," I say. "I've just been busy, that's all."

I can tell he's wondering what I could possibly be so preoccupied with that I would forget personal hygiene when I hear my mother's voice, muffled more from her stroke than from the closed bathroom door.

"Prissy, is everything all right? Who's there?"

"It's okay, Mom. I'll be right there," I shout. "Excuse me," I say to Howie, intending to retrieve my mother and bring her straight to bed, but then Mom chooses this moment to wheel herself with her one good arm into plain view. I don't know what to expect from my mother and I hold my breath in anticipation.

When she lays sight on Quentin and Howie, her face lights up with the pure joy of a child discovering the toys left by Santa Claus on Christmas morning, and I think this must be the moment Mom loses her mind. Her physical incapacities were evident immediately, but the loss of her mental faculties has taken a longer and more convoluted progression. Ever since her stroke, my mother's facial expressions have been limited to either a scowl or a frown that belies the depths of her sadness. Part of me even assumed the stroke must have rendered her facial muscles incapable of smiling at all, and yet my mother's face now appears younger and more at ease than it has in months.

"My squishy boy," she slurs at Quentin. "C'mere and give your Nanny a kiss."

Quentin hesitates and I can tell he's afraid of his grandmother. "What's wrong with Nan?" he asks, as if he might catch whatever horrible thing has happened to her.

"It's okay," I say encouragingly. "She's been sick and she needs some extra help to do things, but otherwise she's fine," I assure him. "She really misses you." Once again I can feel Howie's eyes on me, but I refuse to meet his gaze, instead focusing my attention on Quentin, silently coaxing him to embrace his grandmother, which to my huge relief, he eventually does.

"Clara," Howie says politely. "It's good to see you." He looks uncertain how to approach his mother-in-law under such circumstances and I can hardly blame him. This is the woman who fabricated the story of his death, arranged his memorial service, and called him every name in the proverbial book, and now here she sits in a wheelchair, frail and thin and pitiable. He looks to be steeling himself for another verbal attack, but instead Mom is positively beaming at him.

"Howard, look at you so handsome," she says. "I was beginning to think you'd run out on us, but I know you'd never do that." She smiles as if it were the most far-fetched thing in the world. "Now c'mere and let me give you a hug too."

I am torn between a desire to laugh at Howie's confused expression, and a moral code which says that it's plain wrong to laugh at my mother's dementia. Howie is obviously as taken aback by Mom's sweetness toward him as he is at her physical deterioration. He looks at me for clarification, but I am hiding a smile behind my hand. Howie leans forward tentatively and obliges his mother-in-law's request for a hug. He looks stiff and cautious.

"I'm so glad you're here," Mom whispers in his ear, loud enough for everyone to hear. "Prissy misses you so much."

I feel my cheeks redden and turn hot under Howie's gaze, and I long for my mother to call him a bastard again.

Once I get my mother settled into bed for the night and Quentin has fallen asleep in the old daybed in the hallway, Howie signals for me to join him in the kitchen. I hate the way he summons me, and I want to ignore him entirely, but I follow him into the kitchen anyway.

"Why didn't you tell me?" Howie asks.

"Because it wasn't really any of your business," I respond coolly.

"I could have helped you out."

"We don't need your help."

Howie shakes his head in disbelief as if he still can't quite comprehend what's befallen his mother-in-law. "What happened?"

"She had a stroke," I answer matter-of-factly. "She suffered some paralysis along the left side of her body, and in addition to the job it did to her muscles and her speech, it also affected some aspects of her memory. She doesn't remember what happened between us and I didn't really feel like telling her all over again, especially after everything else she's been going through. That's why she's being, well, nice to you. I would really appreciate it if you just, you know, let it go for now anyway."

"Of course." Howie nods in understanding, while I go on to recite the details of Mom's medical condition. I am detached and business-like, mimicking the tone of all the medical professionals I have spoken to over the past several months. I use words like ischemic and aphasia — words I was blissfully unaware even existed, and yet now I am an overnight expert on them.

Howie rubs his forehead with his fingers during most of my speech, removing them only to intertwine them and rest them on the back of his head like he is about to begin a regimen of sit-ups.

"I'm sorry you've had to go through all this alone," he says, "especially with … everything else going on. You should have told me." He sounds almost annoyed that I chose to keep him in the dark about an issue that's none of his concern.

"You're the last person to tell me what I should have done," I shoot back, and he acknowledges the barb by letting it go.

"Look, Quentin wanted to stay here until we go to the hearing, but I have a hotel in St. John's. We would have gotten here a lot sooner but the flight was delayed more than two hours and just about everyone on the flight was trying to rent a car." He gets up to go and I hate myself for wanting him to stay. It is almost one in the morning and a full hour back to St. John's.

"You can crash on the couch for this evening," I offer. "In my mother's dementia, she'll probably be looking for you in the morning anyway." I wonder if this is true or if she'll have forgotten that Howie was here at all by the time she wakes up. I get up to go to bed myself, not waiting to hear whether he has decided to stay or make his way back to St. John's.

CHAPTER THIRTY-ONE

Prissy

The morning after Howie and Quentin suddenly show up on my doorstep, I awaken on my own for the first time in weeks. It's nearly seven thirty and I'm panicked by the lateness of the hour. I did not hear my mother call to me to get her to the bathroom as I have every morning at six. Sometimes it is 5:55, and other mornings she has waited until 6:10, but never later.

I run down the stairs barefoot, yelling out to her. "Mom!" I reach the back bedroom only to find her bed empty, the sheets neatly pulled up and tucked under the pillows. I stare at the empty bed in confusion while I hear what I think is my mother's laughter emanating from the kitchen.

Although I was vaguely aware of the smell when I first awoke, I am now overpowered by it. Coffee, bacon, maple syrup all swirl together like the inviting smell of a greasy spoon on a Saturday morning. I follow the scent and the voices into the kitchen where I see Mom sitting at the table in her wheelchair with a cup of tea before her. Howie is cutting her pancakes into bite-size pieces and dribbling thick syrup over the top. I watch as Howie proffers one on a fork to my mother while she accepts it with an open eager mouth. She actually laughs giddily when the syrup dribbles down her chin and I stare in dismay as Howie wipes the sticky liquid away with a wet cloth. I stand in the doorway, the outsider now, while my estranged husband and my disabled mother connect in a way I could never have imagined in my wildest dreams.

Howie smiles when he sees me, and waves me inside the kitchen, plopping a mug of bitter coffee in front of my customary seat at the kitchen table. I have been drinking mostly tea since I arrived, and only when I breathe in the aroma do I realize how much I've missed my morning coffee. He makes me a plate of pancakes, tops them off with a spoonful of blueberry preserves and a pat of butter. I regard him warily while my mother sings his praises.

"You are quite the catch," Mom says as Howie clears away dishes and washes them in the sink. I have never known him ever to wash a dish, even so much as place one in the dishwasher.

"He's only good at pancakes," I point out, feeling petty, and yet I can't help but elaborate all the same. "He burns bacon and his eggs are always overcooked in the middle."

Everything seems to have changed overnight. My mother no longer seems depressed, having pulled herself from the abyss of darkness by virtue of Howie showing up unannounced. I barely even hear the slur in her speech, and wonder if she's improving or if I'm merely accustomed to it now. She is saying something but I can't hear the words because I'm too absorbed in listening for the slur. I am ashamed to admit that I want to hear it.

"Prissy? Are you listening to me?" Mom's voice sounds small, distant.

"Huh?"

"I was just saying that Howie is being such a dear and you ought to appreciate him a little bit more. These pancakes taste like heaven."

They were Aunt Jemima. Any idiot could add a bit of milk and egg to a prepared mix, but I stop short of saying so. I am spared at having to respond at all by Charlie's arrival. He doesn't look at all surprised to see Howie, and helps himself to a stack of pancakes.

"How ya been, b'y?" he asks Howie. I think it must be nice to be as adaptable as Charlie, to wander in on such a scene and yet think little or nothing of it. "Pass me the fuckin syrup, will ya, Priss?"

"What are you doing here, Charlie?" I ask. It's eight o'clock in the morning and these days Charlie hardly ever makes an appearance before three.

He shrugs. "Thought shithead might need some moral support today. I could be a character witness or something."

No wonder he wasn't surprised to see Howie. He knew today was

Quentin's hearing with the judge. I feel completely inadequate as a parent since I'm the only one who seems not to have known about Quentin's court date. At the same time I think it's a sweet gesture, and one that should please Quentin very much.

I barely recognize my son when he joins the rest of us for breakfast. He is dressed in khaki slacks and a button-down shirt, and his hair is combed neatly to the side in an exaggerated part. Since the last time Quentin wore a dress shirt was for his first grade portrait, I assume Howie must have purchased the outfit in preparation for Quentin's court date.

Charlie laughs outright at Quentin's appearance. "Hey shithead, where you off to? Choir practice?"

"Shut the fuck up, Charlie," he shoots back.

"Watch your mouth, Quentin." It is Howie.

"But he just called me a shithead!"

Charlie can barely contain his laughter, and Quentin smiles back reluctantly.

"Come on, shithead, you know I mean it as a sign of respect."

My son looks pale and nervous and I take pity on him.

"I think you look handsome," I say, smiling at him.

"I look like a douchebag."

"We don't have to leave for another hour," I say. "Why don't you have some pancakes?"

"I can't, or else I'll puke."

I take mild pleasure in seeing my cocky teenage son humbled by the law, but mothering is an instinct and I hug his shoulders and tell him everything is going to be okay and that I will be right there with him the whole time. I feel Quentin stiffen under my embrace.

"You can't come," he says. "Just me and Dad, and Uncle Charlie."

I try to mask the hurt in my face. "Of course I'm coming."

"Look, Mom, no offense, but you can be a bit emotional. What if the judge throws the book at me? Decides to make me an example? The last thing I need when they're taking me away in handcuffs is to hear my mother scream, 'Noooooo!' and then faint."

I hide a smile. At fourteen, Quentin is a young offender, and this is his first, and I hope his only, encounter with the law. Nor is it a violent crime he was accused of. That he would be handcuffed or sent to prison at all is an impossibility. At most, I imagine he'll get handed a suspended sentence with probation. There is also a chance he will be asked to perform community service or attend some sort of educational program on youth crime.

"Okay, I'll wait right here for you," I say stoically. "Be brave."

I tell my mother they are all gone to see a movie in St. John's, but I don't know if she believes me or not. She nods in acceptance of my explanation in such a way that I have to wonder who is humouring whom.

It takes five impossibly anxious hours of scrubbing the grout in the bathroom and cleaning out the refrigerator before Quentin, Charlie and Howie return from youth court. Quentin shows all the exuberance of someone who has just been acquitted after a lengthy murder trial.

"I'm a free man now, Mom," he says, as if he's just been paroled after serving ten years behind bars.

"You should have seen him, Priss," Charlie says, grabbing a beer from the fridge. "He was white as a fuckin sheet. But he kept it together. Told the judge how sorry he was."

As anticipated, he received his suspended sentence and one year's probation. He also received a stern lecture from the judge on respecting other people's property and the dangers of substance abuse. He was also ordered to attend a youth seminar in St. John's for troubled teens and I'm slightly taken aback at having this label placed on my child. Howie tells me all of this as if he were a lawyer I hired to represent Quentin's interests, and not the father of my child.

"The seminar is scheduled for two weeks so it makes more sense just to wait it out," Howie adds authoritatively. "I've already spoken to Quentin's principal and his lesson plans are being couriered here tomorrow."

"Okay." I am looking forward to having Quentin home with me for two weeks and feel almost grateful that he committed the delinquent act in the first place. "When are you taking off then?" I ask. "You can stay for dinner if you want, assuming it doesn't interfere with your flight back." I am trying to make the best of the situation since Howie seems to have made an effort to do the same, particularly with my mother, and now giving me two weeks with my son.

"That'd be great," Howie says, smiling at me in a way that pierces through my heart. "Actually, I thought I'd wait it out here with Quentin."

I am about to object when Mom calls out to Howie to ask if he could pick up fish and chips, and before I can tell him that she's not allowed to eat it, he's already on his way to Dee's.

CHAPTER THIRTY-TWO

Lottie

I recognize Roger Parsons from the instant he walks into Lawlor's and sits down at the counter even though he isn't wearing a suit or travelling with an assistant or a reporter. As the representative for Paradise Bay and surrounding communities in the provincial government, Roger Parsons is something of a local celebrity. He is known for campaigning tirelessly for things near and dear to the hearts of local residents — paved roads, employment, and accessible health care. He attends weddings and 50th anniversary parties at the Legion. He dances with the brides and toasts the young couples with wishes for health and happiness.

He attends the opening of the flea market every year, wandering the booths and admiring the creativity and entrepreneurship of our residents. Georgia says he buys two bricks of fudge from her on opening day every year, claiming it to be the best treat he's ever had.

Someone told me he attended Ches' funeral, although I don't remember seeing him there. I don't remember much of anything about the funeral except that it was a beautiful summer day and I remember wanting it to be overcast and drizzly, to match my mood. When I saw the bright streaks of sunlight I remember thinking that God must have been pleased that Ches was dead, and I couldn't understand why since I thought suicide meant your soul would be condemned to hell for all eternity. For some reason, seeing the sun made me feel that maybe Ches' soul had been spared after all, and it made me feel lighter, almost weightless.

When I see Roger Parsons, my mouth goes dry. He takes a seat at a stool at the front counter and I approach him with a fresh pot of coffee. My hand shakes a little and I don't know if it's because the pot is heavier than usual since it's filled to the brim or because my stomach is nervous and my limbs feel weak. I can't help feeling that his unexpected appearance here the day after I receive the grant proposal from Dr. Dunn is a sign from above, and I get that weightless feeling again.

I want to speak with Roger Parsons about the grant, but I'm nervous, filled with doubt and uncertainty. I don't know why. Dr. Dunn has put together a wonderful proposal that she couriered to me the previous day. It uses all the language the government is always using. It contains the phrases *improved coordination amongst government agencies, community outreach, improving the quality of life of rural families in transition, providing economic and social supports to families in need,* and so on. These are exactly the same phrases I hear politicians say on the evening news and in the paper all the time.

I have memorized everything and yet I'm afraid I will say something foolish and ruin my chances if I approach Mr. Parsons. I'll be just like the woman working at the Purity Factory who attracted guffaws from all across the country when the Queen of England visited. When Her Majesty asked the woman what she was making, the poor thing didn't say she was making jam jams or peppermint knobs or molasses kisses or any other sweet confection for that matter. Instead she said she was making seven dollars an hour and it was reported everywhere with great humour.

I am about to take his order when I see Fred enter the diner and plop himself next to Roger Parsons. Fred places a friendly arm around him and the two embrace like long-lost friends. Fred told me he had some friends in Confederation Building but he failed to mention they were elected and influential.

"Roger," Fred says, pointing at me, "this here is Lottie. She's the one I was telling you about."

"So you're one the widows who wants to start up a support group," Mr. Parsons says.

I stare at him with my mouth open as I try to process what's happening, that Fred has purposefully arranged the visit and the fates had nothing to do with it at all. I nod. "Yes, sir," I say.

I wait reluctantly for him to ask me questions about Ches, but he spares me the discomfort. "How's your daughter holding up?"

I picture Marianne. She is already prettier than I was at the same age, lean and athletic where I was round and soft. Sometimes I think she is managing okay without her father, but most of the time I worry about her. I wonder if there's such a thing as a gene for depression and if Marianne has inherited it, and if so, is it lying dormant in her brain waiting for the right moment to send her spiralling into a deep depression? I ask her all the time if she ever feels sad, or overwhelmed, if she's tired a lot or if she has trouble sleeping. She always sighs, rolls her eyes at me and says she's not going to kill herself. Still, if Marianne sleeps late, I wonder if it's typical teenage behaviour, or the precursor to something more serious. If Marianne complains of having too much homework, I sit next to her at the kitchen table and tell her to take a break and relax.

"I'm worried for her," I answer truthfully, "but I think she's a brave young woman. She invented her own line of air fresheners and perfume, and I think she's going to try and sell them at the flea market next year. Who knows?"

Mr. Parsons smiles warmly at me. "I'll look for her there then. How can she go wrong with a mother like you?"

Roger Parsons has no idea what kind of mother I am, but he sounds sincere when he says it, which is probably why he continues to be re-elected.

"I believe you have something for me?"

"I haven't taken your order yet," I say uneasily, "but the kitchen is quick. Would you like to hear the special?" He chuckles in response but I don't know what's so funny.

"I'm talking about your grant proposal," Roger says by way of explanation. "Fred told me you had it."

I breathe a sigh of relief and retrieve the proposal from my bag. It looks professional and polished with its cardboard cover and crisp white pages bound together by black spirals. I feel that I've accomplished something important, regardless of whether or not we get funding. Mr. Parsons good-naturedly speaks to everyone in Lawlor's before leaving to go back to his offices in Confederation Building. They tell him of potholes, poor road signage, and snowmobile trails.

"I'll be in touch, Lottie," he says. "Keep your fingers crossed that we can do something."

"I didn't know you knew Roger Parsons," I say to Fred when the excitement dies down.

"Roger helped me out a lot when I was getting the flea market off the ground. He's a good guy, means well and has the district's best interests at heart."

I feel an outpouring of gratitude to Fred for all he's done to help out, and at the same time I feel I might have lured him into this whole thing unwillingly. I wonder if Fred expects Georgia to fall all over him with gratitude when she finds out, like he's a saviour come to her rescue. The truth is, if Georgia knew Fred played a role in the grant, she'd probably run as fast as she could in the other direction.

"I didn't tell Georgia that you're helping us out with the grant."

"That's just fine by me," Fred says, smiling.

"I thought you wanted to do this for Georgia. So she'd be all happy and grateful, and even a little indebted to you."

"Jesus, no," he says, shaking his head.

"Then who are you doing it for? Certainly not for me?"

Fred, who had taken off his wool cap for the breakfast with Roger Parsons, now pulls it back over his head. He shrugs. "Joseph, I suppose. I kinda think he'd want me to watch out for his wife instead of wishing she'd just go away somewhere."

"So what are you going to do now?"

"We'll just wait for Roger to get the ball rolling." Fred hands me a crumpled twenty-dollar bill from his pocket. "He'll probably need a few weeks. This ought to cover breakfast," he says before leaving.

But I wasn't referring to the grant or to the process or to Roger Parsons at all, but to Georgia.

CHAPTER THIRTY-THREE

Prissy

"*D*id you want to spend Christmas with Quentin?" Howie asks me this before he leaves to bring Quentin to the seminar the judge ordered him to attend, seemingly months earlier.

I think this is a question of such monumental stupidity that I wonder if it might be a trick: if I reveal the obvious answer then I must be admitting to something else. I know my hesitation annoys Howie because he sighs. "It's a straightforward question, Prissy."

Is it? I ask myself. The past two weeks with Howie have played out like a calculated game of chess. I analyze his every move, he mine. For instance, I presume Howie must be overcome, not necessarily with guilt, but something akin to it, maybe a sense of duty. Why else, I wonder, does he feel the need to get up with my mother every day, make sure she's clean, dressed and fed? He shovels the driveway at the mere hint of snow. All my bills are paid before I even retrieve them from the mailbox, and the cupboards and the fridge are freshly stocked with Mom's favourite biscuits, jams and jellies. After my mother waxed philosophical about some obscure British tea that she used to be able to buy some forty years ago, Howie immediately found it online and had it couriered the following day. He didn't even seem to mind that she took one sip of it and declared it just wasn't the same as it used to be and asked for a cup of Tetley instead.

He sits with my mother in the kitchen after supper, listening to her stories as if he hasn't heard them all one hundred times before. He doesn't correct her when she talks about my father as if he was still alive, or refers to Quentin as the baby. I sometimes wonder if she even knows who Howie is. These episodes come with greater frequency now, but they dissipate almost as quickly as they come. In one breath she asks for Artie, and in the next she is coherent and aware again. The only thing she seems to have erased from memory altogether is my marital woes and I'm almost envious of her for that.

"Of course I want to spend Christmas with my son," I say finally. "What's the catch?"

"For God's sake, Prissy, there's no catch. Your mother's ill and it's not like you can get away right now. The holidays are less than two weeks away; we're already here so I figured it might be just as well to stay until they're over."

"We?" I ask. "You don't have to stay here, Howie."

He shoots me a look of annoyance. "I'd like to spend the holidays with my son too."

"I promise you he won't get into any trouble."

"And what about your mother?"

I am exasperated with Howie's attentiveness to Mom's needs. It's not that I don't appreciate the effort, but I can't help thinking about what's going to happen when Howie does leave.

"What about her? She's not your problem, so stop pretending that you care. We both know that all of this is about assuaging your guilt. All you're doing is trying to make yourself feel better, but you're just making it worse for my mother and for me. When you do eventually leave, I'm going to have to try and explain to her why you're not here anymore. So the sooner you leave, the better off we'll both be."

Howie scowls, clenches his fists but says nothing more. I don't think I'm being harsh or ungrateful, just truthful.

When Howie returns from Quentin's court-ordered seminar several hours later, he has a Christmas tree tied to the roof of the car, which he leans against the side of the house to dry off. He spends the next hour and a half in the attic, bringing down boxes of Christmas decorations. He retrieves plastic candy canes, oversized snowmen that light up and wave, a Santa that says, "Ho-Ho-Ho, Merry Christmas" when you press its nose, wreaths with shiny plastic holly berries, and an assortment of other gaudy decorations and ornaments. He goes about the evening as if I'd suggested that it was such a good idea for him to stay we ought to have a Christmas party to celebrate.

When he starts stringing Christmas lights along the roof of the house I am truly perplexed since he's never wanted to do it on our own home, even when Quentin was little and eager to help. The wind is howling loudly, blowing snow in all directions, and I shudder against the draft that seeps in through the windows and cracks in the old house. I think of Howie out on the ladder and feel a momentary pang of empathy. Howie is not used to the ferocity of a Newfoundland winter. Our visits home have been mostly during the summer when the air is a refreshing change from the humid Toronto summers. I imagine Howie's hands must be numb and his ears raw.

I turn my attention to Quentin, who is sitting on the couch sipping soda from a two-litre bottle, his hand orange from a crumpled bag of cheese doodles in his lap and his attention riveted to a wrestling match on television.

"Oh my God, this is so fake!" he exclaims. "He didn't even hit him and the guy falls," he declares in outrage, throwing his hands in the air.

"Why don't you get on your coat and help your father with the lights?" I suggest, leaning in the doorway of the living room. Quentin looks at me as if I'd just told him to hike to the top of Mount Everest.

"It's friggin freezing out," he says.

"All the more reason to help then," I say, more firmly this time. "Get your coat on and go help your father. I am not asking you anymore. I am telling you."

"Why do you give a shit about Dad anyway? He's the one who left you."

I feel my cheeks turn hot with embarrassment. It's all bad enough that it's true in the first place, but it feels especially hurtful coming from my own child. "That's none of your business," I snap.

"No, I s'pose it's not. I'm just the kid who has to grow up in a broken home."

"Seriously, Quentin, aren't you getting too old to play the broken home card? Did you not learn anything from your seminar?"

"No, actually, it was such bullshit I almost died from boredom. I think I would have preferred being locked up. Bunch a freaking losers."

"I don't want to talk about this right now," I say, weary with the direction nearly every conversation with Quentin veered off in. "Can you please just go out there and give your father a hand?"

Quentin rolls his eyes and sighs but rises from his perch on the couch all the same. "You're only going to take them down in a few weeks anyway," he mutters, putting on his boots and zipping up his coat. "He'll probably be gone again by then anyway. Such a friggin waste of time," he says to himself as he slams the front door.

I hug my arms against the chill, silently concurring with my son. I'm not in much of a Christmas spirit and I don't know why it seems so important to Howie right now. You could decorate the house however you wanted to, but inside, there would still just be a distant couple, an unruly teen and an old woman too out of it to notice.

I decide to get out and walk to the pharmacy to get my mother's prescription refilled. I hate sitting around, feeling useless, staying in the background while Howie does everything for my mother and the upkeep on the house. I throw on my coat and boots and head outside. The wind blows my hair around the top of my head.

"Where you are going?" Howie bellows from the top of the roof.

"I'm just going to take a walk to the pharmacy and get Mom's prescription refilled," I shout into the wind, annoyed that I feel obligated to tell him where I'm going.

"I'll get it for you." Howie begins to climb down the ladder.

"Sweet," Quentin mutters, dropping the tangled mass of Christmas lights from below and then going back inside.

"Just let me do one God-damned thing," I yell over the howling wind. He hesitates but then backs off.

"Just be careful, okay. It's getting stormy."

I laugh outright. He has never wintered here, and yet he thinks nothing of dispensing advice to me.

At the drugstore, I am vaguely aware of the stares, not just from customers, but from the employees too. It seems everyone is looking at me, whispering and gesturing. I make an effort to smooth my hair, check to make sure my boots match and my coat is not inside out. Everything is in order, but still they stare and whisper. It isn't until the checkout girl sneers at me while swiping my container of Metamucil with far more force than necessary, that I become aware that something is amiss.

"I'm sorry, is there a problem?" I ask when my purchases are thrown haphazardly in a bag and my change is strewn on the counter despite my having had my hand out.

"It's just that your husband usually comes in to do the shopping," the cashier says.

I really don't understand why me being here instead of Howie matters one way or the other. "So?" I say, annoyed.

"So I guess he's not so dead after all, is he?"

I've never fainted before but I think I might come close when I hear this because the buzz of the store grows suddenly quiet and I feel myself grow unbearably hot. I feel the prickle of heat on my skin, but my body seems incapable of producing sweat to relieve the discomfort. I blink stupidly while I process what's happening. I am vaguely aware of the people behind me watching me, waiting for my reaction. It hadn't even occurred to me to hide Howie. Fake death notices and deception are Mom's specialty, and she doesn't even remember taking out the obit in the first place. I am mortified and embarrassed beyond what I imagine is possible, and I bolt from the pharmacy, leaving my change on the counter. I think that I will have to move someplace where they don't know me, perhaps St. John's, where there are too many busy people to care about my own foolish business.

I trudge home slowly, listening to the sound of my boots crunching the snow. I can feel the anger building inside until my head begins to throb. I hate my husband and my mother both. I've done nothing wrong and yet my cheating husband and my deceptive mother are perceived as innocents, whereas I am the one who's vilified.

It's nearly dark by the time I make it home. There is a festive glow from the red, orange, green, yellow and blue lights on the roof, a plastic snowman waves at me, and candy canes light the way to the back door. It is in stark contrast to my foul mood and I slam the door in anger, prepared to have words with my husband and demand he leave me alone at once. I storm into the living room, only to find him underneath the Christmas tree. Mom is telling him to move it an inch to the left and then an inch to the right. She is telling him to tilt it forward, then back, and then rotate it about thirty degrees, all of which he does dutifully until my mother is satisfied. Quentin is rifling through the boxes of ornaments, claiming them to be as old as Christ himself. The smell of fresh balsam fir mingles with the scent of burning wood in the fireplace. It looks and smells like Christmas but I don't feel like part of the celebration. I don't even feel like part of the family. I feel as if I've accidentally stumbled into the wrong house and all of the people inside are strangers to me.

"Prissy," Howie says brightly when he emerges from underneath the tree. I've been standing here, unnoticed, for what seems like an eternity. "You're just in time to help us decorate the tree."

"I have a headache," I state flatly, noticing the snowflakes in my hair have melted into puddles of water on the wood floor.

"You should have worn a hat," my mother says, but I barely hear her because I am already halfway up the stairs.

It is almost midnight when I sneak back down for a cup of tea, but I run into Howie in the living room. It's easy to forget that he's sleeping on the couch since he gets up so early and conceals all traces of his sleeping arrangements from Mom, as if she would know anyway.

"Can't sleep?" he asks. He is wearing a plain white t-shirt and brown plaid pyjama pants. I notice that his hair is getting long by the way it sticks up and off to the side. I resist the urge to try and smooth it back in place.

I shake my head no.

"What do you think?" he asks as he plugs in the lights on the Christmas tree and a jolt of colour bursts from every branch. It's beautiful, it really is, but I can't bring myself to say so.

"What's the matter, Priss?" he asks and I want to wince at the ease with which he shortens my name.

The question is so vast I don't know where to begin. I could start with his affair and his request for a divorce but it seems like that moment has passed. I could tell him that I find his insistence on being here suffocating, that he makes me feel like an outsider amongst my own family, that when he leaves I will be left alone again to care for an elderly parent who will have more questions than I can answer. I could tell him that I will miss my son so much when he leaves that I can already feel the emptiness in my chest. I could answer the question with any one of those responses but instead I reveal only the latest personal affront.

"Everyone in town knows you're not really dead."

I expect a satisfied smirk or a serves-you-right glare, but to my astonishment he throws his head back and laughs heartily. "No wonder everyone around here keeps looking at me so strangely. Shit." He laughs, obviously remembering something of great amusement. I think about some of the looks he must have attracted. I picture old women blessing themselves at the sight of him, children pointing, and others tentatively reaching out to touch an arm to see if he was transparent.

"Maybe we could just tell everyone I'm my twin brother," he suggests. "Separated at birth, perhaps? You could say you didn't even know I had a twin brother."

I can't help but laugh with him at this suggestion. Certainly if my mother were in her right mind, she'd have already put that story in motion. "I don't think so," I say, although I'm smiling.

"Maybe I was cryogenically frozen and they revived me?"

I shake my head playfully. "Uh-uh. Too sci-fi for folks around here."

"I faked my own death to collect the insurance money?"

"Hmmm." I smile, placing a finger on my chin as if I were seriously contemplating the plan. "You know you might be on to something there."

"Did your mother really tell people I had testicular cancer?"

"Yeah, she really did," I admit. "She told everyone they had to remove both your balls."

Howie laughs out loud again and shakes his head. "Your mom is a piece of work."

"She is that." I stifle a yawn. "I think I'm going to turn in," I say, stretching my arms cat-like over my head.

"Night, love," Howie says, and I stop mid-stretch and stare at him. The endearment sounded so easy and natural that I wonder for a moment if all the heartache over the past few months has been some sort of horrible dream.

His face grows red when he realizes his slip. "I'm sorry," he says awkwardly. "It just came out ... I ..."

I long to tell him, *Night, hon,* like I always used to, but instead I turn away and head back up the stairs.

CHAPTER THIRTY-FOUR

Georgia

*I*n the days and weeks after Joseph died, he continued to receive mail as if nothing had happened to him. Telephone bills, cable and electric bills, bank and credit card statements all arrived with his name on them until they formed a sizeable stack on the dining room table. Everything was in Joseph's name and they didn't know he was dead because I hadn't told them yet. I hated to change it over since I liked seeing his name printed so formally on all the envelopes. It made me forget for a moment that he was not going to walk in the door after a hard day's work and rifle through the mail complaining of having too many bills.

Switching things over to my name did not put an end to the mail Joseph received, albeit less frequently. He received special offers on credit cards, flyers for home heating and new windows, and on the 26th of every month, his *Hockey News* came in the mail. When he received his renewal form, I filled it out and sent it back. I did this for three years before I eventually cancelled it. After a while, things came addressed to him in dribs and drabs. A card came reminding him to make an appointment to have his teeth cleaned. The garage in Carbonear sent a reminder to have his snow tires put on. Each time I retrieved something for him from the mailbox, my heart jumped in hope and for a split second I would think that maybe he wasn't dead.

When Joseph receives a letter from Avalon Ford offering great deals on a trade-in for his truck, I don't feel hope or longing or despair. Instead I feel nothing but anger. How could they not know that his truck had been totalled five years earlier? Didn't they keep track of such things? I make the call, the same one I have made many times in the past, and hope and pray that it's the last. *Joseph Reid is deceased. Please remove him from the mailing list.*

I think about the truck that Joseph died in. It was brand new, the first car he'd ever bought new, and I chastised him for it because it wasn't appropriate for families. *Where will I put the car seats?* I asked him this as if we had a brood at home ready and waiting to be carted about town. *We'll cross that bridge when we come to it,* he assured me. I knew he wanted that truck so he and Fred could traipse off into the wilderness to fish and kayak and camp.

And then my heart stops for a second at the realization of something so obvious that I've overlooked it for five years. It was Joseph's truck that was totalled, but Joseph was not in the driver's seat. Joseph had left a few minutes before four o'clock that afternoon because he told me he was picking Fred up on the way. Why Fred was driving Joseph's new truck that night seems strange to me now, since Joseph didn't let anyone drive it. He hardly let me move it if it was blocking my car in the driveway, and yet Joseph had allowed Fred to sit in the driver's seat and take it out on the highway. Suddenly it is the most important thing in the world for me to find out why.

In an instant I am racing to Fred's house. The road is unpaved, but the frozen ground makes the ride smooth. Fred has a vast quantity of land, left to him by his grandfather, but his house is modest, a tiny two bedroom bungalow that looks more like a garage on such a large property.

I know he's home because his truck is in the driveway and I can see the reflection of the television on the living room window. I knock on the door but I don't wait for him to answer and I let myself in. Fred is sitting in the living room, alone, with a Molson in one hand and an opened box of pizza, with three slices missing, on the coffee table. There is a heap of mushrooms piled on the cardboard and I want to ask him why he wouldn't just ask them to make the pizza without the mushrooms. Lottie says he orders breakfast as if he was putting her out, apologizing for stopping by if it's busy or crowded. She would say he would just as soon pick out the mushrooms than ask someone not to put them on in the first place.

Fred is watching a hockey game and I can tell from the uniforms that it is Boston and Montreal. I don't know much about hockey, but I know enough from Joseph to know that these two teams have a great rivalry and that it is the only time Joseph roots for the Bruins. Fred looks at me in surprise and offers me a beer and a slice of pizza, which I turn down.

I decide to come right out and ask the question directly. "Why were you driving that night? Joseph never let anyone drive his truck. It was brand new."

Fred places his beer on the coffee table and breathes deeply. "I've been waiting for you to ask me that question for the last five years and now that you've finally asked me, I'm not quite sure how to answer."

"He wasn't drinking," I say in a measured tone. "The autopsy and toxicology reports found no alcohol in his blood."

Fred nods. "I know. We were going to go out after the game was over and grab a beer. The only thing either one of us was drinking that night was water and Gatorade." Fred takes another deep breath and I have to refrain from yelling at him to get on with it already. "In the sixth inning, Joseph made this diving catch out in right centre. It was one of those great catches — the kind where everyone on the bench is up on their feet cheering. But he came down hard on his arm and when he got up he favoured his left wrist. It was so bad he couldn't even bat the next time up and had to sit out the rest of game with an ice pack on it. By the time the game was over, it was swollen and bruised. I knew he'd broken something and I insisted on driving him to the emergency room for an x-ray, but he accused me of acting like you, the way I was fussing all over him."

I smile sadly thinking this is just the kind of thing Joseph would say.

"He just wanted to go home, to you, so that's where I was taking him. His wrist was too beat up to drive so he asked me to take him home, and I made him promise he'd go see a doctor the next day. We were talking and joking about the game when I caught sight of something running in front of the truck, an animal, I guess. It was an instinct to swerve to avoid it. I just reacted. It happened so fast. I'd like to tell you everything that happened after that, but I don't really remember. I think I blacked out just for a couple of minutes before the ambulance got there. The rest of the night was a horror show. You were there. You know."

I feel ashamed for harbouring so much resentment toward Fred, for blaming him outright for Joseph's death. Joseph would be so angry with me if he knew, and I feel the weight of having disappointed my husband in the pit of my stomach. I want to make things right between me and Joseph, but more than that, I want to make things right between me and Fred.

"Joseph was your husband, but he was my best friend, more than my best friend," Fred continues. "He was like my brother. I ask myself every day why Joseph was killed when nothing happened to me. If I could change it, I would."

"I know," I whisper softly because I believe him when he says this. "Did you at least win the game?" I ask. It never seemed to matter to me one way or the other, but it suddenly seems important. "I think if he won then at least he would have been happy — more than happy — before he died."

"Yeah, we won and he was happy, sore wrist and all," Fred admits with the hint of a smile as he remembered their final moments together.

"I'm pregnant," I say and I don't know why I've said it at this particular moment. It is such a change of subject, from one earth-shattering event to the next. "Nearly four months now," I add lest he think it is some new development. "It's yours," I say when he doesn't show any reaction except to stare as the Bruins fight off a power play as if I wasn't in the room at all. In fact, the only indication that he's heard me in the first place is the sudden pallor to his skin and the beads of perspiration forming on the top of his bald head.

"Fred? Are you okay?"

He looks sad and angry at the same time. "I'm sorry, Georgia," he says coolly. "But I don't know what you want me to say. I can't …"

His words hang in the air, unfinished thoughts. I don't expect this reaction and it confuses me. Impending fatherhood is supposed to be filled with promise and hope, albeit nervous excitement — all of the things that I am feeling about impending motherhood, however un-orthodox it might be. But judging from Fred's reaction, I half expect him to offer to pay for the abortion.

"I'm not asking you to do anything," I say. "I'm just telling you because I thought you had a right to know. I thought you'd be happy."

"Why the hell would I be happy?" He is practically shouting at me now. "First I kill my best friend, but that isn't enough, because then I sleep with his wife and now this, now we're supposed to have a baby together? Why should I be so fucking blessed that I get all the things Joseph never got a chance to have?"

He can hardly conceal the self-loathing in his voice. I think that Fred is the farthest thing from blessed there ever was. I can only imagine the burden of being responsible for taking someone else's life, only to have it thrown in your face at every turn. I'm about to tell him that Joseph would forgive him, but that's not what I really want to say. I think about the people on the news who publicly forgive convicted murderers for killing their husbands, wives, sisters and brothers, even their own children, and I wonder why it's so hard for me to say it to Fred.

"I'm sorry for being so awful to you for so long," I whisper. "I forgive you for what happened that night." The buzzer goes off to end the second period and I let myself out.

CHAPTER THIRTY-FIVE

Lottie

$\mathcal{R}$oger Parsons asks me to come to Confederation Building much sooner than I anticipate. Since I'd only handed him the proposal two weeks earlier, I am expecting exciting news. I don't imagine he would ask me to come all the way out to his office to deliver bad news, but I am cautious and nervous all the same.

I want to bring Prissy and Georgia along as a show of support, but I think better of it. Prissy certainly has the time to come with me. After nearly three months of being holed up looking after her mother, it seems Prissy has more time on her hands than ever before. She visits me at Lawlor's almost daily during that slow period between two and four to complain about her husband's attentiveness to her needs. I love Prissy like a sister but I can't imagine anyone complaining about a husband that pays bills, looks after your mother, clears the snow off your car, and does all the shopping. Listening to her go on and on about how Howie makes her feel useless makes me want to scream at her in frustration. If Prissy were dealt my hand in life, she wouldn't be long thanking her lucky stars for Howie, affair or not.

When I ask if she wants to come to Confederation Building with me, she snorts in protest and then tells me about her visit to the pharmacy that ended in her complete mortification. I knew Howie had been seen around town and that people were talking about Prissy, wondering why she lied to everyone. Some people even claimed they knew it was a hoax all along since they hated to admit being fooled. I overhear things when I pour coffee or bring the bill, but I didn't have the heart to tell her, since with everything else going on in her life, she seemed to have forgotten that she pretended he was dead in the first place. She claims to be embarrassed beyond what she imagined possible and swears that she will never show her face around town ever again, but day after day she walks through the doors of Lawlor's, perhaps the most public place in all of Paradise Bay. I tell her that people will soon move on to talk about other things. If they've stopped talking about Ches, they'll stop gossiping about you, I assure her.

I decide not to tell Georgia about the summons since she isn't aware I've already met with Roger Parsons. If she so much as suspects that Fred has helped in any way, I'm afraid she'll flat out refuse funding of any kind, or refuse to be involved in this endeavour altogether. I still don't understand why Prissy and Georgia hate that people want to help them. I wish I had the luxury of being so particular about who comes to my aid.

I have not visited Confederation Building since a grade eight field trip, when Prissy and I sat in the gallery, giggling every time a politician said the word ferry during a debate on transportation.

As I walk into the open lobby, I feel instantly intimidated by the scene. Men and women in suits rush to get to meetings, shuffling their papers and talking on their cell phones while they check their watches. Each time someone says excuse me so they can pass me without bumping into me, it undermines my own importance, and I feel my confidence wane a little more with each hesitant step I take toward the information desk. I am more aware than ever that my shoes are stained with the salt used by snow-clearing crews and that my coat is missing two buttons. I quell the urge to run back to Paradise Bay and forget all about forming a widows' support group in the first place.

By the time I arrive in Roger Parsons' office, I am convinced he's brought me here to tell me why the government can't fund us. I silently rehearse arguments for the creation of a widows' group in my head, citing what I think are key points Dr. Dunn incorporated into the proposal.

Statistically, young widows may be insignificant, but this is a group that can no longer afford to be ignored. Grief is a necessary and natural part of the healing process, but, as is too often the case for young widows, grief must be placed on the back burner while these women struggle under the pressures of being a single parent, a sole provider, a caregiver for aging parents, and a positive role model. Funding this group is going to yield benefits in the long term, ensuring that women and families in need get the services necessary to become productive members of the community.

Of course I know this is a futile exercise. Once I am given the bad news, I know I will simply thank Roger Parsons for his time and be on my way. I am surprised to see Dr. Dunn already seated in the boardroom, conferring with a young man with square glasses and a laptop in front of him. Dr. Dunn smiles encouragingly when she sees me, waving me inside with a broad sweep of her hand. I realize I'm standing in the doorway, knowing I'm in the right place, but uncertain of whether or not to enter.

"Hello everyone," Roger Parsons says enthusiastically when he makes his grand entrance into the boardroom. He carries a thick black binder, which he drops on the conference room table, making a loud thud. "Well … congratulations, Lottie."

"I'm sorry?" I feel my heart beat faster, and hope swells inside my chest.

"We got the grant," Roger Parsons says, smiling. "Widows Helping Other Widows is about to become a reality." I want to act reserved, to show my appreciation sincerely and respectfully, but I can no more control my emotions than I can stop myself from breathing. I clap my hands and jump up and down with delight like a child on Christmas morning. Then I clasp my hands together and hold them to my lips as if I were giving thanks to God.

"Thank you so much," I whisper, and I hug Roger Parsons and Dr. Dunn and even the man seated at the boardroom table. I have no idea who he is, but I assume he's someone instrumental to either getting WHOW funded or getting it up and running. "What do we do now?" I regret the question almost as soon as I say it. Since I was the one who came to the government seeking financial assistance, I think I ought to know what to do with it once I've gotten it. I wish Georgia were with me since I'm almost certain she'd have something important and meaningful to say.

But thankfully no one seems to think the question is inappropriate.

"There's not a lot of money, but enough to support one full-time position, get a website up and running, and create some marketing and promotional materials," Roger Parsons says. "I don't know exactly how many of you are out there since the statistics are unreliable, but if you've managed to find eleven of them by calling up a radio program then there must be plenty of others like you. Unfortunately, they're not so easy to track down, so they're going to have to find us."

"How?" I have visions of young women in funeral garb knocking door to door in search of me and Georgia.

"Through the internet," Dr. Dunn explains. "We've found social marketing to be particularly effective in such endeavours." She says all of this as if I understood every word and I nod in agreement even though I have no idea what she's talking about.

"A website dedicated to the organization and the resources you have to offer seems like the most rational way to spend the money, at least to start. Anyone can access the information, which will help women find other young widows in their area, find out about meetings, links to grief counsellors, financial assistance, or more importantly, just to start a dialogue with people they might never have had the opportunity to connect with."

The young man uses this moment to reveal his purpose here at the meeting, showing me a variety of web designs of WHOW for me to choose from. There are backgrounds of all different colours with headings that explain what WHOW is and how it came to be, but I don't know anything about graphic design. I don't even know anything about computers since Ches refused to own one. I think it was because he was afraid he couldn't fix it if it broke. He liked machines and cars that were put together the old-fashioned way, with screws and motors instead of memory chips.

Roger Parsons is talking about launching the project in January. He talks about arranging a press conference where there will be a demonstration on the website. He talks about how women's groups will praise the announcement, mental health groups will gladly show their support and social advocacy organizations will herald the funding as a breakthrough. He contends that no one can possibly say anything negative about the initiative, not even the Opposition, but I think he's wrong. I think Ches would have all sorts of awful things to say about it. I can picture him reading the paper and rolling his eyes at the government throwing money at a crowd of whiny women so they could bitch and moan to one another.

I can even picture my response as he says this. I imagine drinking tea and telling him that I'd be the last person to be needing a support group if he did me the favour of dying, because that's just the type of thing I would say to him. It's not so much that I've managed to start a support group or chase down government funding that leaves me speechless; it's that I might actually need the services in the first place.

CHAPTER THIRTY-SIX

Prissy

I awaken to what can only be described as a commotion in the wee hours of the morning of Christmas Eve. I race down the stairs to find my mother and Howie engaged in some sort of heated discussion. Mom is upset and she looks as though she's been crying.

"What's going on?" I ask, breathless partly from running down the stairs and partly from seeing my mother so distraught. Every light downstairs is burning bright and I have to blink my eyes several times to adjust.

"Your mom had a dream."

"It was not a dream." My mother seems angry with Howie's explanation, the first time I've seen her snap at him since he's returned. "She was here."

"Who was here?" I ask in confusion.

Howie sighs in defeat. "Your mother says she saw the Virgin."

"The Virgin Mary?"

"The one and only," Howie replies, throwing his hands in the air.

"Oh," I respond since it's all you can really say when someone tells you they've seen the Virgin Mary moments earlier. I want to refute her claim by pointing out that she's not even Catholic, and as far as I can tell, the Virgin only visits Catholics, devout ones at that.

"My time is near," Mom says and I get goosebumps all along my arms and my neck. She doesn't look or sound anything like herself and the effect is unnerving. It takes nearly an hour to settle her back down, after which neither Howie nor me is in the mood to go back to sleep so we sit in the kitchen drinking tea at four in the morning.

"Jesus, you'd think the Virgin would have the manners to visit at a decent hour," Howie says, rubbing his neck. "I haven't had a good night's sleep in ages."

I know he's joking, trying to make light of an uncomfortable situation but something about it incites me.

"Nobody asked you to be here in the first place," I snap. "Why don't you just go home already and you can sleep all you want."

I can tell by the look in his eyes that he's angry. "All right then," he says coolly. "If that's what you really want, I'll make the arrangements."

"It's just like you to leave when things get difficult, isn't it?" I hear the slight tremor in my voice and I'm afraid I'm going to start to cry, although I have no idea why. I've wanted Howie to leave ever since he got here; I go to great lengths to avoid him, but I know that I'll miss him when he's gone all the same. I cover my eyes with my palms and take a shaky breath.

Howie looks at me, exasperated. "Jesus Christ, Prissy, what do you want from me? I thought you wanted me to leave."

"Of course it's what I want."

"Then why are you so upset?"

"I'm not upset."

"Do you want me to stay? Just tell me and I'll stay."

There is a plea to his voice but I refuse to give him the satisfaction of begging him to stay. "I want you to do whatever you want to do. Isn't that the way you've always done things?" It's the kind of remark that usually angered him throughout our relationship and it still holds the same provocation.

"What the hell is that supposed to mean, Prissy?" He stands up and walks to the kitchen sink, looking out the window, although it's still pitch black, and in the light of the kitchen, there is nothing to be seen save for his own reflection. "All I wanted to do was be here for you right now, and you've done nothing but push me away."

"You don't want to be here for me. You feel obligated to be here, but you're not … obligated. You can go whenever you want," I say, less confrontational now because I am resigning myself to the inevitable.

"We could take her with us," Howie says, turning to face me. "We could convert my office into a room for her and move my computer and things upstairs in the spare bedroom. I'll get twenty-four hour care for her. She won't want for anything."

I can scarcely believe my own ears. "What are you saying?" I whisper.

"I'm not sure." He seems as surprised as I am by his own words. "Maybe we could pick up where we left off."

When we left off Howie was having an affair, carrying on with another woman and telling me he didn't want to be my husband anymore. I am shocked, partly that he's suggested I go home with him, but mostly because I have not readily accepted the offer. For months I've prayed and dreamed of this moment and now that he's asked me, I realize I'm no longer the nineteen-year-old girl who blindly followed Howie years earlier.

"Why did you have an affair?" I ask, the pain and sadness almost palpable in my voice. I realize I've never asked this question yet. I've asked who Howie slept with. I asked for painful details that I didn't want to hear, but I've never asked why before now.

Howie's face is flushed, and I know he's embarrassed by the question, but at the same time he must have known I would ask it eventually. He sits back down and traces the outline of a rose on his teacup, and it looks ridiculous that Howie, who has always been the very picture of masculinity to me, is sitting here sipping tea in a delicate and proper English teacup complete with red and pink roses and a gold rim. He doesn't even drink tea. It's a taste he's acquired only since my mother keeps insisting he drink with her.

"Because I had a moment of weakness," he says, and I stop myself from telling him that I think his explanation is complete and utter bullshit. A moment of weakness is when you order the hot fudge sundae or pay full price for a pair of shoes you know you'll hardly ever wear.

"I didn't think you loved me anymore," he adds. "Ever since I first married you, I was afraid that it might happen someday. You're younger. You're beautiful and fun and ... I know it sounds hokey, but, magnetic. I kept waiting for the day when you looked at me differently, when I wasn't the best thing in your life anymore. I saw it in your eyes every time I looked at you."

If he expects me to find such a speech sweet and endearing, he is mistaken. He's put me through too much to wipe it away with an answer like that. How typical, I think, for a man to cheat and then blame it on his wife. "So it's my fault you had an affair?" I am angry and extremely close to breaking down and I don't care.

"Jesus, Prissy, you couldn't stand to be near me anymore." It is his turn to become defensive and frustrated.

"Did screwing someone else make you feel better?" I don't really expect him to answer but he does.

"At first, yes," he admits, and it's the first thing he's said that I don't take issue with, even as I find it the most painful to accept. "But then it just made me feel awful all the time. I wasn't happy and I knew you weren't happy either, so I did what I thought I had to do, for both of us. I knew it would be hard in the beginning but then I thought it would get easier. But it didn't." He sighs, a sad, depressing sound.

"Look, I'm not saying it's your fault." Howie leans his stubbly chin in the palm of his hand. "I'm the one that messed up. I wish I hadn't done it, but I did."

I want more. I realize he hasn't even apologized to me and I wonder if he would have said anything at all if I hadn't brought it up. I long for a tearful, unshaven version of Howie to get on his knees and beg me to take him back, but the image before me is nothing like that. He is calm again, composed, as he gives me an apologetic half smile, as if he's forgotten to take out the garbage, instead of break my heart.

"What do you think? About coming home?" Howie is looking at me expectantly.

I think of my mother and how much this house and this place means to her. She has never been off the island, not even to come and visit us. We've always been the ones to come home, year after year. To take my mother away from her home now, so she can die amongst a group of nameless, faceless home health-care aides is unthinkable. I don't think Howie is being insensitive; he just doesn't understand.

"I think," I say, "that I'm already home."

Christmas Eve night is awful. My mother has been talking about her visit with the Virgin the entire day, claiming this to be her last Christmas ever, in the way Quentin might say it was his last day of school ever. After her initial shock at her so-called vision, she seems almost relieved at the prospect of dying. By the time dinner is over, she's exhausted, sleeping in her wheelchair with a small pool of saliva spilling on her pyjamas like a toddler on the night before Christmas.

Howie is sipping scotch, of all things, relaxing in my father's old armchair, while I flip through the pages of an old copy of my mother's *US Weekly*. The tension from our earlier exchange stays between us the entire day, an invisible fortress that can't be breached. His words keep echoing in my mind and I wonder if he too is still going over all the things we said to one another or if he's already forgotten them and is planning his return trip back to Toronto.

Burl Ives is singing "Holly Jolly Christmas" on the radio and on television a weather forecaster is providing updates on Santa's whereabouts. When Santa's sleigh is spotted somewhere over the Alps, Quentin asks his father for a drink of scotch.

"Come on, it'll make a man out of me. Please, Dad."

"No," Howie says abruptly.

"Come on, Dad, could you possibly make it through this night without booze?"

Howie laughs at Quentin and it reminds me of the way he used to laugh at all the cute things Quentin uttered as a little boy. "Probably not," he concedes.

"Then think of how I feel. I'm so freaking bored I wanna die. Just one sip. I won't get drunk, I promise. Would you rather I drink here with my parents or out with a bunch of strangers?"

Not for the first time today I regret the decision to have Quentin here for the holidays. I don't know what I was thinking. That we would all sit around the tree laughing and basking in the glow of the holiday? Quentin is not a child anymore, and gone is the lure of Santa Claus, new toys and candy canes, and with it, my own exuberance for the holiday.

When Charlie arrives unexpectedly, we are all thankful for the interruption, none more than Quentin who lights up at the sight of his favourite uncle.

"Jesus Christ," Charlie says upon entering the dark room. "You all sure know how to have a good time, don't ya? I think I'd kill myself if I had to spend Christmas Eve with the likes of you. Break out the fuckin booze or a deck of cards or something."

"Charlie!" I greet my brother with more fanfare than necessary. "Come in, come in. Have a drink. I didn't think you were coming by tonight."

"I just want to drop off Mom's Christmas present. It's out in the fuckin truck. Give me a hand, will ya, shithead." Quentin jumps up, eager to help his uncle.

"Come on, b'y, you too," Charlie says to Howie, who rises slowly, a look of wary hesitation on his face. I wonder what Christmas present requires the strength of two men and a teenage boy.

When they return carting a coffin with a big red bow, I stare at it in defeat. I want to summon enough anger and outrage to give Charlie a proper thrashing, but I am tired of fighting — with my brother, my mother, my son, my husband. I'm tired of telling Mom she isn't going to die any time soon. I've told her fourteen times since this morning, and still she insists that the visit by the bloody Virgin leaves no doubt. Charlie eyes me warily, as does Howie. I know they are both expecting me to start yelling, but I refuse.

My mother is awake now in all the commotion and she wheels herself closer, inspecting the coffin as if she were contemplating purchasing a large piece of furniture. She runs her wrinkled hands over the smooth dark-stained wood, even knocks on it with her swollen knuckles as if testing the wood's strength and durability.

"It's beautiful, Charlie," she says, as if he's given her a rare flower or a sparkling jewel. She asks Charlie to open it, which he does, revealing a sight that takes even my own breath away. Painted on the inside of the coffin is the view from my mother's kitchen window. It is a beautiful mural of sloping hills, winding pathways, wildflowers and the distant sea. "It's beautiful," she tells Charlie.

"The mural was shithead's idea," Charlie says. "He helped me a lot with the painting."

We all look to Quentin, who is embarrassed by the attention. I had no idea my son or my brother was so talented.

"Now help me in," Mom says, and this time she's looking at me.

"I'm not helping you get in there," I say, shaking my head.

"Well, how am I supposed to know if I fit?"

"What difference do it make if you're dead?" Charlie asks.

"I just want to make sure it's big enough."

"You're four eleven," Charlie points out. "You could probably fit in one of my shoeboxes. Of course it's big enough."

Quentin volunteers to try it out, and before I have an opportunity to object he is lying comfortably inside my mother's coffin/Christmas present, assuming a Dracula pose. Seeing my son in a coffin is so unnerving that I get chills down my neck and the hairs on my arms stand tall.

"Get the hell out of that thing right now," Howie says sternly, and I think it must be having a similar effect on him.

"This place is like, so frigging boring," Quentin complains. "No one knows how to take a joke."

I can take a joke just fine. It's the harsh reality that bothers me so much.

CHAPTER THIRTY-SEVEN

Lottie

Our first Christmas together, I asked Ches if we could have my parents over for dinner. I was six months pregnant and already we knew that we weren't ever going to fall madly in love. Still, we were trying to make the best of a bad situation, hoping that love would soon bloom with the arrival of our child. Ches told me he'd rather have a quiet day together before our lives got upended with a baby, which sounded better than it actually was. Ches spent the day napping on the couch and watching television, while I tried not to throw up while removing a neck and a bag of giblets from inside a turkey.

Our second Christmas together, Marianne was just starting to crawl and I suggested we go to my parents so they could spend the holiday with their only grandchild and I wouldn't have to cook. It was about four months after we'd reconciled and Ches was trying to make good on all his promises. My parents made one disparaging remark after another about Ches' job, his ability to support his family and even the state of his clothes, which were wrinkled. I didn't necessarily think it was fair to comment on the latter since I was the one remiss in ironing clothes. Ches seethed in anger the entire time, although he never made a single comment in his defence. By the third Christmas I didn't dare bring up the subject of my parents, and by the fourth, they had left for Calgary to live with my sister and enjoy her Jacuzzi tub.

Year after year, Christmas was just me, Ches and Marianne. There were no cousins, no aunts and uncles or brothers and sisters to create a festive mood, which was precisely why I tried, perhaps too hard, to make it a special day. I insisted on a real tree so the evergreen scent would circulate throughout the house; I mulled spices and sipped hot apple cider; I stuck a bow on every present even though Ches insisted bows were a waste of money; I cooked turkey faithfully each year even though a chicken would have sufficed; I talked about Santa Claus long after Marianne stopped believing, and I hummed along to all the Christmas songs on the radio until Ches yelled at me to shut the hell up because he couldn't hear the television. Despite my best efforts, the day dragged painfully on without people to visit and no one stopping by.

With Ches gone, I lack motivation to pretend that Christmas is different than any other day. I pass the lots selling Christmas trees without stopping. I ignore the sales and specials and steer clear of the aisle at the drugstore with shelves filled with garlands and wrap and boxed chocolates with creamy centres. It makes me sad to know that I've given up the appearance, which is precisely why, at the last minute, I decide to host Christmas dinner for Prissy and Georgia. I want to celebrate with friends instead of dwelling on the fact that after seventeen Christmases together, Ches is gone and Marianne would rather be with her friends than with her mother.

I set the table using my best linens and light-scented candles, and haphazardly put up a tree, although the lot was picked over and the tree has uneven branches with wide gaps. The dried-out needles fall off and litter my living room carpet, but I don't mind. I buy an eighteen-pound turkey, the biggest I've ever attempted to cook, and hope I have a pan big enough to hold the bird.

I don't have a blender so I pull the stale bread into tiny pieces by hand to make stuffing. It's a tedious process and my mind wanders. I think about what Ches might think of our guests if he were here. I wonder if he would get up out of bed and join us, maybe engage Howie in a discussion about the Leafs, perhaps the only common ground the two shared, but at least it would be something. Or would he just get up only to drink himself sick again, as he had in the last few weeks before he died?

I think about my meeting at Confederation Building and I can't wait until everyone is here so I can tell them about the good news. I can't wait to see the expressions of disbelief when I tell them how we pulled it off, and I decide to wait until we are ready to eat, maybe when it's time to say grace. Before long the smell of roasting turkey is circulating throughout the house.

Prissy arrives first, together with Howie, Quentin and Clara. Charlie is spending the holiday with a girl from Bay Roberts, which is just as well, Prissy says, since he already ruined Christmas Eve. She hands me a bottle of sparkling wine and tells me she needs a drink of it sooner rather than later. She is clearly more agitated than normal, although I don't know why. She downs the contents of the bubbly drink from her glass in two mouthfuls and asks for more.

"You'll have to excuse my mother," Prissy says. "I did buy her a nice outfit to wear today, but she insists on wearing that thing instead."

Prissy says this the way an embarrassed parent might apologize for a child who refuses to take off his superhero cape or her princess crown. I look at Clara and notice for the first time that she is wearing pyjamas and a housecoat.

"What odds, Prissy," I say. "So long as she's comfortable, what difference do it make?"

"She won't wear the outfit I got her cause she says she wants to be buried in it instead. I shopped all day for that outfit so I'd have something nice to give her for Christmas and this is what she says after she opened it this morning. 'It's lovely, Prissy. I'd love it if you would bury me in it.' Do you know what she said when I asked her what Quentin could get her for Christmas this year? A pair of insoles," Prissy says before I have a chance to guess. She is now on her third drink and I can tell she's going to be completely smashed within the hour.

"She asks me to buy insoles and she doesn't even walk anymore. She hardly even wears shoes."

I look to Clara's feet, which are clad in a pair of worn slippers.

"It would have made more sense for her to ask me for a pair of ice skates than insoles, which are a stupid gift in the first place, even if you could walk. Not like a coffin. Now that's a fabulous Christmas present."

I have heard all about the dreaded coffin during Prissy's frequent visits to Lawlor's. I know she despises the very idea of it and I can only assume that it must be finished now.

Prissy giggles while she pours another glass of wine.

"Prissy, maybe you should wait until you eat before you drink that," Howie interjects, but Prissy turns on him.

"Why don't you mind your own business since you're leaving soon anyway."

Howie's cheeks burn red with anger and he looks like he wants to throttle his wife, but he remains tight-lipped while she downs another glass, almost to spite him. Prissy was usually all right so long as she stuck with a couple of beers, but she never could hold her liquor. I have seen her drunk only a handful of times and none of them has been pretty. The first time I witnessed Prissy drunk was the night Ryan Hiscock stole a bottle of Lamb's from his parents' liquor cabinet. She spent the first half of the evening laughing and hugging Ryan and the latter half throwing up in the bushes behind the hockey rink. I fear this evening might end the same way for her.

When Georgia arrives, she is carrying a cellophane bag of peppermint fudge and apologizing for being so late. Prissy does her best to cajole Georgia into having a drink with her, but Georgia declines with a shake of her head.

"Come on, it's Christmas," Prissy says convincingly.

Georgia smiles. "I can't because ... well it won't be a secret for much longer. I have some important news everyone." She pauses for dramatic effect while we sit, waiting. "I'm pregnant!"

She smiles enthusiastically, waiting for the rest of us to jump up and offer congratulations, but no one moves because we are all too shocked. Georgia has made the announcement as if she were a blushing bride fresh from her honeymoon instead of a grieving widow. I almost think I might have heard her wrong, but her hands move to her belly to frame just the tiniest swell to her abdomen.

"The father?" I ask in confusion. I'm assuming it's Fred but Georgia looks too happy for that to be the case, and I wonder if she's been hiding someone from the rest of us.

"Who do you think?" Georgia snaps impatiently, as if she doesn't want to repeat that she's been intimate with Fred.

"Maybe it's the Immaculate Conception," says Prissy, giggling. "The Virgin is very busy visiting this time of year."

Georgia looks at Prissy in confusion and shoots me a questioning look, but I have no answers. Obviously, Prissy is going through something either with Howie or her mother or both, but I have no more idea of what's upsetting her than anyone else. I shrug my shoulders at Georgia and look to Howie, who I assume knows exactly what's setting off his wife, but he shakes his head as if to say we are all better off just letting it drop.

"Have you told Fred?" I ask.

Georgia nods. "He needs a little time to get used to the idea. I think I might have scared him."

I think about the day I told Ches of my own pregnancy. I'll never forget the terrified look in his eyes, but neither will I ever forget the tenderness in his expression the first time he held Marianne.

"He'll come around," I say reassuringly.

I have outdone myself. There is turkey, salt meat, potatoes, carrots, peas pudding, dressing, gravy, corn, boiled beets and mustard pickles. Everyone admires the table, compliments me on how delicious everything smells, and just as we have finished passing all the dishes around the table, Clara proposes a toast. I had almost forgotten my own good news with everything going on and I suddenly can't wait for Clara to finish so that I can make my own announcement.

"This is my last Christmas," Clara says, holding her wine glass up in the air. Her hand shakes and wine spills onto the tablecloth but everyone pretends not to notice. "I had a vision the other night of the Virgin and she told me my time is near. So here's to the end of a long and happy life." Clara takes a sip of her wine.

Prissy, who has been drinking all afternoon, now refuses to take a sip. "I'm not drinking to your death."

"It's not my death, it's my life," Clara protests.

"What makes you so God-damned sure you're going to die soon? Because you had a dream about the fucking Virgin?" Prissy leaves the table abruptly and goes into the living room. The rest of us don't quite know what to do. I don't know whether to follow her and see if she's all right or to let her have some time alone and continue eating. I pick at my mashed potatoes, navigating them around the turkey and peas in a sea of gravy while I think about what to do. Everyone, I think, must be feeling the same way since we all look at our plates, but no food passes anyone's lips.

Prissy returns after what seems like an excruciatingly long absence but is probably no more than a minute. She is carrying my Nativity scene in her arms, struggling to keep all the figurines safely tucked inside the manger, and I get a bad feeling in the pit of my stomach. She picks up the ceramic figurine of Mary and tosses it in front of her mother's plate, where it lands on its side. Everyone at the table looks in horror at the figurine, in a kneeling pose, hands folded in prayer, and wearing a solemn expression.

"There," Prissy says. "There's your fucking Virgin. Take her. And why don't you take the baby Jesus while you're at it? Here," she says, tossing the next figurine, an infant swaddled in blue blankets that lands face-down in a plate of stuffing. Before long, she has tossed the Joseph, all three kings, a camel, and a lamb onto the table. Prissy has a crazed look about her, straw from the manger dangling from the ends of her hair, and Clara is looking heavenward asking the Virgin to forgive her daughter, for she knows not what she does.

"Shut up, Mom," Prissy screams. "Shut up! I know exactly what I'm doing!"

"That's enough, Prissy," Howie says sharply. "Please, you're making a fool of yourself."

"You're the one who's made a fool of me," Prissy shrieks back. "Just leave me alone," she says more quietly. "Do us all a favour and leave me the hell alone."

Howie winces against Prissy's outburst, looking pale and unsure of himself. "I am not having this discussion right now." He swallows hard, silently pleading with Prissy. "I'm sorry, Lottie. Thank you for your hospitality, but I think we ought to be leaving."

But Clara insists on finishing her meal since she's sure it's the last meal she will ever have. By the time she finishes her rum pudding, goes to the bathroom, and Howie has her settled in the car, Prissy has passed out on the sofa. She does not protest when Howie gently shakes her, or when he drapes her sweater around her shoulders and effortlessly lifts her from the couch. I have a fleeting picture of Ches carrying Marianne to bed.

Later, when we are cleaning up the kitchen, Georgia asks me if I would forgive Ches if he had an affair. I smile a little bit at this question since I recall thinking that Ches was off to cheat on me the morning he took his own life.

"Would you?" I ask Georgia since I imagine she would be completely devastated by Joseph's infidelity.

Georgia stacks my plates, careful to put the chipped ones on the bottom. "I was always jealous," Georgia admits. "Joseph dated a girl once who worked at the supermarket and I kept running into her every time I ran out of sugar, and it used to drive me crazy because I kept imagining them together until I wanted to tear my hair out."

I personally think that jealousy can be a good thing. People always say that if you're secure and confident in your relationship then you shouldn't have to be jealous, and at weddings someone inevitably will read that love means never being jealous or angry. I don't necessarily think this is true since I hadn't really been jealous or angry with Ches in a long time, because most of the time, I felt nothing. It was only in the beginning when I cared the most about him that I would get angry if he was out late or if I thought he stared too long at the girls who came to the rink to watch their boyfriends or their brothers play hockey. I remember feeling downright livid the day the girl behind the counter at Dee's winked at him when he called her sweetheart, as if I wasn't even there. I think about the more recent years of our marriage when there was no more jealousy, no more anger and no more hurt feelings. It's when you're not jealous and when someone no longer has the power to incite you — that's when things are the most desperate.

"So would you?" I ask Georgia again.

"I never thought I'd say it, but I think I would," Georgia admits, tracing a finger around the rim of her teacup. "I know that Howie cheated on Prissy, but they still have the rest of their lives to make things right, and that's a lot more than everybody gets."

CHAPTER THIRTY-EIGHT

Prissy

$\mathcal{I}$ wake up shortly after midnight, my head throbbing and my mouth so dry my tongue feels like it's glued to the roof of my mouth. I sit up and hold my head in my hands, recalling my awful behaviour at Lottie's Christmas table. A glass of water and two Tylenols are on the nightstand and I gulp up both greedily. Another one of Howie's considerate acts that makes me resent him all the more. Flashes of my own madness play out in my head. I see myself yelling at my mother and hurling religious relics at her dinner plate. I see myself laughing at Georgia's miraculous announcement. There is no one I don't owe an apology to, and I feel my cheeks redden with embarrassment.

I try to fall back asleep but after forty-five minutes of tossing and turning, I give up. I wonder if my mother is right. What if she really is going to die soon? I can not shake the mental image of Mom, dead in her own bed, all alone, and I creep down the stairs to check on her.

The rise and fall of her chest lends me some comfort, although not much. Looking objectively at my mother, I realize that she is old, weak, shrivelled, and near death. Her hair is thinner, the lines in her face deeper and her frame much smaller than it was six months earlier when I first came back to Paradise Bay. I find it hard to imagine this is the same woman who could instil the fear of God in me and Charlie. I remember my mother, an imposing presence, chasing us up the stairs with a slipper in one hand and a newspaper in the other as we scattered, our hands holding our behinds protectively, as she swatted away at our backsides.

I climb in bed next to Mom and grasp a wrinkled hand, tracing circles with my fingertips over her knuckles. I inhale the smell of lavender although I can't understand why since it's been years since she drowned herself in Yardley talcum powder. I comb a lock of white hair between my fingers, and it turns golden in my grasp. I see the lines on her face disappear and her fingernails are no longer stained yellow from years of smoking, but are pink now with rounded white tips.

"I don't want you to die," I whisper, feeling the flow of tears down my cheeks. "You're my mom. When my world fell apart, you were the only person I could tell the truth to. If I didn't have you I don't know what I would have done or where I would have gone. If you die, then where am I supposed to go?"

My mother stirs and opens her eyes, which are focused and steady for the first time in months. "Forgive him, Prissy. He loves you so much." I don't know if this is a final moment of clarity before her death or if my mother has been pretending all these months since her stroke, because she has fallen asleep again so suddenly I wonder if I imagined her words.

When I awake the sky is grey and it's almost nine thirty. I think it strange that Howie does not have my mother up out of bed yet since by this time breakfast is over and they are usually watching television. It's Boxing Day, and I wonder if Howie might have already left, might already be on a plane flying over the Atlantic Ocean right now. I can't imagine he would leave without giving me a chance to say goodbye to Quentin, even taking my awful behaviour into account.

I shake my mother gently. "Come on, time to get up, go to the bathroom." I hurry up because I want to check on Quentin, but my mother still doesn't stir. I shake her harder this time, but she doesn't respond. I wonder if she's already dead, but although she is pale, her skin still has colour and she is warm to the touch. I breathe a sigh of relief at the slow rise and fall of her chest.

"Come on, Mom," I say again but her eyes remain closed, and I know instinctively that something is wrong. I grab the telephone and dial 911 but I hang up as soon as I hear the operator's voice. I think of the way my mother smelled of lavender, the way her hair became shiny and golden for me and her fingers smooth and pink once more, and I know that she's been right all along about her imminent death.

I vow that I will let her die on her own terms. I don't want my mother to die in a nursing home, hooked up to feeding tubes and unable to recognize anyone.

I leave her for a moment and enter the kitchen where Howie is sitting, sipping coffee and reading *The Telegram* from two days ago. I'm relieved to see him still here, especially now.

"How's your head?" he asks me lightly.

I am aware that I am still wearing my black skirt and blue sweater from the previous day and that my hair is tousled and I have mascara smudged under my eyes.

"Fine. Thanks for the Tylenol." I take a deep breath. "Mom is going to die today."

I wait for the news to sink in but I can tell he thinks I've gone just as crazy as my mother. He raises a suspicious eyebrow while he clutches his coffee cup. "Have you been visited by the Virgin too?" he asks.

"Something like that," I say calmly. "Can you call Charlie for me please? He should be here. But that's all. Just immediate family." I am pleased with my calm demeanour. I will not be the person I was yesterday, the one to throw objects at a dying woman because I can't stand that she might leave me soon.

Howie looks at me with a mixture of scepticism and surprise. I think he might be questioning my judgment, but thinks better of vocalizing his opinion. "Okay. I'll let Charlie know. Are you all right?"

Oddly enough, I am. "Uh-huh." I head back to my mother's bedside to begin the vigil.

Charlie arrives around ten thirty, his long hair still wet from a rushed morning shower. Looking down at the pantyhose I donned some twenty-four hours earlier, I am mildly resentful of the luxury of taking a shower. I'm afraid that the minute I step inside the tub, it will be at that exact moment that my mother will die, revealing an important family secret or imparting some last-minute words of wisdom, and I will have missed it while rinsing shampoo from my hair. Charlie throws his coat on the sofa and gestures towards the coffin, still in the living room under the Christmas tree.

"Told you it wasn't a dumb idea," he says.

"Of course it was a dumb idea. Maybe if you hadn't made the stupid thing, she wouldn't be dying right now." I know I sound ridiculous, but the fact that its completion coincides with my mother's imminent death can not be overlooked.

All Charlie can muster is a, "What the fuck, Prissy?"

We sit and watch my mother for what seems like days, hanging onto each breath as if it might be her last gasp, although only two hours pass. Sometimes her eyelids flutter and she mumbles unintelligible things in her sleep. I wonder if she knows where she is and who is here with her. I trace the raised blue veins on the back of my mother's hands, smooth her white hair and adjust her blankets every ten minutes.

Charlie sits in our mother's wheelchair next to the bed, wheeling himself forward and backward an inch at a time. The repetitive motion grates on my nerves and distracts me from concentrating on my mother. I shoot my brother a warning glance, which he either misunderstands or ignores since he continues to move back and forth an inch at a time on the hardwood floors.

Howie hovers near the doorway, offering to make tea or coffee. I sense he thinks this is a bad idea because he's asked me several times if he should call an ambulance or get in touch with Mom's doctor. He has also offered to bring my mother to the hospital himself, and I suspect he thinks that what we are doing is somehow illicit or unlawful.

Quentin sits cross-legged on the rug at the foot of the bed, looking uncomfortable. I don't necessarily think he should be here watching and waiting for his grandmother to die. He's still a child after all, although older than Charlie and I were when our own grandfather died.

I remember Charlie and I sitting at the kitchen table playing Go Fish and Old Maid because it was raining outside. I was ten, Charlie seven, and in the middle of taking him to task for making an incorrect match when the telephone rang. Mom, who was cleaning that day, stood at the wall phone in the kitchen with one yellow rubber glove on and the other tucked under her arm, soapy water dripping on the linoleum floor. When my mother began to cry silently I remember knowing that something awful must have happened because I'd never seen her cry before, not even when she skinned her elbows and knees after tripping on a rock on the way home from Hayward's.

Mom took one look at the terror in mine and Charlie's eyes, and she smiled at the both of us and took us out for ice cream and told us we were going to have a special party for our grandfather. She told us everyone would be there, aunts and uncles and all of our cousins.

Years later, I thought it must have been hard for my mother to have to do that as soon as she heard the news, but I realize now it wasn't hard at all. I lay a hand on Quentin's head. "Come on, let me get you some lunch."

"Now?" he says, looking up at me as if I was crazy. Of course Quentin is fourteen and fully aware of what's happening, whereas Charlie and I were too young to understand. "What if Nan dies when I'm eating?"

I don't know what to say to this since this is the same reason why I haven't taken a shower yet, or changed my clothes. I can't tell him she won't die the minute we leave the room, nor can I let him continue to sit at the foot of the bed for what might amount to hours.

"Get the fuck out of here, both of you," Charlie says. "If she wakes up and tells me she's got a million dollars under the mattress, I'm keeping it for myself."

The vigil goes on into the evening. With every passing minute that my mother hangs on, Howie becomes increasingly nervous. He doesn't say anything but I know he thinks we ought to call someone in a position of authority for reassurance that what we're doing is acceptable. "Just give me a few more hours," I insist.

I concentrate on planning the funeral because it gives me something to do besides watching and waiting. I select the hymns and passages that Mom likes best and smile wryly when I think that her funeral will mirror almost exactly the memorial service she planned for Howie. I select pallbearers, and begin writing my mother's obituary, first in my head and then jotting it down on a paper bag from the pharmacy. I try to remember all of my mother's living relatives, but my mind blanks and I can't recall their names or faces since I haven't seen any of them in years. I realize that I have no idea how to reach them to tell them about Mom's passing, and I think about all the places where her address book might be kept. I should probably have asked her on Christmas since I knew then she would be dying soon.

"Shouldn't we start calling people?" I ask in the silence, although it's specifically directed at Charlie.

"Like who?"

"I don't know," I reply. "Our relatives. Aunt Sade and Uncle Tommy," I suggest, finally recalling the name of my mother's older sister and her husband. "And Aunt Eileen and Uncle Ed."

"It's Uncle Ted," Charlie clarifies. "And Aunt Sade died three years ago."

"She did not."

"Yeah, she did."

"What did she die from then?" I think Charlie is wrong since Sade was always my favourite aunt and I would have remembered hearing this news.

"Cancer."

"What kind of cancer?"

"I don't know, Prissy, the kind that kills you."

"You're talking about Aunt Luce." It's a forgivable mistake. They're sisters with similar features. I know it's Luce because I can picture my mother at my father's funeral. *First Luce, now your father. I s'pose I'm next.*

Charlie rolls his eyes at me but doesn't say anything else and once again the room grows silent save for the quiet breath of my mother.

By midnight, everyone is bored, tired and uncomfortable from sitting in the same room with one another all day long. I have given up my chair next to the bed and sit cross-legged on the carpet with Quentin's sleeping head in my lap. I am torn between wanting to savour every moment of Mom's final hours on earth, and then just getting on with it all. I am tired of sitting here in my clothes from the previous day, and I just want to do something other than wait. I think again about all the phone calls I will have to make. It's always the daughter who accepts responsibility for this task although I don't know why.

"Do you know how to reach Aunt Sade?" I ask Charlie.

"She's dead, I told ya," Charlie answers back. "Why don't you call Dad while you're at it?"

I sigh in annoyance but think better of revisiting the same argument. "What about Uncle Ted then? We should tell someone, no?"

"Tell him what?" Charlie asks, barely masking his irritation. "That Mom is dying? Then you got to call him back again when she's dead. Just wait already and tell him all the one time."

"He has to come all the way in from Halifax so we should probably give him the courtesy of putting him on alert, no?"

"Jesus, Prissy, at this rate he can walk to Paradise Bay on his one good leg and still be here on time," Charlie says, mimicking my own frustration. "Maybe she's in one of those vegetative states where she can stay alive for years without moving," he adds.

"You can't be in a vegetative state unless you're on life support," I say smugly.

Charlie sighs, looks at his watch again. "Jesus, why is this taking so fuckin long?"

"What do you want me to do, Charlie? Put a pillow over her head?"

"I wasn't talking to you, okay?"

"Why don't you just shut up."

"You shut up."

"Asshole."

I think that if Mom could, she would tell us both to shut up. We are behaving so poorly, bickering and squabbling at her deathbed. We should be celebrating her life, sharing stories of a happy childhood and honouring the person she was and the choices she made. I slip a pillow under Quentin's head and stand, stretching out my legs, arms and back muscles.

"Do you remember the time Mom caught you egging Mr. Hickey's house?" Mr. Hickey was Charlie's grade ten teacher. Not only did he give Charlie a D in English, but he doled out detention when Charlie made his objection to his grade known in a profanity-laced outburst in third period.

Charlie's face softens and he smiles. "Jesus, yes," he nods. "That sonofabitch had it coming though. Mom got me good that time."

Indeed she did. My mother sweetly sent Charlie to Hayward's to pick up a dozen eggs and a bottle of Windex. Then she sent him out in the yard where she proceeded to pelt him with the eggs. He was too shell-shocked by his mother hurling eggs and epithets at him to move until he was dripping with the sticky yolk. When all the eggs were gone she handed him the Windex and followed him to Mr. Hickey's house to supervise the cleaning.

"I don't think I've ever seen Mom that upset," I add, smiling at the memory.

"I have," says Howie, who enters the room now and sits at the chair I vacated hours earlier. Howie has been in and out of the room all day, offering tea, snacks and advice, but mostly he hovers near the doorway and lets Charlie and me argue without getting involved. Howie's face is covered in stubble now, a reminder of exactly how long this vigil has gone on.

"I had just proposed to you, and I was full of myself that you wanted to come to Toronto with me and be my wife." He is speaking to me but he is looking at Mom's pale skin and wrinkled face. "You couldn't wait to start planning the wedding and you ran off to ask Lottie if she'd be your matron of honour. As soon as you left the house, your mother ... she was different. Sad, upset, crying in the kitchen when she thought no one was looking. I asked her what was wrong, but she couldn't even speak to me. She picked up a plate of jam jams that had been left out from breakfast and hurled them into the sink, plate and all, and then started crying like it was the end of the world because she broke the plate in half. Your dad told me it was hard for her to pretend to be happy when she was about to lose you. I felt guilty about it but there was no way I wasn't going to marry you. I promised her you'd be in good hands, that I'd look after you, and make you happier than you ever imagined."

Howie leans forward in the chair, with his back to me, still looking at Mom. I sense this is hard for him and I know he wouldn't be able to get anything out if he looked at me. "I don't know what happened to us. The only good thing that's come out of any of this is that you were able to come home and be where you needed to be."

I see a tear slide down Howie's cheek and then another, and then I feel my own eyes pool with tears.

"I'm sorry, Clara, for breaking all those promises," Howie says shakily. He bends forward and kisses her forehead. "Peace, Mom," he whispers.

It's the tearful apology I've always wanted. It doesn't matter that it was uttered to my mother instead of me.

CHAPTER THIRTY-NINE

Georgia

Fred shows up at my house the day after Christmas with a bassinet embroidered in green and yellow gingham, and a rectangular box wrapped in a festive pattern of red and white snowflakes. His appearance is unexpected and I greet him at the front door, unsure exactly of how to approach this situation.

"I stopped by yesterday, but I guess you were out," he says, handing me the bassinet, although he still holds the wrapped present in his hands.

"It's beautiful," I say of the tiny bed. Inside, it is filled with baby blankets, rattles and a plush teddy bear. "Thank you."

"I don't know if you're having a boy or a girl, so …" he explains awkwardly, "that's why everything is green or yellow or white." I imagine Fred shopping in the baby section of department stores and the thought of his large rough hands holding up delicate baby clothes makes me smile, and I look forward to seeing my baby cradled in those big strong hands.

"I don't know what I'm having either." It doesn't matter to me one way or the other. "If it's a boy, I'm going to name him Joseph and if it's a girl, she'll be Josephine."

There's a hint of a smile on Fred's lips. "That sounds perfect. I got you a Christmas present." He hands me the box and I sit and unwrap it, careful not to tear the paper. I don't know why I am so tentative in opening the box other than I'm just afraid to see what's inside. I'm afraid that Fred is interpreting our relationship as a romantic one and

I don't know how to react to something personal and feminine like jewellery or scented bath soaps or terry bathrobes, even though the shape and size of the box assures me it is none of those things.

But my fears are unfounded. My gift is a framed picture of Fred and Joseph as children, maybe about nine or ten years old, each of them wearing rubber boots and holding a fish by the gills. Joseph is wearing a baseball cap that covers most of his face but his golden mane is unmistakable. I hold the picture, study it and try not to weep. Looking at the two boys with not a care in the world, I can't help but feel sad knowing how things would ultimately turn out for them.

"Thank you," I say. "It's perfect. I feel bad, I didn't get you anything for Christmas."

"You got me more than I ever imagined," he says. "I've been thinking a lot about things and I decided I want to be a proper father. I know Joseph would damn well kill me if I left you to raise my child on your own. I'm not sure how this is supposed to work, but I think we can do it." Fred's eyes are pleading with me and I don't know exactly what he wants, but I know I owe him the truth, however hurtful it may be.

"I can't love you," I say. I don't mean it as a personal affront to Fred and I feel bad saying it since he's been good enough to try and make amends. "It's just that I've already experienced the love of my life and you don't get that twice. That's what makes it so special. I am incapable of loving anyone else the way I loved him. I can forgive you for what happened that night. I can raise a child with you. I can find friendship with you, and one day maybe even companionship. But I will never love you."

I sound cold, especially in light of his peace offering, but I'm not interested in creating expectations that I will have to quash in the future.

"I'm not looking for love, Georgia," he says, putting his hands in his pockets. "I'm just trying to get from one day to the next day, and that makes us kinda the same, doesn't it?"

CHAPTER FORTY

Prissy

*C*harlie awakens me with a gentle shake just before five in the morning to tell me Mom is awake and asking for me. I jolt upright from my place on the rug and chide myself for having drifted off. At once I'm wide awake, every muscle and every nerve fuelled by a sudden burst of adrenalin. This is what I've been waiting for; this is why I am still wearing the clothes I donned more than forty hours earlier, complete with a run in my stockings that's travelled the length of my knee all the way to the reinforced toes. It's why my mascara and eyeliner are smudged in half moons underneath my eyes and why my hair is pulled back from my face in an uncombed ponytail. I did not get the opportunity to witness my father's death and I am determined to be awake and alert for my mother's. I don't know if she'll impart last-minute words of wisdom or whisper some meaningful truth on her deathbed. I just know that I need to witness her final moments and to hold her hand as she leaves me. I sit next to her on the edge of the bed, take her hands into mine and bring the tips of her fingers to my lips.

"Mom," I whisper. "I'm here."

"Prissy," she says, although her voice is hoarse and she coughs slightly with the exertion. I think about telling her not to talk, but I want desperately to hear what she has to say. "I'm glad you came home," Mom says, and I nod, wondering if she is still confused, if she thinks I've just arrived in the nick of time.

"Me too," I say, playing along.

"When are you coming home for good?" she asks me with a hint of a smile and I feel the start of the tears prick my eyes. It is the same question my mother has asked me at the end of each and every visit back to Paradise Bay over the years. *One of these days, Mom,* I always tell her. *I s'pect I'll be long gone by then,* is her customary response. *Sure, I'll be back before you know it,* I always assure her. It's become a ritual between us, the way we banter back and forth as suitcases are packed with souvenirs and plane tickets retrieved from carry-on bags in the corner of the living room. It's the way we both avoid having to endure drawn-out, tearful goodbyes. I think this is very clever of her to resurrect this conversation on her deathbed so we are spared the pain of having to say the ultimate in goodbyes.

I am about to recite my line, *One of these days, Mom,* just like I always do, but my mother has one final surprise up her sleeve and I don't get the chance.

"Promise me you'll stay," she says quietly. "Promise."

This is the last thing I expect and I hesitate with my response. I don't know where I'm going to land when all of this is over, when my mother is gone and when the minutia of my divorce is resolved. I can tell my silence bothers Charlie because I can feel his eyes bore a hole in the back of my head and I can hear him rub his hands together as if he were physically holding himself back from grabbing me by the shoulder and forcibly extracting the promise. I know he wants me to say whatever Mom wants since she'll have no way of knowing whether I keep the vow or not, but he is not being asked to make such promises. He is not about to burn in the fiery pits of hell for a promise he isn't certain he can follow.

I steal a sideways glance at Howie. I don't know what I'm looking for in his expression — maybe a silent plea that if I don't return to Toronto with him he will wither and die — but he sits stone-faced in the far corner of the bedroom. He can no more ask me to deny a dying woman's last wish than I could deny it, even if I wanted to.

"I promise," I say and I feel relief wash over me like the tide's waves jutting out to coat my feet and ankles before they recede and then return again, submerging even more of me. "I promise," I say again, this time without hesitation because I'm certain that this is where I'm supposed to be, even if I don't yet know what it is I'm supposed to do.

Mom looks at me, her blue eyes lighter than I remember, like a favourite pair of jeans faded from wash and wear. She smiles at me, content, and then closes her eyes once again. I lose her about half an hour later because her fingers fall limp in my grasp and the rise and fall of her chest slows and then stops just moments after I see and hear her final breath. I continue to hold her hand until Charlie pries her fingers from mine and places my mother's hand on her chest.

In some ways, I am relieved that the vigil is finally over and ashamed for feeling that way, but I think Charlie and Howie are also relieved. We are all exhausted waiting for it to happen. Howie calls the funeral home and makes arrangements for someone to come and take her, and to my own surprise, I instruct him to have the coffin removed from the living room and delivered to the funeral home.

"Are you sure?" he asks and I nod yes. It was what she wanted after all, and in the sober light of the morning I can see it for the fine quality craft it is instead of the fear it represented to me. It's solid construction, plain and yet ornate in its own right. I think of Quentin painting the ocean and I am sure my mother would roll over in her grave if I buried her in anything but.

"Is it true you shit yourself after you die?" Quentin asks me after Mom has been taken away to be prepared. I don't know if it's true or not, although I've heard the same thing too.

"She shit herself when she was alive," Charlie says, "so I don't imagine she has any better control now that she's dead." He is crass beyond even what I expected he might be capable of and yet it's entirely forgivable under the strain of the past several days. Quentin laughs at Charlie's joke, but I get the sense it's because he thinks he ought to and not because it's actually funny.

"What are they going to do to her?" Quentin asks. "I mean to get ready?"

My knowledge of funeral parlour procedures is sketchy at best. I don't think I quite want to know what they're going to do to her. I think they drain her blood and replace it with formaldehyde but I don't know for certain. "They'll put makeup on her," I say, like my mother is off to the beauty parlour instead of the funeral parlour.

I locate Mom's address book near the telephone desk upstairs in the hallway and begin the process of calling people. With each call I find it harder and harder to emote. Each person I telephone asks the same questions and offers up the same reaction. *At least she died at home surrounded by her family. That's the way she always wanted to go — nice and peaceful.* I provide details on the wake and the funeral and then move on to the next person on the list.

When Aunt Sade answers the phone, I say her name louder than necessary so Charlie will hear me. "Aunt Sade! Hello!" I repeat my spiel about my mother's death, being careful to recite the hours for the wake, along with the funeral details that I know so far. I expect her to comment on Mom's death in the same way everyone else has. I expect her to tell me my mother would have wanted to die at home, but instead she shouts in triumph.

"I knew it," Aunt Sade says emphatically before I have finished reciting the funeral details. "I had a vision of my dear sister this morning and I knew right then and there she had passed."

I wonder why I am the only female in the family who does not have visions. I think psychic abilities are supposed to be passed on, or maybe you just have to be old and crazy to get them.

"Be strong, Prissy," Aunt Sade says. "I know it must be hard for you, first to bury your husband and now your mother, all in the space of a few months. We'll be there as soon as we can, and in the meantime, you try and take care of yourself."

"I'll try," I groan and then hang up. I feel as if Mom is sabotaging my life even from the grave. Howie's absence from my mother's funeral seems unthinkable to me. I find Charlie and point out not only that Aunt Sade is very much alive but that she thinks Howie is dead.

Charlie sits at the kitchen table, laughing. "How the fuck you gonna explain that one? He's a pallbearer, aint he?"

"I don't know, Charlie. I'm too tired to even think about that now." I pinch the bridge of my nose to fight off the growing headache.

"Can he grow a beard by Thursday? Maybe if he grew a beard and wore dark glasses no one would recognize him. We could say he was a cousin from Halifax."

I ignore Charlie's plan because somewhere in my mind I actually think it makes sense, that it could work, which makes me fear I'm becoming as crazy as Mom for even thinking it.

"Where is Howie anyway?" I haven't seen him or Quentin since my mother was taken away to the funeral home.

"He took Quentin into town with him to place the obit in tomorrow's paper. Then he said something about having to go to Hayward's to run an errand. Said he'd be back in a few hours. He told me to tell you to get some sleep and that he'd bring back dinner."

It seems strange to me that I should do things like sleep, eat, shower, wash dishes and so on after my mother has just died. It doesn't feel quite right sitting at her kitchen table when I know she will never occupy her place here again.

"I miss her," I say.

"Me too."

To my surprise my mother looks good. I had been worried Mom would be unrecognizable underneath layers of makeup applied by an undertaker who was unaware she never wore makeup to begin with. I had visions of seeing her laid out with a face thick with pink rouge, blue eye shadow and painted lips, but she is nothing like that. I can hardly believe it is the same person who was taken out of her bed little more than a day and a half earlier. Her cheeks have a rosy glow that looks almost natural and the lines around her eyes and mouth have been softened. Her hands are folded neatly together and she is wearing just a hint of a smile, like she's up to something mischievous but no one knows what. I take a few moments longer to gaze at her before the viewing hours officially start. Charlie stands in the doorway, legs apart and hands clasped behind his back in the habit of a bodyguard. I hardly recognize him in black dress slacks and a button-down shirt. His hair is tied in a ponytail and he's shaved his goatee, making him look more like the little brother I remember. Howie is speaking with the funeral director about the details of the funeral service and the burial. Quentin is sitting in a plush chair, wearing the same outfit he wore to court and looking deathly afraid of his grandmother's body.

"C'mre, and say goodbye," I say, motioning him closer. Quentin reluctantly gets up from the chair and stands next to her, peering inside the casket.

"She doesn't look dead," he says, stuffing his hands in his pockets.

"They made her look real good, didn't they?"

"Yeah, kinda like a wax figure."

"The coffin came out nice, didn't it?" Quentin shrugs his shoulders in response.

"I love the detail that you painted. I mean, it's beautiful. I know she really loved it." In the furthest reaches of my imagination, I never thought I'd be praising my son's role in the construction of my mother's coffin, but it really is like nothing I've ever seen before. I don't know how it's going to be received by all the other mourners since it's such a bold statement, but I think it suits Mom's very essence.

I am thankful when the doors finally open and viewing officially starts. Georgia and Fred arrive, together with Lottie and Marianne. Then Aunt Sade and Uncle Tommy, Aunt Eileen and Uncle Ted, my mother's physician, Dr. Ferguson, and my grade ten teacher, Mr. Newman. Soon, just about everyone in Paradise Bay is milling about the room, chatting and laughing, the buzz of conversation so loud that I have to strain to hear some of the things being said. I hear my mother's name being mentioned over and over again, and always it is accompanied by laughter. I find my spirits lifting with the energy in the room, greeting old friends and family members like the celebration of life it was meant to be. When I observe Georgia tilt her head back in laughter at something Fred whispered to her, I shake my head in wonder that Georgia can laugh inside the walls of a funeral home.

Charlie is basking in all the compliments paid over the casket. I notice he is handing out his phone number to several uncles and cousins and other locals. I don't know what's worse, shopping for a coffin at someone else's wake or soliciting business at your own mother's funeral. I keep quiet about it though since I've said enough negative things about Charlie's endeavour in the first place, and I know he deserves the praise.

"Look at you," Aunt Sade says, hugging me close. "How are you holding up?" She looks like my mother, only heavier and with different coloured hair.

"I'm fine, Aunt Sade." I smile and wonder what my mother would think about her wake, about all the people on hand to pay respects.

"I'm just thinking it's sad that Mom is missing this. I mean it's a shame she can't see and hear everyone coming together for her. I think she would have loved it."

"How do you know she can't?" Aunt Sade says softly, and I force a smile.

I think that my mother's initial idea of a handmade coffin being simple is the very thing that is drawing the most attention to her. "The coffin is beautiful," Aunt Sade says, as if reading my mind, and for a moment I think she really might be psychic. She takes her camera out of her purse and begins snapping pictures of my mother's body like she's a crime scene investigator. Each time the flash goes off, I blink and pray it is the last, although no one thinks anything of it. Aunt Sade is a holdover from another generation when you wouldn't think of going to a funeral without a camera. My own mother shot an entire roll at my grandfather's funeral, which she had the audacity to put in a photo album alongside our school pictures and vacation photos. When I see Aunt Sade delete three shots of my dead mother from her memory card, I note with irony that the older generation is moving forward. I can't help but think it isn't fair since it isn't as if my mother was looking away or not smiling at the right moment. When Aunt Sade asks me to get in the picture with my mother, I comply, albeit reluctantly. I don't know whether I should be looking at my mother's dead body or the camera, to pose mournfully or to smile.

I catch Howie's eye from across the room and he shoots me a smile filled with amusement at my discomfort and embarrassment. I smile broadly, our own private joke. I see him make his way through the crowd, but just before he reaches me, I notice my Aunt Sade's face grow pale. She is staring directly at Howie with a look of shock and dismay, and I feel my stomach drop as I try to come up with an explanation that won't make me look too horrible.

"Are you okay, Aunt Sade?" I place a hand on her arm to steady her.

"He watches over you."

"Who?" I ask, confused.

"Your husband," Aunt Sade says in a serious tone. "He's here. I just had a vision. I saw him clear as day."

I smile. "I know. I can sense his presence too."

CHAPTER FORTY-ONE

Lottie

I received the best news of my entire life a full week ago, and I still haven't had the chance to share it yet. Ever since I found out about getting the grant for WHOW, I have been bursting with excitement at the very notion of revealing our good fortune. I had planned to tell everyone at Christmas, but after Georgia announced her pregnancy and Prissy destroyed my Nativity set, it hardly seemed appropriate. And with Prissy's mother's death, it didn't seem right to bring it up at the funeral parlour either.

But there's an urgency now to tell Prissy and Georgia since I anticipate we will be losing Prissy soon. We are sitting in Clara's kitchen drinking tea, Prissy and I, while Georgia makes room in the fridge and in the cupboards for all the leftover cakes and crackers following the burial. Georgia is rummaging in the cabinet by the fridge and removing a handful of things to stack them more efficiently. She stands with a large jar of Metamucil in her hands.

"Do you still need this?"

Prissy's eyes are still red and slick and I think Georgia, of all people, should be a little more sensitive, considering it took her five years to get rid of anything belonged to Joseph. The burial was difficult on Prissy. I know firsthand that the moment when the coffin is lowered into the ground, it smacks you right in the stomach with the finality of it all. Prissy shakes her head and smiles. "I hope not," she says.

"I have some good news," I say. Georgia continues to rummage in the refrigerator, although she is eating more than she is putting away.

"We received a grant to start the support group."

Georgia stops fussing in the refrigerator and Prissy looks at me in disbelief. "Are you serious?" Georgia asks.

"Why would I joke about something like this right now of all times? I met with Roger Parsons, Dr. Dunn and a computer expert. They want to use most of the money for internet stuff. Create a website, chatrooms, and so on. I'm not all that well-versed in computers, to be honest with you, but if we say we're young widows, then I guess we have to act like it. Marianne says she can teach me."

Georgia screeches with delight and hugs me and then Prissy. "This is fantastic news," she squeals and then begins peppering me with questions about my meeting. I insist Georgia take the one full-time position and Georgia insists I take it. In the end, we agree to split it into two half-time positions after Prissy nixes being part of it.

"I'm not a legit widow," she insists, but I suspect there's more to it.

Prissy will be gone from here soon, even if she doesn't know it yet. As they lowered Clara into the ground, I watched Prissy's shoulders shake with the sobs that coursed through her body. I watched as Howie drew Prissy close to him, his wool coat absorbing the wetness from her tears as she cried into his chest. I watched as his hand smoothed her hair and he whispered something in her ear, while his lips brushed her brow. Howie had been so tender, and Prissy so open and trusting for someone who'd professed a desire to be widowed not several weeks earlier. Watching them, I felt something stir in my chest, knowing that Ches had never held me in such a fashion.

Marianne asks me all the time if I loved her father and automatically I say yes because I feel as if it's the right thing to say, especially under the circumstances. If I close my eyes and concentrate really hard I can see Ches the way he used to be, before he started drinking heavily, before his accident left him bedridden for long periods, and before he took to sleeping most of the time. We got along okay. We did things together. But I don't think I loved him the way you're supposed to, certainly not the way Georgia loved Joseph or the way Prissy loves Howie.

When Marianne asks me why her father killed himself, the answer comes more easily and truthfully. I think about the day I told Ches I was pregnant and how he ran after me in the tall grass. I remember

Ches shivering in the freezing cold, hoisting Marianne on his shoulders so she wouldn't miss anything at the Santa Claus parade in the streets of downtown St. John's. I remember his enthusiasm to try for another child when Marianne was three, even though it wasn't meant to be, and I remember his conviction to get a second job after I'd left him when Marianne was an infant. The memories are few and far between. Mostly, I remember Ches lying in bed, unshaven and unkempt and unable to make it through the day. The answer, I think, is simple. "Your father always wanted to be a good man. He always wanted to be better, but as much as he tried, he just couldn't be the person he wanted." I tell her that Ches loved her very much, but that something was wrong inside him that made him very sad. I know it sounds overly simplistic, but sometimes the most complicated things in our lives are that way.

I think about this when I reflect on the fact that Georgia has finally found her peace with Fred, and Prissy has found love again in the man she'd never really stopped loving. I feel a tinge of jealousy, but more than that, I feel guilty knowing I will miss Prissy when she leaves Paradise Bay, maybe even more than I miss Ches.

CHAPTER FORTY-TWO

Prissy

$\mathcal{I}$ have no idea what to do with all the junk my mother has accumulated throughout the course of her lifetime. I sit amongst boxes, piles of papers, bound issues of *Reader's Digest* and stacks of supermarket tabloids, feeling completely overwhelmed by the range and variety of Mom's belongings. Earlier, I packed up all of her clothes and sent them to the thrift shop, even the cashmere wrap I mailed as a Christmas present just four years ago. I came across it on the top shelf of her closet, still in its box and neatly wrapped with the Holt Renfrew tissue paper. I don't know what I was thinking, sending my mother something so fancy in the first place. I just thought she'd never owned anything so luxurious and that she deserved to wrap herself up in the soft warm fabric. I suppose it was too over-the-top for my mother since it never made it out of the box, and yet her quilts bore patches in several places, and her woollen sweaters were stretched to the point they barely resembled the shape of a sweater.

I have divided things into three piles: keep, discard and undecided. The discard pile is the biggest by far. Newfoundland Light and Power bills from as far back as May of 1984 are piled on top of a 1979 calendar from Irving and a 1982 calendar from Scotiabank. I rack my brains wondering about the significance of those years and then scoff at the notion my mother could possibly be that organized. Most likely, she had simply thrown the calendars wherever she happened to be, and they'd wound up in places that never got organized.

The keep pile is the smallest, containing bank records, medical records, receipts from the funeral home and newspaper clippings, including my own wedding announcement, as well as Quentin's birth announcement. There are postcards from relatives long gone and faded photographs of people I barely recognize without their grey hair and wrinkled skin.

It's the undecided pile that proves most daunting. There are copies of mine and Charlie's report cards through the years, a macaroni necklace I made in Brownies for Mother's Day, a clay ashtray Charlie had fashioned way back when ashtrays were an acceptable school project, and a Happy Birthday Nanny card Quentin had made out of blue construction paper. Aside from the momentary burst of nostalgia, they mean nothing to me, but I'm reluctant to throw them out because they had meant something to Mom. I still keep Quentin's baby clothes in a box in the attic, along with the first lock of his hair I cut and the first tooth he lost. They are in a box next to my framed wedding invitation and my wedding album, both of which had been exiled to the attic years ago. I picture a grown-up Quentin going through those boxes, smiling at old memories after I die.

I hear the floor creak and I see Howie watching me, leaning easily against the doorframe, one hand in his jeans pocket, the other holding an envelope. His overcoat is draped over one arm.

"Hey," I say in acknowledgement. Since the funeral, we are both guarded towards one another, as if the ordeal of the past few days has left us emotionally spent. I'm surprised at how easily we've slipped into our old ways, making small talk, exchanging insignificant bits of information about the weather or the tools in my dad's workshop or how many minutes a quarter gives you in a parking meter on Water Street, or countless other things I couldn't care less about.

"You don't have to do all this right now."

"I want to," I say. "It's keeping me busy."

We don't speak for several moments. I continue to rifle through my mother's things and Howie continues to watch me.

"I'm taking an early flight out tomorrow," he announces. "I'm staying at a hotel by the airport tonight so I can make the flight."

"Oh," I mouth, although no sound comes out. I don't know what to say, although every second he stands in the doorway becomes more uncomfortable for me. I am surprised by the announcement, but perhaps I shouldn't be. There were no fits of passion between us throughout the wake or the funeral, just the comfort of something familiar in the way Howie held my hand throughout everything. It's not that I didn't expect he'd leave to resume his life in Toronto, just not yet. But seeing him in the doorway, his overcoat folded over his arm, it makes perfect sense. Howie is all about obligation, and with my mother's burial, his duty is complete.

"Quentin?" I whisper. His name is both a plea and a question, and I'm afraid to look up.

"Quentin's not going anywhere."

I wonder if this is my consolation prize for the dissolution of my marriage and my mother's death, and if I'm supposed to thank him. I wonder if it's a temporary reprieve and if he expects Quentin to head back to Toronto with him in another couple of weeks.

"Prissy," Howie says, as if trying to explain himself, but I don't want to hear it and I don't want to tell him either, so I sit cross-legged on the floor and stare at the papers in the discard pile until their edges are blurry.

"I've been gone a long time and I have to take care of things. I have to sit down with my partners and work something out and I have to talk to someone about putting the house on the market."

He is selling our house. I wonder if a lawyer advised him to sell the house and split the profits. I hear of such things happening all the time and yet all I can think about is how excited we were the day we moved in. I'd never imagined living in anything so grand.

Howie crouches down on the floor before me now, the way he used to with Quentin when he was a little boy lining up all his toy cars and trucks in a miniature traffic jam. He hands me the envelope and I take it with an unsteady hand, wary of the contents. The last time I received an envelope from Howie, it contained divorce papers.

"I got this after your mother died, but I wanted to wait until after the funeral to give it to you."

Inside, I find a deed to a building. I've seen hundreds of them in Howie's office over the years, but this one has my name on it. The address I recognize instantly. "You bought me Hayward's?"

"Yeah," he says, smiling. "Hayward, that old sonofabitch, drove a hard bargain too. I think he knew we fooled around in his store and he wanted to give it to me as payback."

My thoughts are reeling under a cloud of confusion. "But why?"

"Because I would make a lousy fisherman. Because the last time I went to pick up milk, Mr. Hayward told me he wanted to retire. Because I can't let you break your promise to your mother. Because I love you."

His voice is trembling and I don't have time to digest what he's saying because Howie is holding me in his arms, caressing my hair and crying into my neck and shoulder. I have never seen Howie so out of control and it unnerves me just the slightest. He has always been infallible to me, strong, decisive, steady, and seeing him so emotionally distraught takes me by surprise but only for a moment. In an instant I am crying tears of relief.

I feel his lips on mine and my mouth opens in response. The sensation is at once familiar and new. My heart beats faster and I feel my legs weaken, but then it doesn't matter because Howie is carrying me up the narrow stairway into my bedroom. He does not let me down until he is lying on top of me, pressing his body into mine. I don't care that I didn't brush my teeth after lunch or that my bra and panties don't match. There is a sense of urgency in the way he makes love to me. He does not stop and savour the moment of our bodies touching again after such a long absence, but instead, he is rushed and hurried, making love to me as if I might disappear at any moment. It is the same way he made love to me the first time we met at Hayward's, and for a moment I am just a young girl again, swept away by a handsome stranger. I am as rushed as he is, enjoying the feverish pitch of his body on mine. I feel the intensity of his climax, feel him convulse and shudder before collapsing next to me.

We make love once more before I find myself drifting off at four in the afternoon in the crook of my husband's arm. I don't know if the next time he makes love to me, I'll think about him holding another woman or not. It still stings, it might always sting. I don't know if it will be easier to maintain a happy marriage here in Paradise Bay, but I do know that we will both try harder.

In the fading sunlight of late afternoon on the first day of the New Year, I have my first and only vision. It is of my mother and she is looking out the kitchen window, the same view painted by Charlie and Quentin on the inside of her coffin. She is smiling and satisfied that she's finally brought her family home to stay.

Acknowledgements

Thank you to my husband, Roberto, who encouraged me to write creatively, supported me throughout the process, and then pushed me to cross the finish line even when it seemed so far away.

I will forever be grateful to Annamarie Beckel at Breakwater Books for her warm and personable reception, her utmost professionalism, and for guiding me throughout every step of this process. Thank you to Rhonda Molloy for her wonderfully creative cover design, and to Alison Carr for transforming my word document into a bona fide book. Thank you also to the entire team of talented professionals at Breakwater Books for your enthusiasm and dedication. Finally, I'd like to express my appreciation to the individuals, organizations and agencies that support independent book publishers everywhere.